The Fell

Lyndsey Harper

CRIMSON
EDGE
PRESS

Printed in the United States of America

First Printing, 2017

ISBN-10: 1-945397-90-X
ISBN-13: 978-1-945397-90-5

Cover art by The Dust Jacket.

Acknowledgement

Matt—my best friend, my patient husband, and my biggest cheerleader. He continually forgives me for my lack of a domestic side (especially when writing), listens to me blab for hours, gives great hugs, and makes a mean Mexican casserole to help keep me alive.

My Momma and Daddy—my real life superheroes. They have never failed to give me their invaluable love, wisdom, and support for my entire life, even now while they are busy kicking cancer's butt.

My awesome siblings—Becky and Alex. They have put up with my middle child brand of crazy for this long without killing me, and they never fail to show their love to me, especially in their teasing.

My entire extended family—my loud and loving crew. You guys keep growing all the time, which means I am continually blessed.

My friends—a conglomerate of the most nerdy, snarky, and golden-hearted people from all walks of life. They aren't related to me and still, surprisingly, haven't blocked me on Facebook yet.

Nathan Jarmusch—the clever writer and warrior who will remain forever the Great Dragon in my heart and on these pages.

And finally, Crimson Edge Press—the wizards behind the curtain. Thanks for taking a chance on me, and replying to my tweet years ago, even though I didn't really know what I was doing then on Twitter (and still don't).

Dedication

For my daughter, Chloe.

You're the reason Mommy writes.

Table of Contents

Chapter One 1

Chapter Two 17

Chapter Three 23

Chapter Four 41

Chapter Five 52

Chapter Six 62

Chapter Seven 72

Chapter Eight 87

Chapter Nine 101

Chapter Ten 115

Chapter Eleven 131

Chapter Twelve 146

Chapter Thirteen 158

Chapter Fourteen 173

Chapter Fifteen 186

Chapter Sixteen 196

Chapter Seventeen 209

Chapter Eighteen 216

Chapter Nineteen 228

Chapter Twenty 242

Chapter Twenty-One 250

Chapter Twenty-Two 262

Epilogue 271

About the Author 277

The Fell

Lyndsey Harper

-1-

Leer Boxwell cracked his worn knuckles inside the opposite hand, the skin on them dry from the chilled air that chapped it over time. A squint of a dark brown eye narrowed his focus. There was no need to rush. Despite knowing his opponent's overwhelming eagerness for battle, he remained still, calm. He would make his move, but only in time.

A lock of blond hair drooped past his brow. He ignored it, silently pondering the vast number of choices before him. The loud vibrations in his ears pestered him. With a subtle shrug, he closed off his surroundings and honed in on the task. He could feel the growing impatience of his enemy emanating toward him. Leer drew his bottom lip inward and nipped at it, surveying his situation, effectively destroying the scab that had formed on it in response to his previous abuse.

Patience. He smirked to himself, his tongue running behind his top teeth as he rotated his left hand. *It will all be over soon anyway, my friend.*

He widened his lopsided grin at the gentle, firm words of advice from his mentor, Finnigan Lance, which echoed through the stillness of his mind.

Count carefully. Steady and balanced.

A rigid chill in the air ran across his shoulders despite the sweater layered over his tunic. Flickering candles crusted over with boonwax drippings dimly lit the dank, meager battle zone. The hewen-wood stool he sat on could hardly be considered comfortable. A solemn tune washed over the crowded room from the fiddler tucked in the corner. The aged yellow nim antlers mounted on the wall cast ghostly shadows over the weathered planks of the inn, while stringed banners of colorful feanet hens bound upside down by their feet seemed to peer down at him with disapproval.

Yet, Leer never felt more at home.

"Are you plannin' to make yer move within my lifetime, Boy?"

The surly voice of Leer's opponent sliced through Leer's concentrated focus like a knife. His dark eyes flicked upward, taking in the man seated across from him with barely concealed disdain.

"You believe me to fail, Bilby," Leer remarked, a dark, thick brow arching as he eyed his competitor.

"I believe you to be backed into a corner like a whelp," Marcus Bilby replied, giving a small, dark-toothed grin. "I believe yer with no place to go but down by my boots, beggin' for mercy."

Waves of chuckling ensued around them, Bilby's supporters clanking their mugs of ale together in agreement.

Leer idly stroked his stubble covered jaw with a smirk, wetting his lips. "Hmm," he said, still holding the older man's gaze. "Two games in, you should know me better than that by now."

He raised his hand slightly as Bilby drew a breath he failed to hide. Leer smiled as he felt Bilby's gray eyes lock on him, watching his every move with renewed interest. On the right side of the beautifully detailed cylas wood tafl board stood an unassuming game piece. So far, Leer had managed to prevent drawing Bilby's attention to this strategically important, but yet unused pawn. Leer now thoughtfully thumbed this piece, planning his next move. The path he chose to shift the pawn surprised Bilby, who watched with his lips pressed together, perched on the edge of his seat.

As Leer withdrew, Bilby excitedly moved his chosen piece, sliding the pure white painted bone a block closer to his goal of reaching the board's edge.

"Hah!" he squealed, leaning back and folding his thick arms over his plump stomach. "I can see the apprentice still has much to learn from the master."

Leer was more than aware of his current position within the game. Two of his three remaining black pawns were on the approach to Bilby's white king pawn. Leer hoped he could use his rogue from the right to block in the king, but there was still a distance to go. Early on in the game, Leer executed a flamboyant line of attack, knowing he could find himself in such a precarious position. He reasoned that if he were successful, his victory would taste that much sweeter.

"Steady, Bilby," Leer advised.

Leer watched the older man's wiry brow lift in doubt. "Yer blinder than my papa if you think you've room for escape."

"Aye, that's true for two of my men at present."

"You mean to tell me that you put yer hope in one piece on the wrong side of the board?"

"I don't have hope. I'm sure of it."

The thick stench of hops and musky sweat enveloped Leer as Bilby leaned in; Leer's nose wrinkled. "It's impossible," Bilby challenged. "There isn't a hope under the sun for yer rogue piece to catch my king before he reaches the corner."

"Are you certain?" Leer countered in an even tone.

The candlelight flickered as the surrounding patrons of the inn shifted their positions. A murmured hum of questioning rose from the crowd, buzzing with curiosity.

Bilby squared his shoulders, his fat knuckle brushing against his right nostril with a quick swipe. "Of course I am."

Leer gestured to the board as he pushed up his sleeves. "Then shall we continue the game so I might rightfully congratulate you?"

"As certain as Hiline is the greatest nation, he'll lose," a man snorted in the back, raising his ale mug victoriously.

"Gentlemen," Leer said, keeping his eyes on Bilby, "what's life without risk?"

"Show him, Marcus," another smaller man encouraged. "Let the daft boy have his lesson."

"Mop the floor with him, at's what you'll do," another agreed.

"Stupid whelp is askin' for a loss."

Enthusiastic cheers in Bilby's favor erupted from the crowd. Leer gripped the twisted silver handle of his ale mug and took a casual sip.

"Alright," Bilby shouted, raising his hand to silence the audience. His tongue ran over a chapped bottom lip surrounded by dirt-streaked gray whiskers. "Yer move."

Leer set his cup down with a growing smile. "Aye," he agreed, clearing his throat. "But you should know, I'm a man who simply hates to lose."

"Then yer also an idiot, because losin' is all you'll do now, Boy."

Leer shrugged. "I'd just hate for you to be disappointed."

"Disappointed how?"

"Disappointed by me breaking your clean record in this inn."

Bilby laughed throatily. "Boy, I'll lay three extra coins on yer failure," he declared, fishing the worn currency from his waist pouch and slapping it on the table, the game board rattling in response.

Leer glanced down at the money. "It's not your coins I want as my prize."

"My wench, then?"

"Nay."

"Go on, then—what will you 'require' should you win?" Bilby asked with a chuckle.

Leer swallowed, keeping his eyes locked on the older man's in front of him. "Everything you know about the Grimbarror."

A hush fell over the inn; the fiddle music screeched to an abrupt halt.

Bilby's eyes narrowed. "What did you say?" he asked.

"I said," Leer repeated, "I wish to know everything you know about the Grimbarror."

Callous laughter exploded through the men and few barmaids present, ripples of mockery piercing Leer's ears.

"You well-washed loon," Bilby cackled, slapping his knee through his amusement. "You wish to hear fairy tales, is that it?"

Leer's jaw flexed as he clamped his molars together. "I seek the truth."

"Hah!" Bilby screeched. "Would you like a cup of warm milk to go with your bedtime story, Boy?"

Leer squeezed his eyes shut briefly, trying to push away the reverberating voices around him. "Are you, or are you not, the Marcus Bilby that Finnigan Lance spoke of?" he demanded. "The one whose life he saved?"

Another wave of eerie silence fell over the inn. Bilby leaned in, gripping the table with white knuckles. "What name did you say?" he asked.

"Finnigan Lance," Leer enunciated.

"Curse you for speaking that name," Bilby snarled, spitting on the ground.

"Cheating scoundrel, he was," a man bellowed from the rear of the crowd.

"Nothin' but a drink bloated habbersnitch." another agreed.

"You'd better have good reason for speaking that name in this place, Boy," Bilby warned, leaning forward.

"He *wasn't* a cheat," Leer snapped. "You peddled furs with him. You worked with him, and he saved your life from insurgents. And I do believe you owe him a favor."

A murmur trickled through the crowd, sending Bilby into visible panic as his peers reacted to the revelation.

"And what?" Bilby retorted with a scoff. "Lance has come back from the dead to claim it?"

Leer's jaw flexed. Finnigan's death was still fresh in his mind; it had not been long since he found his bloodied, mauled corpse. "Nay. You'll pay your debt to him through answering my questions."

Bilby's eyes narrowed. "And just who are *you* to lay claim to any favors?"

Leer held his gaze. "His son."

"Liar!" Bilby screeched, smacking the table. "He never had a child, you daft boy." He took up his mug and knocked back a long swig of ale. "Whoever you are, yer sorry arse needs to make yer move," he encouraged with his chin after setting the mug down. "I shan't be owin' you a single bit once this game is through. Instead, you'll be muckin' my stalls for free for the rest of the winter."

"Aye, well, just in case, my winnings will be all he told you about the Vei."

Bilby chuckled. "Sure, Boy. Go ahead. Make yer move."

Leer shifted his focus back down to the board. With much less hesitance, he slid his last rogue pawn toward Bilby's unguarded king, only pausing as Bilby took his rightful turns to expectantly move his king further toward Leer's far left corner of the board. Leer could hear Bilby's breath quicken in anticipation.

I tried to warn you.

His careful calculations had not betrayed him. Leer saw Bilby's eyes grow round as their game pieces met. Through his haste to reach the border, Leer had pinned Bilby's king between two of his already trapped pawns and his rogue from the right, automatically winning the game.

"Ahhh!" Bilby shrieked in disgust, throwing his arms up as he stood abruptly from the table.

"Careful," Leer warned with a smug grin, crossing his booted feet at the ankles. "We shouldn't want the entirety of Enton to know of your defeat."

"You whoreson," Bilby snapped, raising a bowed knife he retrieved from his belt toward him. "You cheated."

Leer sprung back, his hands in the air as he stood and moved away from his stool. "I did no such thing," he insisted, eyes narrowed. "It's not my fault you weren't focused."

"You should think this is quite amusing, shouldn't you?" Bilby sneered, coming around the table, knife outstretched toward Leer. "Stickin' around, makin' a fool of me, just like that habbersnitch, Lance…"

"Actually, all I had in mind was collecting my information and being on my way."

"The only thing you'll be collectin' is yer guts from the floor, you dillyburt."

Bilby slashed the knife in the direction of Leer's abdomen with a shrill battle cry. Leer jumped away from the swing, cursing under his breath. *No sword,* he reminded himself with a grimace. He quickly calculated the distance he'd need to cover before reaching the door: *Too many bodies. They'll never let me pass.*

A swirl of panic began to build in his mind. *How? How do I get out?*

To his right, he heard the fireplace crackle and pop behind him as the raging flames ate through the dried timber. A stream of collected thoughts coalesced, giving him startling clarity. *Well, if this loon wants a challenge, then a challenge he shall get.*

"Steady now, Bilby," Leer taunted with a grin. "I'm but a single unarmed man. Surely, as favored as you are here, you needn't worry so." Leer sidestepped to his right, noting the expression on Bilby's face. "Unless, of course, you consider me superior. Then I suppose there would be cause for worry." He chuckled. "And judging from the scowl you're wearing, I assume you don't."

Leer reached behind himself, his hands brushing against the cold stone of the fireplace edge. *Steady and balanced,* he reminded himself, the pads of his fingers digging into the textured surface. *Where is it? Maybe just a bit further...*

He continued to shift right until his shoulder collided with the edge of the fireplace wall, his fingers brushing against a piece of rope. *There you are.*

He had arrived.

"Well then," Leer said with a grin as he clamped down on the rope behind himself, "I do believe that this is where we part ways."

"You ain't goin' anywhere, habbersnitch," Bilby growled.

Just as I expected, Leer thought as he watched Bilby charge at him. He dove low between Bilby's thick legs, entangling him using the timber sling he yanked from the hook on the wall behind him. Leer grunted from the sheer effort it took to bring the much larger man down to his knees. Bilby groaned as Leer pulled him down flat on his stomach. Leer kept his left knee pressed on Bilby's back, bracing against the bigger man's grunted straining.

"Sorry," Leer apologized curtly, snatching Bilby's knife from his sweaty palm.

"You cod-boiled snitch," Bilby screamed. "I'll skin you like the dillyburt you are."

"Aye, I'm sure you'd like to," Leer agreed as he caught his breath. "You do surprise me, Bilby. I wouldn't have taken you to be such a spry fellow, but rather one more fond of meals than combat practice."

Leer could feel the eyes of the patrons on him. "I won fairly," he stated with resonance, sensing their hesitance at challenging him. "And by the agreement we made, I require my winnings, and then I'll be on my way."

"As sure as the sun sets to the left of the Fell, Boy," Bilby seethed under his breath, "I'll have yer—"

"You know," Leer interrupted, gritting his teeth against the struggling man he kept bound, "let's discuss that. Let's discuss the Fell, shall we?"

"I ain't tellin' you a mite."

Leer grimaced, annoyed at the phlegm Bilby spat onto his right boot. "You *will* tell me what I wish to know," Leer reminded him in a low tone, bending closer to Bilby's ear. "Otherwise, it'll be *your* hide skinned."

"Be damned to the underworld."

"Tell me what you know about the Grimbarror."

A gust of winter wind ripped through the inn as the front door swung open. Leer kept his focus on Bilby, even though the skin on his hands burned from squeezing the ropes.

"Tell me," he demanded, pressing his knee into Bilby's back.

"Release him," Leer heard a man bellow behind him. He ignored him, his heart thumping against his ribs, adrenaline coursing through his veins.

"Tell me!" Leer shouted, saliva flinging from his mouth through his rage. He heard the heavy thudding of boots filling the space behind him as the horrified crowd shifted to make room.

"Release him, Boy," the man demanded again; Leer heard the distinct ring of a sword being unsheathed.

The guards ripped Leer upward from Bilby. Leer growled and shrugged against them in protest, which resulted in his neck pulled taut by a hand gripping his thick blond hair.

"He owes me information," Leer protested, wincing as the guard braced him.

Leer felt the slick blade of a sword against the right side of his throat.

"This arse brought it on himself," Leer argued. "I want my information," he snarled, struggling against the guard who held him as he watched Bilby brush off his sweater in disgust.

"You will show the proper respect," the guard warned.

"And you'll let me be to settle my own business."

The guard holding Leer kneed him in the back. With a groan, Leer crashed to the ground on his shins.

"Show the proper respect, you rind," the guard who held him snapped.

Freed from the blade to his neck, Leer countered the attack of his captor by pulling and flipping the guard over his own body. The guard landed with a thud in front of him. As Leer stood, the second guard, seemingly more important in rank, seized him, pressing his sword against Leer's jugular. From the quick glimpse he saw of the man's tunic and sashes, Leer knew exactly who was clamping his fingers around him.

"Citizens," the guard began. "My name is Lieutenant James Shelton Doyle. If anyone has any objection to this man's arrest, or information to support his innocence, speak now."

The thick wall of patrons remained silent.

"Know that King Gresham does not condone such unwarranted violence," Lieutenant Doyle continued. "This...mongrel...will be dealt with according to the law. As you were."

"Damn near broke my ribs, he did," Bilby whined, his gray eyes squinted as he glared at Leer.

"I can assure you, Sir, that he will be dealt with. As you were," the Lieutenant barked.

Hummed conversation rose from the onlookers as Lieutenant Doyle yanked Leer to his feet. Leer's worn boots scraped against the floor planks as he fought his forced exit.

"This isn't over, Bilby," Leer warned, fighting to look back at Bilby. "You will pay your debt to Finnigan."

The bitter winter air assaulted Leer's face as Lieutenant Doyle shoved him outside. With a grunt, the Lieutenant threw him forward into a waiting wall of bodies. Snarling like a wild animal, Leer twisted and thrashed, trying to release himself from the guards' iron grip.

"Your name," Lieutenant Doyle demanded.

One of the guards to the Lieutenant's rear threw Leer's coat and scarf at him. Leer turned his cheek, the clothing slapping against his face before it dropped to the ground by his boots. "Screwley of Ewe," Leer replied curtly.

Lieutenant Doyle's eyes narrowed. He stepped closer, examining Leer like a specimen. He nodded once to one of the men who held him, who then punched Leer in the stomach. Leer coughed, spit flying from his mouth in bursts as his abdomen clenched against the assault.

"What's your business with Marcus Bilby?" the Lieutenant asked.

Leer's jaw clenched; he remained silent.

"I would choose to answer, Boy," Lieutenant Doyle warned. "It might be the only thing to save you from box time."

"I wanted to chat," Leer stated. He growled after receiving another punch to his side.

"Show respect, rind," one of the guards who held him ordered.

"I wanted to chat, *Sir*," Leer spat.

"About what?"

Leer's nostrils flared through his silence.

"About what?" Lieutenant Doyle repeated, stepping closer.

"The Fell," Leer snapped.

The Lieutenant laughed, the suddenness of it catching Leer off-guard. "Oh for the love of Hiline, you're Private Boxwell, aren't you?" He shook his head. "Yes, you must be Boxwell." Lieutenant Doyle smirked. "I suppose your time as a scout on the western borders has left you with too much time to think. Although displays of defiance and brazen idiocy in the King's guards aren't rewarded, you've some gall, I'll grant you that much."

"For what, Sir? Not heeling as a dog?" Leer asked.

"For not hiding your miserably paranoid fixations in front of me," Lieutenant Doyle corrected in a sharply edged tone. "You've recently developed quite the reputation among your peers." He paused. "I won't lie and say it's been a pleasure squaring off with you."

"It seemed like you took great pleasure in showing your superiority in front of the peasants, Sir."

The guard struck Leer again in the ribs. Leer grimaced, clenching his jaw.

"My great pleasure would be in ending your miserable, paranoid life," the Lieutenant replied.

Leer drew a sharp breath through his nose, clamping his molars together in heated silence.

"Tell me, Boy," Lieutenant Doyle asked, "what is it that makes you an expert on the Grimbarror? Is it personal experience?"

"…Yes."

Lieutenant Doyle's eyes narrowed. "What sort of experience?"

Leer ground his molars as he delayed his reply, analyzing the Lieutenant. *Why should you care, if you say they are merely tales?*

"Answer your Lieutenant," one of the other guards holding him snarled.

"My mentor, Finnigan Lance, died by it," Leer yelled, nostrils flared.

"Finnigan Lance," Lieutenant Doyle repeated.

"Aye."

"The same Finnigan Lance who served as a furrier to King Gresham?"

"Aye."

"…The same Finnigan Lance who had a reputation for closing a tavern nearly every night of the week?"

Leer remained silent.

"So, you say you know this beast killed him. How?"

"His body was mauled. No decent man could've done what was done to him."

Lieutenant Doyle pursed his lips, eying Leer. "Couldn't it have been a wild beast *other* than your creature?"

Silence enveloped them, the cold winter air punctuating the stiffness.

"So, you believe your mentor, as it were, was mauled by a fantasy creature?" Lieutenant Doyle's brows arched, his lips curving to a small grin. "And why would the creature feel it necessary to travel the distance to Hiline solely to kill a single drunken man?"

Leer chewed on his bottom lip, looking away as he stewed.

"Tell me," the Lieutenant continued, "what could have been so important about a furrier to the king? Did Finnigan slay more than the beast's allotted amount of tragurns?"

"I know what I saw," Leer argued, his gaze returning to Lieutenant Doyle, who laughed, shaking his head.

"Then you deserve the high watch for the rest of your pathetic existence." The Lieutenant's eyes flicked to the men holding Leer. "Let him go," he ordered.

Leer felt the men shift their weight behind him, their hesitance obvious. "Sir," one of them said, "he's outright flitbloached. Shouldn't we bring him to the box?"

"No," Lieutenant Doyle replied. "Surely this little boy has learned his lesson. He's no doubt worn out his welcome in Enton, anyway. See to it that he's posted in the west tower this eve."

"But, Sir—" another began.

"That's an order," the Lieutenant warned. "I've bigger shads to braise. The princess's averil is this eve, and I don't wish to waste any more breath on this fool. The solitude of high watch should be enough to knock some sense into him."

Leer yanked his arms free the instant he felt the guards loosen their grip. He swept his coat and scarf from the ground, glaring at them in disgust as he moved away.

"Private," the Lieutenant said, halting Leer in his tracks. "I'd advise you to refrain from any more shenanigans that reflect badly on the King's army." Leer's chin dipped back toward his shoulder as he listened. "The next time, I won't be so generous."

"Yes, *Sir*," Leer hissed, stalking toward the narrow cobblestone street.

-2-

The cobbled walk marked the beginning of where Leer felt more comfortable. The usually soft and muddy road leading out of Enton—the largest city within the Royal Vale—was hard under his boots. The mud had solidified in the freezing air, now slick from the chipped ice covering it. Peddlers with stocked carts and tents filled most of the precarious paths carved, the rest of the area laden with untouched ice and snow. People navigated it themselves at their own risk. Although in Hiline, if one didn't know how to manage in the snow in winter, he wasn't expected to last long, anyway.

Leer weaved through the pathways, avoiding pushy sales pitches from humble peasant salesmen who lined the street. He shoved his gloved hands deep within his coat pockets, expertly bracing himself against both the cold and the guilt of his inability to help them.

His mind raged despite his outward silence. Bilby had slipped through the cracks. It had taken days to locate him. Leer knew Finnigan must have shared something with him. After all, Finnigan spoke about Bilby a few times. Surely Finnigan must have confided in him.

Then there was the strange occurrence of defeating an armed man with a piece of cloth. How? How had he managed to think to overpower a man with a knife using a timber sling?

Luck, Leer thought with a scowl. *Not that I've much of it other than with that.*

"Boxwell!"

He froze, his dark eyes scanning his surroundings. With his mossy brown scarf wrapped around his head, covering his ears, Leer had a hard time pinning down the location of the voice calling his name.

"Boxwell!" the voice came again ahead of him.

Leer squinted, blinded from the sun's glare off the crisp white snow covering everything around him.

"What should you need now, you oaf? Have you lost your vice again?" Leer called back, spotting the owner of the voice—a stout middle-aged man with russet hair and a blacksmith's apron. With a grin, he crossed toward him.

"Fine," the man said with a shrug, wearing a wrinkled scowl surrounded by a thick red beard. "I shan't care a bit if you freeze to death before the averil this eve."

"If you began to care, Jarle, I'd worry you had taken ill," Leer teased, closing in on his friend.

Jarle cracked a small, gap-toothed grin, tilting his round head to the rickety blacksmith's shop door behind himself. "Get your ezel inside. I've got a bit of Hedda's *surprise stew* left in my tin."

Leer kicked the excess snow off his boots before ducking into the dank space. He moved to the fire, which glowed with controlled rage in the center of the room, simultaneously stripping off layers of outerwear and weaving through piles of tools and scrap iron to reach it.

"I am afraid to know what the surprise is this time," Leer joked, rubbing his palms together with relief. The fire popped as Jarle fed it another log.

Jarle tried to hide the small grin at the corners of his bearded mouth. "Careful, lad. It ain't be Hedda's fault you can't stomach a bit of habbersnitch."

"It isn't the habbersnitches I take issue with, but rather their little pokey bones when I sip my broth."

"Ya," Jarle said with an honest nod of agreement. "It be true Hedda's eyes have dimmed a bit."

Leer's lips curled upward. "A bit? She married a lump like you. I'd say the woman is outright blind." Jarle's eyes narrowed; Leer laughed. "Oh, come on, now. Don't be a lass about it."

"'Least I have myself a wife," Jarle replied indignantly.

"Aye, well I'd rather not be responsible for anyone but myself."

Jarle snatched a large mallet from his workbench in one hand, while using a grip in the other to withdraw a red hot piece of iron from the forge, bringing it to his work surface. He began working the metal, the steady ping and clink of it oddly soothing to Leer.

"You can't keep gallivanting around with courtesans forever, pretending you like empty canoodles." Jarle paused, waggling his eyebrows. "You'll go broke, besides. A fire is nice, but there's nothing like the warmth of a wife, ya?"

Leer sipped the vermin stew broth, relishing how the thick, salty liquid coated his insides with heat.

"Perhaps," he mumbled.

"What ever happened to that one lass?" Jarle paused, his hammer hand gesturing toward his chest. "The one with the straw colored hair and the large *bobbingar*?"

Leer's nose wrinkled. "She…" He sighed. "When she heard what I think, she thought me mad."

Jarle grunted, giving a small nod. "I'm sorry, *mijn zoon*. It's true her teeth resembled my cart mare's, but she still would have made a fair wife."

"You barely knew her."

"Well, she was an unpaid woman and she was with you. It's better than nothing."

Leer rolled his eyes. "I've got more important things to accomplish before I seek out a wife."

Jarle sighed, shaking his head, the red curls poking out from under his navy blue knitted cap. "You have to give it up, Boxwell," he advised with a huff, slamming the mallet onto the metal as he shaped it. "Soon there won't be a soul who will think you right, if you don't."

"I haven't got reason to give anything up."

"Isn't your reputation reason enough?"

Leer gave a small belch. "Nay, Jarle. My reputation is a cause long since lost."

Jarle frowned; he paused over his work. "It's a tale, Leer," he said gently, looking up at the young man across from him, seriousness in his eyes. "Those northerners have no special abilities to conjure. It's rubbish told by Hiline's greatest enemy to scare our armies."

"You deny the possibility, then?"

"Of a scaled beast-man who harnesses powerful magic?" Jarle scoffed. "*Mijn zoon*, I know your heart is

20

heavy. But it shan't be a beast you should pine for. If you want an enemy to hunt, then hunt nature herself."

"Nature." Leer wet his lips. "So nature, then, made a man with eyes that glow yellow?"

"Listen to me," Jarle warned, turning to Leer. "You walk a dangerous path with your beliefs. Not all tales are true, *mijn zoon.*"

Wiping his mouth with the back of his hand, Leer set the emptied tin down on a shelf behind him. "This one is," he assured, his eyes fixed on the shorter man in front of him.

"Leer—"

"I saw it, Jarle."

"I'm just asking you to consider—"

Leer's abrupt, angry shove away from the shelf he leaned against caused several of the materials it housed to rattle to the floor. He ran a hand through his hair, turning away from Jarle as he drew some sharp breaths.

"I saw it," Leer repeated through gritted teeth. "I saw the beast and it saw me."

"You saw a tragurn that eve," Jarle argued. "Finnigan died by a wild animal, not a monster."

"I know what I saw."

"Leer—"

"I know what I saw," Leer spat. "It wasn't at all natural, and it killed the only real family I ever had." His fingers flexed beside him. "All I care about in life is destroying that creature while making it suffer as much as I have. I won't rest until its dead." He smiled ruefully. "Then all of Hiline will know of the power that makes the Grimbarror." He met Jarle's eyes once again. "Perhaps after that, I won't be the madman they think me to be."

With a quick tug, Leer slipped on his mittens and wrapped his woolen scarf around his neck. As he headed for the door, Jarle intercepted him.

"Boxwell," Jarle said, taking Leer's elbow with a firm grip, "I don't think you crazy, ya?"

Leer allowed his face to soften a bit, knowing Jarle spoke the truth. "For now."

-3-

Leer closed his cottage door behind himself, shutting out the bellowing winter air. He sucked a long breath through his nostrils as he shut his eyes. Frenzied thoughts he left Jarle's shop with continued to swim around in his head, and he couldn't seem to rid himself of them, no matter how hard he tried.

With resignation, Leer removed his mittens and snatched a candle and flint from the nearby ledge, expertly drawing out a spark and lighting the wick to see his surroundings. Holding it in his hand, he crossed to his cot, eying the dark tunic that laid over it. His assigned living quarters were meager to say the least; within three strides, he reached the straw mattress. With the candle seated on a shelf, he tossed his mittens, scarf and coat on his bed and swept up the heavy tunic, drawing it over his undershirt. He smoothed it down, the thick cobalt wool feeling unusually oppressive. His guard issued long sword glimmered in the filtered sunlight streaming through the cabin's window slats.

Leer sighed and picked up the sword that rested in its sheath. He noticed how his mind began to clear as he secured the belt over his shoulder and around his waist—the welcomed weight of the weapon on his hip distracted him.

Perhaps I should be concerned that I enjoy carrying a sword as much as I do.

He smirked, straightening up to view his reflection in the splintered looking glass that hung on the wall near his wash bucket.

Or perhaps not.

Nearby shouting distracted Leer from his thoughts, the frenzied voices of castle servants and guards barely muffled through his cottage walls as they passed. The averil to celebrate the memory of Prince Edward Gresham, and welcome Princess Maegan Gresham into her new station as throne heir, was this eve.

Leer sighed, sitting on the straw mattress. Prince Edward had indeed died a terrible death—murdered at the hands of insurgents, a growing ragtag group of mercenaries who had long since fled Hiline to the Cursed Waste of Sortaria in an effort to establish their own kingdom. The ongoing battle between the royal kingdom and the insurgents was seen as a quarrel among brothers, since the insurgents didn't have any true power against the mass of trained army guards. However, in light of Edward's death, the quarrel had become war.

As determined by the law, Princess Maegan would now succeed King Gresham as queen. A fragile and pale creature with less experience in leadership than a stable boy would lead the nation.

The averil will surely be full of eager suitors. Not that any beyond Lieutenant Doyle should truly have a chance at her hand.

Perhaps at one time, Leer would've considered himself one of those suitors. For the present moment, though, Finnigan's death consumed his life.

Finnigan.

The mere thought of his name plagued his mind with horrid images of the older man's sliced body. With a sniff, Leer reached under his straw mattress and fished around until his fingertips made contact with soft leather. He yanked the book from its hiding place and ran his hands over the hide covering it.

Finnigan's journal.

When Leer sorted through Finnigan's cottage just after Finnigan's death, he found the journal to be the only possession Finnigan had worth keeping. The rest he sold for mere pence to fund his trip to the Fell.

Leer brushed his fingers over the cover of the journal, tracing the odd pattern on the nimskin. A rather grotesque face with eyes that made the hairs on the back of Leer's neck stand on end was tooled into the cover. Whether the face was human or animal, he couldn't decide, nor why it should have ever been on the journal in the first place.

Whatever it is, it's certainly vile. He sighed. *There must be some way to discover the truth through Finnigan's words. Why else should he keep them if not?*

Buisines played by court musicians bellowed, interrupting him. Leer looked up, a groan rumbling in his throat. It was the call for all shift changes. With a heavy sigh, he tucked the journal back into its hiding place and stood, squaring his shoulders.

High watch in the dead of winter awaits.

The high tower was the least coveted guard position, usually assigned to new apprentices who had yet to earn their place in rank. As a scout for the king during his travels, Leer abhorred the idea of being trapped in a tower while less competent guards protected the site of the averil.

Too small, he inwardly grumbled, tossing his small gwyd horn aside. *Too cramped.*

Raw winds and swirls of snow sweeping up from tree branches assaulted the sparsely covered tower, which was barely large enough to accommodate a single man carrying a sword and a signal bugle made from a mountain gwyd's crooked horn. Leer grit his teeth as he peered through the small tower opening. Honey yellow rays of the setting sun cut across the landscape. He heard the conflicting melodies of mourning and celebration in the distance, bagpipes and fiddles coming to life under skilled masters. People from all of Hiline's regions would come to the Vale; some of the more remote groups sent small delegations to represent them. Wearing dark cloaks, they would crowd the streets to watch the driving celks escort the cart carrying the prince's body. The celks would solemnly march his body to its final place of rest, the royal family's crypt adjacent to the castle—the same place he found Finnigan's discarded body after returning from a scouting excursion to the northeast upon Prince Edward's death.

Leer couldn't ascertain if the overwhelming chills that prickled his body was from the weather, or from the memories that plagued his consciousness.

He shifted his eyes to the blackening outline of the Fell. The monstrous Sortarian Mountain was rather intimidating despite the blanket of darkness washing over its two tooth-like peaks. His jaw flexed, his throat bobbing as he swallowed back his anger.

Had it not been for such evil, Finnigan would still be here.

Finnigan had told Leer stories of how the Sortarians, Hiline's northern neighbors, had mastered the art of manipulation through the Vei, the ancient practice of channeling both good and evil from within. Only an unselfish mind could protect the Vei's finicky, unpredictable balance. It needed a skilled master with unparalleled focus on good to tame it. Conversely, those who attempted to harness its power for evil would grow in strength and become the Grimbarror.

No one had seen any trace of the Vei's presence for decades. Most believed it to be a long dead art; some even claimed it was a myth altogether. But not Finnigan. For whatever reason, he was convinced that not only was it real, but it was still possible to access.

But Finnigan died before Leer could ever tell him he was right.

Finnigan's eyes were frozen open in shock and horror when Leer found him. Leer tied one of his scarves around the older man's head to give him the peace he deserved.

And that's when he saw a figure in the distance, in the tree line not far from Finnigan's abandoned body—a man, larger than he had ever seen. A glow around him permeated the thick darkness of the night, highlighting the scales he bore on his face and the claws that ended his fingertips. The rims of his eyes were yellow, like the bile that crept up Leer's throat, threatening to escape.

He was the power no one believed in.

As quickly as it seemed to appear, the beast vanished in a ball of white light so bright, Leer's eyes watered instantly.

Leer fished some jerky out from his waist pouch and tore at it with his teeth, his chest tightening as he fought his anger.

Only tales. It's much more than mere tales, Hiline.

Time crept by, while ounces of Leer's patience faded with each passing moment. The sun was nearly shrouded by the Fell on its journey to the rim of the earth when a distant steady, white glow in the sky made Leer's heart stop. It drew closer with each breath, and his stomach sank with familiar dread. He had seen that powerful energy only once before:

The night Finnigan died.

"Shit," he breathed, dropping forward to his knees to have a better look. There was no mistaking what he saw. He knew what the odd light signaled, whether anyone decided to take him seriously or not.

He fumbled about, panicking as he sought the gwyd horn he had rendered useless. When he finally pawed the horn, he licked his lips and brought it to his mouth, his eyes never leaving the haunting white light.

He froze.

He held his breath in preparation to sound the alarm, but he couldn't release it. He was stunned, transfixed by the light as it grew. An orb of pure light, like a dim miniature sun or a vast lit snowflake.

Leer drew another full breath, blowing into the gwyd's horn with power, shuddering as he heard the eerie bellow of the call. Again he sounded the horn, then three times more following in short, panicked bursts until he heard another soldier calling out to him from the ladder on the outside of the tower.

"Private, what is it? Is it insurgents?"

"Nay," Leer replied, squeezing his sword hilt. He turned and left the tower, facing the fellow soldier who had scaled the ladder to the small platform outside of it. "Notify the king's guard. Get the Lieutenant. All of the commanding officers. Immediately!"

"Who are you to—" the soldier began to interject.

"Listen to me," Leer urged, gripping the man's cobalt vest. "Just do as I say should you wish to live this night."

The soldier brushed Leer's hand off himself. "Tell me what you saw."

"Just—"

"Private!"

Leer cringed when he heard Lieutenant Doyle's voice from below. He bypassed the guard on the platform and took hold of the long, thick rope hanging on the side of the tower, sliding to the ground to the Lieutenant's side. The Lieutenant wore his finest tunic, each knob of brass polished, his detailed sword strapped tightly to his side.

"Private, what is the meaning of the alarm?" Lieutenant Doyle demanded, seriousness in his eyes.

"You need to go to the king, the princess," Leer said, his words tripping over each other. "You need to get them to safety. I'll gather the other guards and—"

"Boxwell," Lieutenant Doyle interrupted, grabbing his arm. "I don't take orders from you. Now, tell me what you saw."

Leer chewed the inside of his cheek briefly as he considered his options.

Blast, he inwardly groaned.

With a deep breath, he eyed the Lieutenant. "The Grimbarror," he replied with darkness in his voice.

The delay before Lieutenant Doyle's laughter made it sting Leer that much more.

"I'll be damned," Lieutenant Doyle said with a shake of his head, "you really are insane."

"We don't have time for this," Leer insisted, turning toward the direction of the averil. "If you won't protect our king and princess, then I will."

Lieutenant Doyle snatched Leer's arm, clamping down on his wrist. "How dare you, you scoundrel." He bent it backward as Leer tried to wriggle out of his grasp. "If you think you're setting a single foot near that averil, then you're sorely mistaken."

"Watch me."

Freed by a swift elbow to Lieutenant Doyle's gut, Leer lurched forward, scrambling toward the rising bonfires in the distance. Still, the Lieutenant tackled and pinned him to the ground, pressing his face mercilessly against the cold cobblestone with his knee.

"Guard," Lieutenant Doyle yelled above Leer, keeping him braced against the walk. As Leer fought, he saw a stampede of boots rush toward them. "Seize this man. Shackle him and put him in a cell immediately."

"Yes, Sir," a guard replied.

More hands apprehended Leer, snapping him up from the ground to stand. Cold irons slapped across his wrists, heavy chains laced around his arms.

"You're making a mistake," Leer growled, pulling against his bonds as the guards led him. "Do you hear me? You'll be sorry."

"The only thing I'm sorry about is not doing this sooner," Lieutenant Doyle replied through Leer's angry screams.

Golden dusk light filtered through the single window in Leer's musty cell; the slivers washed onto Leer's face as he tried to stretch himself high enough to peer out of the barred narrow rectangle in the outside wall high above him. He jumped, lunging toward the opening with outstretched arms, his fingers shy of making contact with the bars. He almost tumbled onto the ground before catching his footing, cursing under his breath as he kicked the straw underneath him in rage.

This is madness. I need to get out of here.

A man's voice in the blackened cell next to him disturbed Leer's fit. "I've seen a lot of you guard boys come in here to cool off. For as long as I've been in here, I can't say I've seen the likes of you."

Leer drew a deep breath through his nostrils, sighing. "I've surprised myself with how long I've stayed out of the box, too," he replied, his back still turned, shoulders slumped in defeat. "How long have you been in here?"

"Just about six months, I figure."

"Blast," Leer muttered, his breath visible in the cold air. "Well, you certainly ruffled enough feathers, I gather."

"I suppose being in the Vale will do that to a man," the man offered nonchalantly.

Leer's eyebrow rose. He turned toward the cell next to his, peering into the darkness. "What do you mean by that?"

He got his answer when the man stepped into the light next to the bars that divided the cells.

"You didn't figure I'd be one of your own, did you?" The sandy brown haired man laughed, propping his elbow on the bars that divided them; Leer saw a deep red half moon and triple slash tattoo on the fair skin of the man's left forearm. He gave Leer a small bow. "Bennett Falstad, from the insurgence…though from the look on your face, I'm guessing you already knew that."

Leer's skin crawled, his lips pursing in disgust. "It's not hard to see a roach on the straw."

Bennett sighed, rolling his eyes. "Ah yes, the ol' 'roach' compliment. Lovely. Like I haven't heard that one before. 'Suppose now you won't be telling me your name, hmm?"

"Leave me be," Leer growled.

"Tell me, Blue," Bennett continued, leaning on the bars with a grin as Leer turned away, "what has you stuck in the box this fine evening? You certainly don't smell of drink, though you're acting a bit of a fool." Leer heard Bennett laugh in response to his silence. "Well, I'll share a secret with you—one doesn't sit in a dank place like this for nearly six months without learning a few things about observing people."

"I don't care to hear anything from the likes of you," Leer snapped over his shoulder, spitting on the ground for emphasis.

"I figured," Bennett said. "Ah, well. 'Tis a shame, really. Might have been able to at least give you a bit of comfort to know you're not alone."

Leer shifted his weight, his chin dipping down as he tried to avoid listening to Bennett.

"In fact," Bennett continued, "I'd say it's a true shame Hiline didn't have more faith in you. Had she had trust instead of doubt, she might have only owed you a grand debt after this eve was over rather than experiencing much worse."

With wide eyes, Leer spun around and charged toward the dividing bars. He managed to be quick enough to reach through them and grab at Bennett's tunic, clamping down on the deep hued fabric.

"What do you know of it?" he demanded, shaking with fury. When Bennett refused to answer, Leer slammed his shoulder and side against the rails. "Tell me what you know," he growled.

Bennett's laugh haunted Leer's mind. "You already know, my friend."

"Tell me!" Leer demanded. "Tell me what the insurgents have planned."

"It's not insurgents, and you know it, Blue."

Leer froze, still gripping Bennett's tunic. "then what—"

"The Grimbarror," Bennett interrupted with a smile, snickering as he watched Leer's face change. "Ah, yes. You *are* a believer. I told you I learned a few things down here."

"What do you know of the Grimbarror?"

"Not everyone refuses to believe, Blue."

Leer took a deep pausing breath as he searched Bennett's eyes. "You've taken our prince. Should you wish to take the entire royal family?"

"Stop denying what you know," Bennett snapped. "You know insurgents aren't to blame for what should come this eve." He paused, his glance flicking toward the small window. "It's drawing nearer. I can feel the shift."

The shift?

Bennett's brows furrowed as he looked back to Leer. "Don't you feel it?" he asked.

"What's feeling got to do with anything?" Leer snapped.

"Why do you think I'm down here?" Bennett asked. "Do you think they'd keep me locked away underground for six months for robbing carriages?" He laughed. "It's not merely anything. It's *everything*, Blue. Can't you feel it?"

Nay, Leer thought. *Aye. I don't know.*

Leer loosened his grip on Bennett slightly, trying to quench his dry throat with a swallow. "I saw the orb," he murmured, avoiding the answer.

Bennett's expression grew more serious. "It won't be long, then."

"How much time do we have?"

"Not much, I'm afraid."

Leer released Bennett and combed through his cell for a possible way out, kicking aside the stale straw and running his hands over the cold iron that held him in. "I've got to get out of here," he breathed. Heart racing as he realized there was no escape, he pounded on the bars. "Hey!" he shouted. "Let me out. We need to protect the king."

Nothing.

Leer slammed his hands against the bars even harder. "*Hey! Now!*" He paused when he heard a Hilinian guard who clutched a large club grumble as he came down the stairs and into view.

"Silence," the guard yelled, whacking the club on the rails. "I'll arrange a beating for you if that's what it takes."

"You've got to get the king and princess to safety," Leer begged.

"Whatever for?"

"There's to be an attack—"

"Oh right," the guard interrupted with a growl. "You're the mad one."

"No, wait! Please listen," Leer pleaded, reaching for the guard as he turned to leave.

A deafening crash resounded above them. Stone crumbled against iron and cascaded down with thunderous blasts that shook the ground the three men stood on. Each of them tumbled and fell, cast into darkness as stones doused the guard's torch when it toppled from his hand. Dust and debris shattered inward through the slotted window, while razor sharp pieces of iron and rock cut through the air.

The ground ceased shaking with unnatural suddenness. Both Leer and the guard rose to their feet, coughing as the dirt choked their lungs.

"It's here," Bennett whispered, slumped against the divisional bars.

An intense milky light, as peculiar as the sudden pause, poured into the cell through the window, blinding and painful to Leer's eyes.

"Bloody hell," the guard exclaimed, mouth gaped. "What is that?"

"Don't," Bennett managed between wheezes. "Don't...Don't look at it."

The guard didn't heed Bennett's advice, the man's gaze still trained on the blazing light piercing the dark cells.

"Blue!" Bennett called; Leer turned, watching him pull himself up to stand. "Don't be like your daft guard. See what it does to a man?"

Leer saw Bennett holding a hand over his torso, bright red blood oozing between his fingers from a noticeable wound in his chest. "The debris," Leer murmured, dumbstruck. "You're hurt…"

"Listen to me, Blue," Bennett snapped, knuckles white as he clutched at his torso. "Whatever…you do, do not…look at…the beast's light. It's a…trick. It wishes to…soothe you…before…it kills you." Bennett pressed his head against the iron bars, sliding down the cell wall to his knees onto the straw. Crimson fluid sputtered from his mouth as his hand fell limp from his wound, his eyes fluttering shut in defeat as he slumped over.

Leer's focus shifted to the guard's sudden wail. Leer's eyes widened as he watched raging white hot flames engulf the screaming guard and consume him alive. The guard's flailing hands slid down the bars of Leer's cell door as he collapsed, writhing in pain.

The silenced voices mixed with the smell of odd ash that followed sickened Leer. He swallowed back the bile that pushed up his throat for escape, hands shaking as the moldy straw ignited, fervent blazes licking a path across the block of cells. If he didn't escape soon, he would burn like the guard.

Hot iron, he thought, examining the glowing bars. *I can bend it.*

With a quick prayer, Leer shut his eyes and raised his boot to the iron, giving it a swift kick. He yelped in pain, feeling the burn of it even through the sole. He grunted, slamming his foot into the bar again, wincing against the strike of the heat. Despite the pain, he kept kicking, crying out in agony as the iron slowly spread, producing an opening seemingly large enough to slip through.

With careful urgency, Leer inched his way out of the cell through the meager path he created. The ground rattled from a second explosion, tossing Leer forward. He scraped his left cheek and arm across the hot iron. He screamed, the searing pain gripping him as he tried to steady himself so he didn't fall on the burning straw.

With every ounce of resolve he could muster, Leer leaped toward the stairwell exit. Limp by limp, he crawled up the steps; the terrorized screams of people above him became more pronounced toward the surface.

An agonizing pain like none he had ever felt struck his temples, and Leer cried out, clutching his head as he sank in defeat. Through the barrage of volts that belted him, an image of King Gresham and Princess Maegan flashed through his mind.

The averil.

Pushing through the strange pain, Leer shoved through the door at the top of the stairs. As quickly as he could, he ran through the castle and out onto the icy cobble walk and snowy paths, gasping for breath as frigid gusts of air blasted against him. A burst of sourceless flame surged through the open air in the courtyard; Leer barely missed it as he ducked out of its path. Ash and embers rained from the sky, the earth vibrating under him as he ran.

Close to the site of the averil, Leer tripped over his injured foot, crashing down onto the wet snow face first. With a groan, he slowly pushed his chest up, the cold snow biting through the flesh of his bare palms.

The beautiful glow of alabaster light poured down from above, washing over the fractals and casting an iridescent luminosity around him. Though he heard Bennett's voice in his mind, he couldn't help but gaze, hypnotized at the cleansing brightness.

"Mine," a voice came, its pitch terrifying and twisted, breaking Leer from his reverie. "Mine. I want it, I want what's mine."

Still, Leer couldn't speak; his mouth moved but words failed to form.

The voice moved away, continuing its demands through odd riddles. "To the demon born of days past, the price of power to be paid at last. The blood of the betrayer, spilt in the Fell, the debt of greed be forevermore quelled."

With all the willpower he had, Leer shut his eyes and rolled onto his side, groaning as he pushed himself up to stand. His feet slid on the ice as he scrambled closer to the averil, praying King Gresham and Princess Maegan were in hiding.

"Mine," he heard the voice cry again. "Mine! I want it, I want what's mine!"

As he reached a crumbled wall, a high-pitched scream stopped him in his tracks, his heart dropping.

"Princess Maegan," Leer whispered.

He surveyed the rubble. A quick glimpse of Princess Maegan standing still, red hair swaying, gave him a bit of comfort.

She's alive.

"Princess!" Leer shouted.

Pained and desperate, Leer scrambled onto frozen rock, pulling himself over the top and onto the other side. One failed calculation, and Leer's grip diminished. His body slammed against the icy broken wall as he slid violently downward.

When his body finally halted, Leer moved to stand, groaning as his burned foot made contact with the ground. Several yards ahead, he saw Princess Maegan's curvaceous body motionless, amethyst velvet garments billowing behind her, her gaze lifted toward the dazzling orb.

"Look away, Princess," Leer ordered, stumbling forward. "Look away!" He kept his eyes down, moving sloppily toward her as fast as he could bear.

"Mine, mine," the voice came again from ahead, softer in tone.

Leer's breath caught; he willed his feet to move faster. "Princess, look away! Don't look at the light!" He shuddered as he caught a glimpse of silhouetted horn edged wings arching with eerie grace behind a cloaked upright figure.

"Mine, mine," it snickered, the timbre eliciting gooseflesh across Leer's skin.

Still some distance from Princess Maegan, Leer stumbled as his boot caught on a hidden rock. He cursed, snow pushing its way into his nose and mouth as he fell forward onto his stomach.

"No!" he screamed, back arching as he looked back up toward Maegan.

He was too late.

The earth shook as the ground split open underneath him. Rock and dirt collapsed into itself, consuming everything in its path. Leer clawed at the snow as he tried to move to higher ground, but with a treacherous shudder, the trench swallowed him into its belly.

The last thing Leer saw as snow and ice rained down on him was Princess Maegan rising into the air, vanishing into the light.

-4-

As he woke, he heard familiar, distinct sounds: the clattering of pots, arguing, and the clank of a knife. He smelled habbersnitch stew and boiled herbs. There was no question where he was.

Leer's dark brown eyes slowly opened, making any confirmation of seeing the interior of Jarle and Hedda's small home unnecessary. He wasn't expecting the set of large blue eyes that peered down at him from less than six inches away.

"Mama!" the adolescent girl so close to his face yelled; Leer jumped in surprise. "The handsome man is awake."

Hedda rushed to the girl's side. "Oh *godzijdank*!" she breathed, dipping a rag into a nearby bucket and draping it across Leer's forehead. "Jarle! Jarle! Come quickly."

Jarle joined Hedda's side, panic streaked across his face. Leer blinked heavily under their gaze. "Speak to us, *mijn zoon*," Jarle goaded. "Say your name."

"I should…" Leer began in a hoarse whisper, "think my name to be…Leer Boxwell."

"Ya, ya, and who is your king?"

"King…Calvin…Gresham."

Jarle smiled. "Ya, that's good."

Memories flooded Leer with unforgiving haste. He bolted up from his cot. "The princess!" he exclaimed, grimacing under the sudden pain that struck him. "Ah, blast." Jarle guided him back down with a gentle, stern hand. "Jarle, the princess—"

"Ya," Jarle acknowledged. "'Tis been a while now, Leer. Be still."

Leer winced as he breathed, his fingers reaching slowly to his ribs to feel the various tightly wound bandages. "How long?"

"Five moons, now," Hedda murmured, gently stroking Leer's forehead with the dampened rag.

Leer's mouth gaped. "Five days?"

"Ya," Jarle said with a nod. "You were still as stone when they found you. They thought you were dead. You looked dead." He examined his friend with pursed lips. "You still do." Jarle flinched as Hedda smacked him across his bicep. "Well, he does," he defended, brows furrowed.

"You're just a wee pale," Hedda assured Leer. "Drink." She offered Leer a cup of steaming liquid. With effort, Leer propped himself on one elbow as she guided it to his lips. "Gytha flower tea. Very powerful. It will make you strong."

"Well, I think you're handsome," the girl to Hedda's right sighed dreamily.

"Thank you, my lady," Leer murmured, swallowing the bitter herbal brew with a twisted expression.

"Ya, well he's old enough to be your papa, Emma," Jarle scolded the teen.

Leer examined the blonde girl with an arched brow. "She can't be that young. How old do you believe me to be, Jarle?"

"Old enough to know when to stop looking," Jarle snapped with a glare.

"Aye," Leer replied with an uncomfortable smile, averting his eyes from Jarle's daughter.

"You took quite a spill, they figure," Hedda said to Leer. "The snow must have protected your bones well."

"Maybe the bones, but certainly not my head," Leer muttered.

"Maybe its nature giving you a little reminder of why you should start using some sense," Jarle offered, to which Leer rolled his eyes.

"What would you have had me do, Jarle? Nothing?"

"Don't fuss," Hedda scolded, guiding Leer back down onto the cot. "You still need rest."

"I can take care of him, Mama," Emma offered with a hopeful smile.

"Emma, be off with you," Jarle snapped, shooing his daughter away. Emma reluctantly left, taking one last glimpse of Leer before disappearing into the upper loft.

Jarle glanced over at Hedda, meeting her eyes; she slipped away in silence, removing the cloth from Leer's brow.

"Jarle," Leer said as he lay on the cot, running a hand through his matted hair, "is the king...?"

"Alive," Jarle confirmed, his head tilted down as he gazed at the floor. "Unlike much of his army."

Leer's nostrils flared. "Princess Maegan hasn't been found, I take it?" Jarle shook his head. "How many scouts has the king sent?"

Jarle sighed, delaying his response as his lips formed a thin line. "Nearly as many as he has."

"To where?"

"The Cursed Waste."

Leer leaned his head back with a groan. "Senseless twit, he's sent them the wrong way."

Jarle's brow wrinkled. "Perhaps you hit your head harder than we know."

"He's looking in the wrong place," Leer argued, meeting Jarle's eyes.

"The insurgents have waged war. They've made camps there before. How else should they know where they are keeping the princess?"

"Don't you see, Jarle? It's not insurgents at all."

"My boy, tell me you're not saying it's—"

Leer pushed himself up despite the pain, cringing as he sat upright to face Jarle. "I saw what it can do to a man," he snapped, his voice low. "I heard it speak. It spoke of a debt owed and—"

Jarle's hand covered his face as he rubbed it. "I can't listen to your madness, Leer," he exclaimed, his hands falling to his sides. "I can't. You're gone, Leer. Gone! There is no Grimbarror and there is no debt owed. There is a real army of insurgents from Sortaria who have taken the princess in order to gain control of Hiline." Jarle stood. "But there is *no* monster."

Leer followed suit. Getting to his feet was harder than he imagined it would be but he showed as little weakness as possible to Jarle. "You will deny the possibility when all that has happened is beyond the capability of men?"

"I will tell what I know to be true, and the Grimbarror is not such," Jarle retorted.

The two men eyed each other for a moment. Leer's stomach sank though his anger rose. "Tell me, Leer," Jarle asked, his voice softening, "when will you realize that Finnigan passed from a mere accident?"

"Do not speak to me of Finnigan," Leer snapped, taking a step closer to Jarle.

"You know as well as I that Finnigan wasn't murdered that night," Jarle continued despite Leer's rage. "When will you accept that?"

Without a word, Leer turned and snatched his shirt from a chair back near the fireplace. He yanked the tattered and torn tunic on over his head.

"Where shall you go, Leer?" Jarle asked with a sigh. When Leer didn't respond, he rubbed his eyes. "The army camp was destroyed when the earth split. There isn't much left standing." Leer paused in horror, his back still to Jarle. "I'm truly sorry, *mijn zoon*. The Vale is nothing but a shred of what she once was."

In pain, Leer sat on the edge of the bed, readying himself to put on his half burnt boots. He had to leave. He had to go to his cottage in the barracks.

Finnigan's journal. It has to be there.

The journal couldn't have been damaged. He didn't know what he would do if it were. It was all he had left of his mentor. It was the only material thing Leer cared about.

"Stop, will ya? For a moment," Jarle begged, grabbing Leer's arm as he sat next to him. "Look, I may not understand why you believe it all so, but the least I can do is give you things to wear before you chase after it. Wait here."

Jarle left, and a few minutes later returned with an armful of clothes, a pack, and another pair of boots. He handed Leer a soft, warm cream tunic and evergreen wool sweater.

"Hedda is vexed that I can't fit those anymore," Jarle murmured, watching Leer put the garments on. "At least you'll save me another scolding." He dropped the boots in front of the cot. "Not from the Hiline army, but these should do to keep frost from claiming all of your toes." He then laid a heavy dark brown overcoat, mittens, an embroidered cap and a wide blue scarf in a pile with reluctance, still clinging to the dark bag. "I guess I can't stop you, can I?"

"Nay, Jarle," Leer replied, finishing lacing the tall boots, "but you've kept me going, and that's more than most have done for me."

"Ya, well you've got a few sores you'll need to mind," Jarle grumbled, snagging a small jar near the bedside. "Otherwise, you won't be going far." Tossing it into the sack, he went to the opposite side of the cabin. "See to it you put the yeran bark ointment on your face, arm, and foot every day until it's used up," he instructed.

Leer blinked as he focused on his reflection in the looking glass near the cot. He traced his fingers along the long, red burn that striped his left cheek, swallowing back the memories of the cell. His face was sure to scar, but it would eventually heal. The two men that died weren't as fortunate.

How many more had been claimed by the monster from Sortaria?

He shifted his attention to Jarle, watching him open a few crocks that lined the knotted shelves above the small table in the dining area.

"I won't be giving you more than normal rations," Jarle said over his shoulder. "Perhaps it'll force you to return home to your senses. Where is it you'll be going, anyway?"

Leer shut his eyes for a moment, remembering the haunting riddle spoken by the frightening voice. He rubbed his still sore head. "The Fell," he finally said, yanking on his mittens.

Jarle's eyes widened as he looked back at Leer. "You *are* mad."

"Jarle—"

"Going to the blasted Fell, and in the dead of winter, no less? Have you fallen off the rim of the earth?"

"It's where she is, Jarle. Where it's keeping her."

"But—"

"It's where I must go," Leer interrupted, gritting his teeth as he stood once more. Fully dressed, he sighed deeply as he looked toward the front door of the home that sat on the outskirts of Enton.

"Idiot," Jarle said under his breath with a sigh. "Well, don't be completely crazy and forego a sword. Take the one with the white grip. I know she's the one you favor."

"I can't," Leer protested. The sword was a beautifully crafted masterpiece made with the finest cylas milkwood. Jarle could sell it to any pompous fool in the Vale to feed his family for the entire winter.

"It's been in my home too long," Jarle argued, taking the sword from the wood pegs it rested on above the fireplace. "Besides, if you're going to go on a failed mission, at least I know your death won't be from carrying a poorly made weapon."

Leer wrapped his fingers around the hilt, giving it a gentle squeeze; the milkwood shimmered in the light from the fireplace. He adjusted the leather sling it lived in across his broad back and over his hips. "You don't hold hope for me, then?" he asked Jarle quietly.

"I trust what I see," Jarle replied, not making eye contact with the younger man. "I thought you were a man of sense, of logic."

"I am."

"Nah, only for board games. What you are is a man who just took a blow to his skull that failed to knock any type of sense in him. A man with no room for anything but his own stubborn self."

Leer stepped toward Jarle. "You're angry, Jarle. Afraid for me."

"Ya," Jarle said with a nod. "That we can agree on."

Silence passed between them, thick and lingering as it ate away at Leer's comfort. "Go," Jarle whispered, his eyes fixed on the white grip of the sword Leer held in his mittened hand. "Go before I kill you myself to spare you the trouble of going to the Fell to die."

Leer saw the concern below the surface of Jarle's anger. "Aye," Leer replied, tucking the sword away. "I should hope you'd thank Hedda for me."

"Ya, ya."

"Jarle—"

"Go, Leer," Jarle interrupted, opening the door. The sun still shone, the rays bouncing off the crystals of the surrounding white snow. It wouldn't be long until nightfall, though. "Fortune be with you."

"And you, my brother," Leer replied, looking Jarle in the eyes for a lingering moment before slipping out of his door.

48

The moon hung over the hewens by the time Leer reached the edge of the Vale, where he witnessed what Jarle had warned him of. Pools of frozen water surrounded the charred barracks he once called home. Hiline's crested flag that had proudly sailed above hung with shame, torn in an unusual way. To Leer, it looked like from the claw of a giant tragurn. He knew, though, that a tragurn couldn't scale the slim pole the flag hung on—certainly not without leaving as much as a trace of its presence in the wood.

For all of the destruction, the Vale was eerily calm, few people daring to make eye contact as he passed them down the cobbled walk. They quietly sifted through the rubble of the village with sullen faces, trying to make sense of its existence. The crisp wind blew whispers of secrets through the trees. Nature had been the closest witness to what had transpired five days prior, and she remained as silent as the people she housed. She, too, refused to confess belief in something as horrific as the Grimbarror.

Leer reached his cottage, and not a moment too soon for his liking. The desolation of the town in the dark of night made him sick with dread for the morning. What else might he see when the sun rose? Leer promised himself he wouldn't be in the Vale to know. He only needed the journal from under his cot, and then he would be on his way.

The door hung ajar; the thatched roof had partially collapsed into the cottage.

"It stands," Leer breathed with hope.

He gripped his sword and braced himself as he kicked the door fully open, ready to challenge any looters he might encounter. When he assured himself he was alone, he allowed himself to grimace, the strike irritating his still healing burn.

He began toward his cot with a wince through the freshly fallen snow that managed to sneak in through the holes above. Leer pulled aside what roof debris he could, his muscles and head aching as he wrestled to access the underside of his bed.

Leer's fingers brushed against the binding of Finnigan's journal, and he breathed a heavy sigh of relief. He pulled the book from under the straw mattress, his knuckles whitening as he tightened his grip on it. He opened the pack Jarle had provided and slipped it inside, retying the laces and slipping it onto his back. It was safe.

Sword drawn, Leer spun around when he heard the cottage door open, finding himself facing two guards, one portly with blotchy skin, and the other shaped like an upright trough. Leer tightened his jaw, eyes wild as he readied himself to square off.

"At ease," the taller guard remarked, taking a casual step closer. "We would've killed you already if you were wanted dead."

"Then what do you want with me?" Leer snapped, tightening his grip on his sword.

"I'm under orders to take you to the king."

Leer paused, brows knitting together. "Of what use does he have for me?"

"Who knows," the stocky guard to the rear muttered.

Leer tilted his chin up, examining the lead guard. "'Suppose I shan't be trusting you?"

"Whether you know what he wants or not, it'd be in your best interest to have an audience with the man you serve under," the taller guard replied impatiently. "Besides, it's bloody cold out and I'd like to get a move on."

Stiff silence spread between them for a few lingering moments. With a swallow, Leer lowered his sword, tucking it back into its sheath as he held the guard's gaze. "Lead the way."

-5-

Wall torches lit the southern end of the castle, the flickering light casting elongated shadows over the dark halls. The damp air was thick with the same tension Leer felt in the streets when he first returned to the Vale, the usual reckless haughtiness replaced with tangible fear.

Leer followed behind the taller army guard, the shorter guard parallel to his right. Leer could feel his eyes on him, but he kept his focus forward. Though no one spoke, Leer couldn't stop the rush of questions from surging through his mind.

How does the king now deem me useful? Is this a trick? Does the king think me responsible for what happened to Princess Maegan?

Leer wiped his sweaty palms on his pants as he walked, drawing an inconspicuous breath. *Breathe, Boxwell,* he coached himself. *Steady. Just breathe.*

"How many perished?" Leer asked, taking a glance at the guard next to him, noting his solemn expression in response.

"Nearly three hundred with the army men, we figure," the guard replied. "Most burned to death."

Leer's lips parted. "Women and children, too?"

"Yes. A great deal of those attending the averil perished."

Leer swallowed back the sickness that grew inside, instead focusing his attention on the finely detailed portraits displayed in the hall. He caught glimpses of stiff-faced people through the flickering of torch flame, each seeming to stare at him with disdain. An image of fiery red hair surrounding a much more delicate, kind face made his stomach sink.

The princess.

He remembered the way she floated above him, disappearing into thin air as he slid down with the rock, unable to save her in time.

"Private."

Leer blinked, refocusing. He hadn't realized the guard had stopped in front of a large sable colored door with iron handles carefully crafted by skilled hands— perhaps Jarle's.

Jarle.

Leer squeezed his eyes shut. He hadn't meant to be so blunt. Leer had trouble relinquishing control and accepting possibilities other than his own. Whether the fight Leer engaged in was needed or not, it would be fought anyway.

"Boxwell," the guard snapped.

Leer nodded quickly, squaring his shoulders as the guard opened the door.

"Come on," the front guard ordered, gesturing Leer forward, "and give me your sword."

Leer froze in the doorway. "Nay," he argued under his breath.

"You will."

"It shan't leave my side."

"Enter," Leer heard the king say with resonance from across the room, the fire silhouetting the tall man draped in an elegant fur cloak. "Private Boxwell would be more useful armed, I think."

"Yes, Sire," the guard obliged without question, letting Leer enter the room before him.

Leer paced himself, his nerves getting the better of him. The sight of Lieutenant Doyle standing in the darkened corner beside the flickering hearth momentarily distracted him. A fire of hatred ignited within Leer. His pulse quickened, his fingers flexing as they hovered near the hilt of his sword.

What the hell do they wish to do to me?

From across the way, Lieutenant Doyle suggestively cleared his throat. Leer grit his teeth, dropping to one knee. He lowered his chin down to his thigh, nostrils flared as he bowed his head. He half expected to feel the cold blade of a sword against his neck.

"Rise, Private," he instead heard King Gresham instruct, to which Leer obeyed, his head still dipped downward. "Private," the king continued, "I need to see the eyes of the man who people say must have seen my daughter last."

Leer tensed; he ran his tongue across the backs of his teeth as he lifted his chin, glancing first to Lieutenant Doyle. Hesitantly, he shifted focus. The king's eyes were soft, warm.

"Private," King Gresham said, tilting his head back slightly. "Will what you speak to me be the truth sworn on your honor and your life?"

"Aye, my lord," Leer replied.

The king nodded. "Then you shall tell me everything you know regarding my daughter's kidnapping."

As Leer drew in a deep breath to begin, Lieutenant Doyle interrupted him. "Sire, if I may," he began with a scowl playing at the corners of his mouth, "this man was detained during his watch. He was manic and directly disobeyed orders."

"I am aware, Lieutenant," the king replied with a curt nod.

"My lord," Lieutenant Doyle objected, aghast, "two men were found dead—a guard, and an insurgent—in the area from which this man escaped. Soon after, your daughter went missing. And we've only just discovered the body of Marcus Bilby, who many witnessed as a victim of Private Boxwell's hysterics."

"His body?" Leer asked, his brows furrowing. "Marcus Bilby's?"

"So you claim to have no knowledge of how the man died, then?" Lieutenant Doyle challenged.

Marcus Bilby is dead. But how? And why?

"Nay," Leer snapped. "I wasn't near that man in recent days."

"Can anybody vouch for your story?"

"Aye, I've two to do so."

"Regardless, Sire," the Lieutenant continued, eying Leer, "this man should be hung for treason."

"Lieutenant," King Gresham replied with audible irritation, "I believe decisions of law and justice are to be made and ordered through me, are they not?"

The Lieutenant bowed his head as a sign of respect to the king. "Yes, my lord."

"Then I should like to hear what he has to say."

"Yes, my lord."

King Gresham turned to Leer. "Private, tell me everything you know regarding my daughter."

Leer drew smoke scented air through his nose, the warmth of the king's fireplace adding to his nervous sweat. "I'm afraid that what I know to be the truth is not what my lord wishes to hear," he admitted.

"Do you think I wish to hear lies, Private?" the king accused, nostrils flared.

"Nay, Sire. My lord seeks truth." Leer's gaze fell on Lieutenant Doyle. "As do each of the men before him."

"Then speak it, Private."

Leer swallowed. "My lord, I witnessed power beyond what Hiline knows to be considered truth, beyond the understanding of all men."

The king lifted his chin. "What power may that be? What weapon do the insurgents hold?"

Perfect. Here we go. "It's not a weapon, nor insurgents, Sire. In fact, it's not of ordinary men at all."

"Why, you infernal scum," the Lieutenant growled as he charged Leer, who drew his sword in defense, their blades clattering as they crossed. Leer couldn't help but notice the unusual purple hue of the Lieutenant's blade. It was unlike anything he had ever seen.

"Lieutenant, Private! Stand down," the king ordered with a snarl, causing both Leer and Lieutenant Doyle to freeze.

Leer panted as he tried to lower his pulse, his grip firm on his sword hilt. After a long moment, he tucked his sword away, his eyes fixed on the Lieutenant.

"Continue, Private," King Gresham said with a wave of his hand while Lieutenant Doyle returned his weapon to its sheath.

"Sire, the creature that has your daughter has taken her through some type of willing control," Leer began again, turning to the king. "I witnessed your guard fall victim to its manipulation. The man died from its power."

"How?" the king asked. Leer caught the Lieutenant's disgusted look out of the corner of his eye.

"I'm not sure I know, my lord," Leer admitted. "The man…simply caught flame."

"Preposterous," Lieutenant Doyle argued.

"Aye," Leer insisted, his eyes narrowing at Lieutenant Doyle. "I saw it with my own eyes. The man caught fire without being touched by nary a spark. And Marcus Bilby knew of what I speak."

"Regardless," Lieutenant Doyle interrupted with a sigh, "shouldn't the guard who came to your box have carried a torch to view you and the prisoner?"

"Aye," Leer replied, "but the fire that burnt the guard was hot enough to shape iron." His mouth tightened as he turned back to look at the king. "My lord, the fire was unnaturally hot. No one in Hiline could rationalize the events which I witnessed."

"So now you speak on behalf of, or even over, your king's appointed researchers?"

"I know what I saw."

"Enough," the king snapped. A hush fell over the room for a long moment, only challenged by the snap of burning timber in the hearth. "Private," he said to Leer, distinguishable doubt clouding his tone, "I asked you to speak to me the truth on your honor and your life."

"And I have, Sire," Leer pleaded, his eyes wild. With a deep breath, he withdrew his sword from its sheath and dropped to his knees in front of the king. Gingerly, he laid his sword at the king's feet. "If my lord doubts so much as a single thing I've said to be nothing but true, then it's his just decision to exact the law which I have sworn to uphold. Lest I be nothing but a deceiver, I should die by the hand of my king tonight without honor."

A long silence stretched before Leer heard the king shift his position. "Rise, Private," the king said in a low tone. "Retrieve your sword, for there shall be no blood shed on my accord. I put my faith in your word."

With great hesitance, Leer reclaimed his sword and tucked it away, his entire body quivering with pent up adrenaline. He swallowed, suppressing a shiver.

"Where does your collective knowledge place the beast?" King Gresham asked, glancing toward Lieutenant Doyle, then back to Leer.

"My mentor, Finnigan Lance, recorded all of his research in a journal. It contains everything he knew about the beast," Leer replied.

"A journal?" Lieutenant Doyle asked, his brow arching.

"Aye."

"We will need to see this journal, then, to see what information we can ascertain."

Leer studied the Lieutenant. "I can tell you the beast's lair is said to be in the heart of the Fell."

"The Fell?"

"Aye."

Lieutenant Doyle crossed his arms over his chest. "So essentially, you suggest going to Sortaria with reduced numbers while insurgents hold the upper hand? Traveling to the Fell in the dead of winter, no less? It's nothing more than the plan of a madman."

"Private, is this where you believe my daughter to be?" the king asked, ignoring the Lieutenant's remarks.

"Aye, it is, my lord," Leer confirmed.

"Then I shall send men there to scout the area and retrieve her."

"My lord," the Lieutenant interrupted, "with most of our scouts at the eastern wood, we have but a few to spare. If we send them to the Fell, should the Vale need protection, we would surely fail to give her it."

Leer watched King Gresham turn to the fire; his own eyes fell on the hypnotizing flames as he drew courage silently.

You needn't an army behind you, Boxwell. This is your chance—avenge Finnigan. Deliver the proof.

"I wish to go, if it pleases my lord," Leer finally announced. He felt the bitter glare of the Lieutenant on him, but kept his focus on the fire. "It's where I meant to travel to before speaking with you tonight."

"For what reason?" the king asked, still watching the fire.

"The same as my lord's."

King Gresham turned, examining Leer. "You plan to go to the Fell alone?"

"Aye, my lord."

The king's boots clicked on the marble as he paced away from the others. "No," King Gresham challenged, looking out through the window near where he stood. "You should not, Private."

Leer shook his head. "My lord, I wish to seek the princess and bring her to safety."

"And you shall," the king agreed. "Though," he added as Leer sighed in relief, "you shall not go alone. The Lieutenant shall accompany you."

"I should very much wish to retrieve the princess from harm," Lieutenant Doyle said with a slight bow.

Leer felt cool dread spread through his veins as his stomach sank. "My lord, I would think one man should be sufficient."

King Gresham faced Leer. "You challenge my command, Private?"

"Nay, my lord," Leer mumbled.

"Then it's settled. You'll both leave at dawn. Private, see to it you have packs readied on two driving celks."

"If I may, my lord," Leer interrupted, "the way to the Fell is certainly not one which a celk of any caliber can manage for too long in the snow."

"And now he speaks for the capability of animals," Lieutenant Doyle remarked.

"You suggest traveling on foot, then?" the king asked, baffled.

"Aye, my lord," Leer confirmed. "We'll be forced to abandon the animals once we've reached the Eyne Wood."

"Then you've been the way to the Fell?"

"Nay, Sire. I have only been as far as just east of Cabryog."

"Perhaps Finnigan Lance made the trip to the Fell before and recorded it within his journal," Lieutenant Doyle suggested.

Leer paused, the weight of the pack he carried heavier than it had been before.

"Did he make the trip, Private?" King Gresham asked.

"Aye," Leer replied after a pause.

"For what purpose?"

Leer thought it an odd question, given the circumstances. The genuine curiosity with which the king inquired rattled him. "Furs, my lord," he replied, holding the king's gaze. "But I'm afraid all the journal holds are records of legend, not a map."

With a soft nod, King Gresham returned his focus to the fire momentarily before walking away toward a rear exit. "Get rest, then. Dawn comes in but a short time."

-6-

First light bore a crimson and purple sky the next morning, the hues majestic as the sun slowly peeked over the tops of the tall hewens. Leer trekked through the snow, the tragurn-skin pack shifting between his broad shoulders with each step north.

Inhale, exhale. The cold air invigorated his lungs as he hiked, the prospects of the journey ahead adding to the excitement that ran through his body. Four days on foot to the base of the Fell, he figured—should the Lieutenant be able to keep up with the ambitious pace he set. Only another half day's journey after that to the heart.

"Mind telling me what you're planning on doing for camp this eve?" Leer heard Lieutenant Doyle ask.

Judging from the softness of the tone, Leer assumed the Lieutenant lagged behind him. A quick glance over his shoulder proved him right.

"The day's just begun, and you're already worried about resting?" Leer paused and asked with a smirk.

"I'm trying to plan ahead so at least one of us can be sensible," Lieutenant Doyle replied as he closed the gap between them. "My guess is, this area is filled with wild beasts, perhaps tragurn, and the winter would seem a time for them to become awfully hungry."

"Well, there are always the trees to nest in. They aren't known for climbing without making a ruckus."

Lieutenant Doyle stopped. "The trees? Surely you must be joking."

"Unless you have a better suggestion, Lieutenant."

"My suggestion would be to have taken driving celks."

Leer watched as Lieutenant Doyle fell in step beside him, his strides firm through the powder. "Tell me, Private," the Lieutenant began, "how is it you knew of Princess Gresham's whereabouts?"

"I went toward the light," Leer replied, adjusting the scarf wrapped around his neck and over his mouth.

"To confront your supposed beast, yes?"

"Isn't that a guard's duty? To protect the kingdom?"

The Lieutenant laughed. "Yes, I suppose it is."

Leer inhaled deeply, pausing as he scanned the vastness in front of them. He hadn't imagined being accompanied on the trek, let alone with someone like Lieutenant James Shelton Doyle. He pursed his lips at the thought of how the next few days would unfold.

No matter, Leer reminded himself. *Company or not, you've a job to do.*

He wriggled his shoulder until the strap slid, the pack swinging around toward his front. He plunged his mittened hand into it, retrieving the small journal nestled between rations and a woolen blanket. As he replaced the pack strap, he began walking again, flipping through a few pages awkwardly. The Lieutenant's steps resumed alongside him.

Their simultaneous crunching of boots through snow was the only sound made between them for quite some time. Reading and walking proved to be quite difficult, and the sun's bright rays bouncing off the pearlescent landscape made it more of a challenge. Leer squinted his eyes, the small swirling script of the journal barely legible.

"Sightings of Vei strength noted around eastern wood just south of Prijar. Locals recall unexplainable events, including strange lights and sounds."

"So," Lieutenant Doyle said with a sharpness that broke through Leer's concentration, "by my calculations, we ought to reach Prijar by nightfall."

"Aye," Leer affirmed, distracted.

"You've your nose in that book for quite some time. Anything you care to share?"

Leer's brow furrowed as he stopped walking; he looked up from the page to the Lieutenant, who paused alongside him, lifting his chin toward the journal.

"There must be something regarding direction," he remarked.

"Nothing of immediate use," Leer replied.

The Lieutenant's brow arched. "But of use later, I gather?"

"Depends on what your interest is."

"My interest, I assume, is the same as yours, Private. Finding the princess."

Leer gave a small nod. "Of course."

Lieutenant Doyle stared at him for a beat before he continued forward through the snow. Leer remained still for a moment, watching his back as he closed the journal. With a deep sigh, he continued after the Lieutenant.

"Tell me more about your beast, Private?" Lieutenant Doyle asked.

Leer's eyes narrowed. "What do you wish to know?"

"What any man would if he were to go on a hunt—qualities, feeding, habitation, and the like."

A small knot formed in Leer's stomach with surprising haste. *What has him so curious?*

"Well," he began, "it isn't so much a beast as it is a man."

"So, it's a man who lost his sense?"

"Nay, it's a man with the mind of a beast."

"And he lives in the Fell?"

"Aye."

"For what purpose might he have to attack during peace?"

"…I can't say. I need to learn more about the power of the Vei it uses before I can conclude."

"Ah, yes," the Lieutenant murmured with a nod. "The Vei. A terribly corrupt influence long since dead."

"If it were, then how did the beast gain its power?"

"Surely you don't believe he's anything more than a man parading around behind the mask of lies?"

"The Vei isn't a lie."

Lieutenant Doyle pursed his lips. "I must say, you're quite a strange man. Did your mother not nurse you at the breast long enough?"

"The Vei exists," Leer continued. "Its power is still attainable."

The Lieutenant laughed. "Of course it is."

"Then how do you explain the Grimbarror?" Leer countered, a heat rising behind his scarf covered ears.

"'The Grimbarror' isn't anything more than a rebel with an army to help do his bidding. A poor excuse for a court magician's cloak and dagger trick."

"I *saw* it," Leer argued, his jaw flexing.

"Look," Lieutenant Doyle interjected, pausing as he turned toward Leer, "I know you think you saw it, but I can assure you, you didn't."

"You believe me to be dishonest, then?" Leer asked, eyes narrowing.

"I believe you to be disillusioned as to what the truth really is."

Leer's grip tightened around the journal. "I know what I saw."

He brushed past the Lieutenant, grinding his molars together to shove aside his irritation. He paused briefly when he saw in the distance the thickening underbelly of storm clouds overhead. Being labeled as a lunatic was the least of his worries.

A storm was brewing.

"How about we call for a ration?" the Lieutenant asked a while later, freezing in place as he scanned the area.

Leer grumbled as he noted how the growing clouds shrouded the lingering midday sun high above them. They were still some distance from his intended goal of the Monu River. The swirling icy air pushed against the bits of warm, bare skin on Leer's throat as he paused to consider the proposal.

"I'd wait until we get to the edge of the Monu River," he advised, adjusting his scarf. "That way we can refill our canteens at the same time."

"That might be the most rational thing I've ever heard you say." The Lieutenant sighed, shielding his eyes from the blinding rays of sun bouncing off the crystalline landscape around them. "And where might the river be?"

"That way," Leer pointed a mittened hand, as he moved around the Lieutenant.

When they reached it at the base of a hill, the Monu River was solid on the surface, the flowing waters under it concealed by a layer of ice.

"Wonderful," Lieutenant Doyle mumbled. He skidded down into the valley, tossing his pack from his shoulders onto the ground before rooting through it. Moments later, he produced a pickaxe. "I think that as the lower rank, you should do the honors." He held it out to Leer expectantly, his eyebrow arched while he waited for Leer to take it.

"Aye," Leer said with a grumble, sliding his own pack from his shoulders. "We wouldn't want to break protocol, would we?"

With a firm grip on the handle, Leer rammed the sharp tip of the axe into the frozen river. "Tell me, Lieutenant," he asked between huffed breaths as he splintered the thick ice with relative ease, "if you had taken this journey alone, would you have waited for a private to come crack the ice for you?"

The Lieutenant shoved him aside from the water's edge, snatching back the pick. "I'll take that," he growled. "I needn't a private to do my work for me."

Leer stretched upward with a smirk concealed under his wool scarf. He scanned the perimeter, drawing a deep breath through his nose. The scent of the air as it weaved between hewen and lingan trees' needles exhilarated him. Despite living the majority of his life in the upper class territory of the Vale, Leer always felt most at home in nature.

"You say you've journeyed through these woods before?" Lieutenant Doyle asked between pings.

"Aye," Leer confirmed, his back to him.

"For what purpose?"

"Hunting. My father sold furs."

"Ah. So I gather that's how you met Lance, then?"

A heavy weight descended on Leer's chest at the thought. "Aye. He and my father were friends."

"Your father," Lieutenant Doyle swung the axe between puffs of breath, "was a furrier for the army, yes? He, Bilby, and Lance?"

Leer's brow wrinkled. "Aye." *What does this have to do with anything?*

"So, your father spent quite a measure of time with them."

"I suppose he did."

"I see." The Lieutenant paused as he watched the ice begin to split. "You didn't wish to take up the family business, I gather?"

Leer scoffed. "His business was the drink, not furs."

The Lieutenant laughed softly. "Sounds like my father."

Leer glanced behind him, watching Lieutenant Doyle work on the ice for a moment. "I suppose we have more in common than we knew."

"Don't get too wetbacked, Boxwell. I don't quite feel like tossing my rations."

As the pickaxe's ping rang through his ears, Leer listened to his surroundings. It was otherwise silent—perhaps too silent.

"Say, it's been a bit since we've heard wildlife in these parts, hasn't it, Lieutenant?" he asked as he continued surveying the area.

"The less wildlife, the better," the Lieutenant replied.

"Could be the sign of a pack of tragurns."

"Lovely." Leer heard him slam the axe once more and triumphantly gloat when he broke through the surface. "Hah! Come on, then. Fill your canteen, Boxwell." Leer's focus remained on the woods. "Boxwell. We haven't got all day."

"In a minute," Leer murmured, his back still turned, eyes narrowed.

He saw something.

"Private!" Lieutenant Doyle yelled.

Leer's brows wrinkled as he ignored him and moved forward, squinting as he examined a hewen's knotted trunk. The bark bore a freshly gouged angular crescent moon line with three distinct slashes across the center. Leer traced the erratic cuts in the tree trunk with his mittened fingertips.

Insurgents.

The woods were likely an extension of territory, their symbol a warning to those who might enter its depths.

"Insurgents," Leer called back to the Lieutenant, still feeling the grooves in the wood. "Be on your guard."

"Oh, wonderful," Lieutenant Doyle replied. "Now I've to add rebels to the list of things intent on killing us."

"The cuts in the wood look fresh," Leer mused. "No more than a month or so old."

"Quit dawdling and fill your canteen."

Leer ignored him, studying the tree line just beyond the tree trunk. He paused, his stomach sinking as he heard branches snapping in the distance.

"Draw your weapon," Leer hissed back to Lieutenant Doyle, creeping backward toward the river as he unsheathed his sword.

"I don't take orders from you," the Lieutenant objected.

"Draw your weapon," Leer repeated hoarsely, pausing when the air went silent. "It stopped," he whispered.

"What stopped?"

"Perhaps if we remain still for a while, it will begin again."

A moment of silence passed; Leer's brow furrowed as he studied the forest's edge.

"Do you hear anything?" Leer whispered.

A flying rock collided with the side of Leer's head, knocking him to the ground, the ice scraping against his face as he slid toward the frozen river. The world went black around him.

A moment later, Leer blinked heavily, his eyes opening to find his face in the snow. He groaned, feeling the tenderness of all of his still healing injuries as he slowly pulled himself to his knees, snatching up his sword. He noted the blood left behind in the area where he fell. With a cautious hand, he touched his hand to his forehead, finding fresh blood on the wool of his mitten.

Trying to ignore the throbbing of his head, he scanned the perimeter.

Damn.

He was alone.

"Lieutenant!" he called, clumsily shifting his weight to his feet. As he picked up his sword, he looked down and noted the disturbance in the snow, multiple footprints visible. The path of the tracks stretched toward the woods.

"Blast," he growled, darting toward the trees.

The sun spliced in thin rays through the thick blanket of evergreens overhead that dimmed Leer's surroundings. The cold air stung his lungs; he paused to catch his breath, coughing as he shuddered from the chill.

"Lieutenant!" he called, hoping to hear something in response. *Say something.*

He hadn't expected the warm whisper of a feminine voice in his ear:

"Come with me."

-7-

The owner of the voice was hooded and masked. Leer couldn't see anything but a set of sharp pale blue eyes belonging to a small young woman, who searched his face for a moment before she grabbed his hand and began racing with him deeper into the woods in the opposite direction.

Her nimble feet caressed the ground with respect and delicacy as she weaved between tree trunks and over exposed roots. Her firm grip challenged that of most of the men he knew.

For a few moments, he followed without question, a fog settling around his mind as if his choice was not his own. He stopped abruptly, the woman's hood falling back slightly to reveal a swatch of shiny dark hair.

"Stand back," Leer warned, readying his sword.

"Come on," the woman sighed with frustration, not seeming intimidated by his display of aggression. "We've got to keep a move on."

"From who?" Leer demanded, still holding his sword out in front of himself.

The woman scoffed. "Are you joking?"

"Why would I be?"

"So what, you believe a village boy aimed that rock for your head?"

"I think it was you," Leer corrected, raising his sword.

The woman pursed her lips. "Are you blind or just daft?" she accused.

Leer's brow wrinkled. "So, it wasn't you?"

She looked baffled. "You're an imbecile."

"Excuse me?"

"Look," she said, her hands finding her hips, "do you wish to live, or to do you wish to die like your friend?"

"He's *not* dead," Leer insisted.

"Like you'd know even if he was," she murmured.

"Well...if he is dead, then *you're* the one who got him killed, because I never said I had a travel companion." Leer eyed her. "So you must have arranged this."

The woman gaped. "Me? First of all, I can't help it if he's a weakling, so it's not my fault what happens to him. And by the way, in case you haven't noticed, *I'm* attempting to save *your* life."

Leer took a challenging step closer to the woman, whose cloak had spread open from the haste of running. He examined her, realizing with surprise that she wore tight riding breeches, a cream tunic and a silver-hued willet fur vest under it instead of a dress, as usually worn by women in the Vale.

The unusual sight both startled and mesmerized Leer, his gaze resting on her toned legs. He felt his chest tighten at the view; his palms grew sweaty in his mittens. Heat rose around his neck, making his scarf almost immediately unbearable.

For the love of Hiline, don't stare at her, you blithering fool.

Leer shifted his eyes to her boots with a hard swallow. "He's a Lieutenant, you know," he noted, still trying to recover.

"And what does that mean to me?" the woman asked indignantly.

"That if he dies," Leer said, looking up at her, "then the blood of King Gresham's army is on your hands."

Her mouth gaped open. "You're absolutely insane."

"I've heard that before," Leer muttered to himself with a shrug.

The pitch of the woman's voice raised. "How do you suppose you can blame *me* for all this?"

Leer looked her in the eye. "Well, this was your set up, aye?"

The woman's mouth dropped open as she put her hands on her hips. "I don't believe it. Forget it. Die then—you and your daft Lieutenant."

As she whirled around in the opposite direction, Leer caught onto her arm.

"Unhand me," she warned, tugging against his hold. "I won't be making the mistake of trying to save your useless life, you can bet your fancy sword on that."

"Who are you?" Leer demanded.

"Who are *you*?" she asked back.

"Private Boxwell. And now you, lass."

She shrugged him off her, glaring up at him. "First off, don't call me 'lass.' Secondly, I don't recall agreeing to divulge my name."

Before he could let out his upset reply, the woman covered Leer's mouth with her mittened hand, yanking him down with her behind the cover of brush.

"Shhh," she warned, her eyes looking over his shoulder. "They're close."

"How close?" Leer asked when the woman's hand slipped away from his mouth.

"Too close for us both to run any further without being seen."

"They want a trade."

"Of course they want a trade. They're insurgents. Which is why I was trying to run."

"Then why 'save' me?"

She hesitated. "I felt sorry for you."

"Excuse me?"

"You're in insurgent camp territory. Alone. Hit in the skull with a rock." She squinted for a moment. "Quite a gash you've got, but you'll live. And you reek of the guard, which means you're likely daft or slow. Call it charity, I suppose."

"How did you know I am a guard?"

She scoffed. "You've practically got it branded on you with your stupidity of entering the area without an escort."

The sound of approaching footsteps snapping crunchy snow underneath quieted them both. Leer's stomach sank with dread.

"Come on out, sprite," a booming voice called through the wood, equally harsh steps accompanying it. Instinctively, Leer's hands gripped around the woman's wrists, one of her brows arching in surprise as response. "We saw you with the towhead, so show yourself. We know your style—I'm sure these two loons weren't traveling without a purse. Can't keep it all for yourself."

A few more resounding paces sunk into the earth. Leer shifted position, causing snow to rattle from the brush, dusting both of them as they hid behind it. As Leer looked back from the approaching insurgents in the distance to the woman he still gripped, his eyes locked on hers, and his stomach sank.

"Let me go," the woman whispered, her eyes piercing as she looked at him. "I'll settle this and get you your Lieutenant back."

"No," Leer argued. "They'll kill you. Or worse."

The woman pulled her hands free. "For the love of Hiline, they don't care a mite about me, you or your friend."

"He's not my friend," Leer corrected.

"Well, whatever he is, they won't hurt him if they don't know you're both guards. They're just big bullies with a hunger for coins—harmless, really."

Leer's eyes widened as the woman snatched the small velvet bag of coins from his belt.

"Hey," Leer hissed as the woman stood, her chin tilted up.

"Over here, boys," she beckoned, jingling the coins in the bag.

"What are you doing?" Leer demanded under his breath, reluctantly coming to stand in view next to her.

"Keeping us all alive," the woman replied matter-of-factly.

He scoffed. "By stealing from the king to satisfy insurgents?"

She frowned, exasperated. "You are quite the details man, aren't you?"

The groan of the crushed snow and vegetation under the feet of the two approaching insurgents interrupted Leer, his focus shifting upward to take in their burly forms. The two men seemed taller than average, though the one in the front was also far broader.

"Got yourself a nugget with your coins, eh sprite?" the front one asked with a hearty laugh as he eyed Leer, gripping Lieutenant Doyle's sword in his fat hand. "I say, he's not much meat on the bone. Not like me."

"Please," the woman laughed. "I already told you, I don't court insurgents. And anyway, this one doesn't belong to me. He's the other's slow page. Felt sorry for him."

"I'm not slow," Leer objected. "Nor am I his page."

"Shut it," the woman hissed, glaring at him.

"What about this one?" the front insurgent asked. Leer's brow rose as he saw the Lieutenant bound and gagged by vines, and in the clutches of the insurgent toward the rear. "Why would you want to stick your neck out for 'im? He a night time companion?" Both the insurgents cackled.

"Certainly not," the woman emphatically replied.

"You meant to take the coins without sharing," the front one tsked. "Not a very cordial way to treat those helping you." The large man took a step forward. "You tried to cheat us."

"If I did," the woman snapped, "then why would I've stopped to offer you two the purse? I could've made off with the slow one and the coins myself."

"I'm *not* slow," Leer argued.

The front insurgent lifted his chin. "How do we know you're not keeping some already?"

The woman rolled her eyes and put her hands on her hips. "I'm not. But does it even matter if I'm willing to give you a remaining portion?"

The two men glanced at each other, then shrugged. "Suppose not."

"Right, then," the woman nodded. "A trade. The purse for the dark-haired one and his weapon."

"Not the weapon," the front man replied, shaking his head as he twisted the sword around, the purple hued blade glinting in the sun. "I like it."

"Both, or no deal," the woman challenged, squaring her shoulders.

"Is that right, now?"

"Yes."

The insurgent in the front laughed after a long moment of silence, his chuckle shaking his thick chest. "You know, sprite, you amuse me. Perhaps I'd let you keep some of the purse if you'd change your mind about courting your own kind."

"Look," the woman eyed him with a sigh, "I'd really like to get on with my day, so either you take the purse or not."

Leer heard the muffled protest from Lieutenant Doyle. He looked to the woman expectantly, seeing her still staring ahead at the brooding, husky figure in front of her.

The insurgent wiped his mouth with the back of his hand. "You first," he said, nodding in reference toward the bag she held.

The woman smirked. "I'm no fool, Rahjin. Let the dark-haired one and his sword go at the same time as I toss the purse. On my count of three. Have we got a deal?"

Rahjin, the front insurgent, pondered the proposition for a moment. "Fine," he finally said, scratching his large stubbled chin. He flexed his gnarled hands thoughtfully. "But if you try anything sneaky, I'll have Teshi snap his spine in half."

"Done," the woman said, eliciting a groaned protest from Lieutenant Doyle. "One...two..."

As promised, on the count of "three," the woman tossed the blue velvet satchel toward Rahjin's far left, who tossed Lieutenant Doyle's sword near her. Teshi shoved Lieutenant Doyle carelessly onto the thick snow covered brush as he bounded after the purse with Rahjin. Leer shut his eyes, breathing a sigh of relief.

"You were truthful, sprite," Rahjin called triumphantly as he examined his prize while pacing away. His laugh chilled Leer and haunted his ears. "There's enough here to be shared, if you change your mind."

"I don't always cheat, boys. But I always refrain from courting insurgents," the woman replied with a wink as Rahjin and Teshi scurried out of sight.

Sure they left, Leer bolted toward the Lieutenant, working furiously with his sword to slice away the vines.

The Lieutenant gasped, "Detain her!" when he was finally ungagged. He stood on shaky feet with a glare. "She's an insurgent who's stolen money from the king!"

"First of all, I am *not* an insurgent," the woman replied sharply. "Secondly, I saved both your lives. And thirdly, I've stolen more than just coins."

"Excuse me?" the Lieutenant asked with disgust.

She smiled, sliding their two packs off her shoulder from under her cloak, holding them up. "Uh-uh," she warned, raising a dagger clutched in her hand. "I'm going to assume these are at least somewhat important to both of you to survive wherever it is you're going, right?" Leer saw in his peripheral the Lieutenant reaching for his sword. "Oh, and your sword." She nodded over toward the weapon to her rear.

The Lieutenant lurched forward. "Why you little—"

"Hey," Leer interrupted, stopping the Lieutenant. He calmly took a step forward toward the woman, examining her still masked face. She trained her bright blue eyes on him with reservation. "Fine," he said to the woman as he approached. "Suppose we agree to another even exchange, just like the one you did with Rahjin and Teshi."

"So you want a deal, then?" the woman asked with a smirk.

Leer nodded, taking another step closer, as if approaching a skittish nim. "Aye. Our packs and his sword for your freedom."

She was silent as she considered his proposal. "I already think that I'm rather free at the moment, Private Boxwell."

"Aye," he murmured. "For now, you are."

"For now?"

Leer shrugged. "You won't be much of a chase."

She laughed. "I could kill you to avoid the trouble of running."

"You could," Leer agreed. "But you won't."

Her eyes narrowed. "What game are you playing?" she asked.

"No games, lass," he replied confidently. "I can just sense it in you." He took another step closer, his grip still firm on the sword lowered at his side. "Do you suppose we can arrange a deal now?"

"You don't negotiate with her, Private," Lieutenant Doyle interrupted from behind. "Stand down."

"I told you," the woman said through clenched teeth, "don't call me 'lass.'"

"Then at least tell me your name so I might address you properly," Leer offered with a smoldering grin.

"That smile of yours might work on other girls, but it bears no weight with me," she replied, with her own small smirk. "Have we got a deal?"

Leer stepped forward, tucked his sword away, and lifted his hand to the woman. "Shake."

"Are you mad, Boxwell?" Lieutenant Doyle asked behind him. "Oh wait, I forgot—you are."

Leer continued to approach despite the Lieutenant's exasperation. He kept his hand out, waiting once he closed the gap.

"Alright, shake," the woman agreed with obvious hesitance, stowing her dagger and lifting her small mittened hand and gripping Leer's, keeping her eyes on his. He held her gaze as she peered into his burnished irises; he watched her lips part and admired their scarlet hue in the moment.

With little hesitation and a slick turn of his wrist, Leer wrapped the woman into a tight lock that she couldn't escape, the packs dropping to the ground as her back pressed into his chest. She growled, wriggling against him as he pinned her arms down.

"You whoreson," she snarled as he held her in place.

Leer inched his mouth close to her ear, catching the faint scent of hewen needles and something else he couldn't place in her hair. It was a bit smoky, a bit sweet. "Never make a deal with someone you don't know," he said in a husky tone.

"I tried to save you."

"You used me," Leer corrected, wincing as the woman's protest irritated his still sore ribs. "I know you were traveling with them."

"So what? And you're not using me now?" she argued.

"This is different."

"How?" she demanded. "How is this different?"

"Because it's not my skin I'm protecting."

"Well, you're one of the king's dogs, so whose skin is it then?"

"The Princess of Hiline's."

Leer was thankful when the woman stopped wrestling. "What has happened to her?" she whispered.

"Have you been in these woods that long?"

"I don't cross into the Vale if I can help it. I can't stomach the place."

"She was taken on the eve of the averil," Leer explained with a short sigh, dipping his mouth to her ear. "Look," he whispered, "if you return the packs and sword to us to without a fight, we'll forget your debt." Leer paused, his warm breath blowing against her neck. "You'll have my protection. Of that I can vow on my mentor's grave to be truth." He took a lingering glimpse of her supple mouth while she thought over his proposition. *Focus*. "What say you? Shall we let him handle it," Leer nodded to Lieutenant Doyle, "or handle it this way?"

"Fine," the woman replied, still compressed against Leer's chest. "Now, I want you to let me go, alright?"

"Not until the Lieutenant has his sword," Leer replied with a grin, walking forward with her.

She stiffened in his arms. "Sure, you're just enjoying the experience."

Leer laughed gently. "It's certainly not terrible, but I'd just rather have him sated first."

"I hope your princess finds you more charming than I do," the woman retorted.

"*My* princess?"

"Why else should a man go through all the trouble to retrieve her without an army if he wasn't seeking the crown?"

The Lieutenant interrupted Leer before he could respond, crossing to retrieve his sword and the discarded packs. "Good work," he said with a satisfied smile. "Now we will have you detained by the men at the nearest Keep immediately."

"Nay," Leer argued, still holding the woman close. His objection got the attention of Lieutenant Doyle. "Her debt is squared. No need to delay us from the Fell by traveling to the Keep. It's a half day's journey east of here one way and frankly, I haven't got the extra energy for that sort of thing."

"The Fell?" the woman asked, aghast. "Are you both mad? Going to the Fell by yourselves, and in the dead of winter, no less?"

"We've business there."

"What business could you possibly have? And anyway, travel on the northern road is bound to be treacherous."

"So then you know the way?" Lieutenant Doyle asked, taking a step closer.

Her eyes narrowed. "Maybe, but why would I tell you?"

"You should if you value your freedom."

Leer interjected, "She's of no consequence to us at all."

Lieutenant Doyle lifted his chin in thought. "The insurgent will accompany us," he murmured, a smile tugging at the corners of his mouth as he looked her over. "After all, she has proven herself to be a...suitable guide for these woods."

"I'm *not* an insurgent," the woman argued, her eyes narrowing.

"Oh excuse me, the thief."

"I steal only when I deem it necessary."

"And what if she deems it necessary to kill us while we sleep for this arrangement?" Leer argued, eyeing the Lieutenant. "This isn't a trip I wish to subject someone to by force."

"I remind you of your place, Private," Lieutenant Doyle warned. "You've no allowance to question my orders." He looked down at the woman as Leer held her. "What say you? Would you rather be taken to the Keep, imprisoned and possibly hanged, or join us and live a little longer to prove your merit?"

"I refuse either," she argued. "I'm not some sort of thing you two can tote around like property."

"Pick one," the Lieutenant growled, his finger snatching her chin and turning her face to force her to look at him.

The woman stiffened, looking down for a moment before replying. "Fine. I'll take you."

"Good," Lieutenant Doyle replied with a growing smirk. "I'd like to get a bit further north before nightfall. But first, we should at least introduce ourselves. I'm Lieutenant James Shelton Doyle." Leer felt the woman suppress a shiver. Her disguise couldn't conceal how her eyes rounded as she looked at him. "And the man clawing at you like a tragurn is Private

84

Leer Boxwell. Now, we should at least know your name, shouldn't we?" He took a step forward, taking hold of the woman's chin and tilting it up to force her to look at him. "And perhaps even see your face?" He paused, the bottom corner of his mouth turning up into a small smile. "You've the most...exquisite eyes I've had the pleasure of seeing."

"How is either necessary?" she asked with challenge as she tried to turn away from his hold.

The Lieutenant accepted it. "We wouldn't want to have to call you 'sprite' for the next few days, should we?"

"I could live with it, I suppose."

Lieutenant Doyle clearly wasn't amused. "Tell me your name."

"Mildred O'Malley Flannigan," the woman smirked.

"Bloody little—"

"Easy," Leer warned the Lieutenant, pulling the woman back instinctively.

"Stand down, Boxwell," Lieutenant Doyle instructed, his voice dark. "Your name," he demanded, shifting his focus to the woman.

"Gerta Strude," the woman mocked, her lie obvious through her angry tone.

With strength Leer hadn't expected, Lieutenant Doyle grabbed the woman and ripped her hood from her head, exposing her dark wavy hair as it fell over her shoulders.

"Your name," he yelled at her.

"Lieutenant!" Leer protested, surging forward.

"It's alright," the woman breathed, pushing Leer away with an outstretched arm, her mittened palm pressing gently against his chest. After a beat, she lowered it, shaking the Lieutenant off herself and studying the dark-haired man. After removing her mittens, she slowly raised her hands to the back of her head to undo the ties of her mask, revealing her face.

Leer swallowed as he caught a glimpse of her freckle-dusted ivory skin. Her features were pale and soft, delicate. Understated.

"Astrid," she whispered. "Astrid Browne. Are you satisfied?" She tossed the dark felt disguise at Lieutenant Doyle, turning away as it dropped to the snow.

"Quite," the Lieutenant replied with a smirk. "Well, let's be off, then," he added, nodding to Leer. "I'd like to get that hot supper in Prijar."

-8-

The lilt of the Grimbarror's voice haunted Leer. With each burdened step through the snowy wood, he rehashed the fateful eve of the averil over and over in his mind. Still, it wasn't the fearsome events that made him push forward for hours as he trudged through the snow. It was the mystery of the beast's words, the rhyming puzzle laced with gruesome promise that drove Leer mad.

This past week was the most chaotic period of his life. Stress and strange occurrences mounted at incalculable speed. First, he discovered Finnigan's body after the prince was killed. Then, he witnessed the attack of the Vale that took so many lives but somehow spared his own, not to mention the peculiarly accurate compositions of his mind during his escape from Bilby, or the demon's haunting yellow-rimmed eyes plaguing his sleep.

Guilt spread over him as Leer caught the orange rays of the setting sun through white-tipped hewens.

Nearly seven days, now.

Could she be…?

He squeezed his dark eyes shut with a low growl that rumbled in his throat.

Maybe this is without merit. After all, why would the beast keep her alive?

When he opened his eyes, he saw Astrid and Lieutenant Doyle walking a few paces ahead. He could hear the tension in their voices.

"Quit dawdling," the Lieutenant snapped over his shoulder at him. "I won't have you slow our pace."

Annoyed, Leer lengthened his strides to come alongside Astrid. He caught a glimpse of her from beneath her hood. She stared straight ahead, her expression chilled like the air that reddened the tip of her nose.

"All I'm saying is, you should consider the possibilities, Lieutenant," he heard Astrid argue.

"I have," the Lieutenant snapped, pausing next to her. "And I have concluded that I will keep going until I know for certain."

"Know what, exactly?" Astrid asked, his lips pursed.

"As I've said before, the truth regarding the princess."

Astrid protested, "It's not my fault you wish to deny what is obvious."

Lieutenant Doyle eyed her through a moment of thick silence. "You should tread carefully, breedbate," he growled.

"Hey," Leer interjected, stepping forward. "Leave her be."

"Please," Astrid sneered, "He doesn't frighten me."

The Lieutenant shifted his focus to Leer. "Mind your tongue, Boy," he warned, his lips twitching. "I'd just as easily have you imprisoned at the Keep with the thief."

"Then why fight your urge?" Leer challenged,

"Because under that sad excuse for a hairstyle lies a brain that has information I need. So long as our princess is missing, you will serve your purpose under me. Am I clear?"

Not waiting for a response, the Lieutenant passed them both. Leer turned his head toward his right shoulder and blew out the excess spit that lingered in his mouth. In silence, he stalked away toward the slices of amber setting sunlight, a chill deeper than the air flooding his lungs.

"So where are you from, Miss Browne?" Leer asked, breaking the thick silence that had grown between them.

"Astrid," Astrid corrected in reply without stopping. "Hiline."

"Really? Gee, we wouldn't have figured," Lieutenant Doyle remarked.

"*Where* in Hiline, Astrid?" Leer continued.

"The east."

Leer sighed. "Alright, what is it you do, then?"

Astrid smirked. "You mean, besides thievery?"

"Aye."

"Nothing worth discussing."

"Surely there is."

She glanced toward him. "Well, I can assure you, there isn't."

"Well, there is your peculiar dress."

Astrid laughed. "You try trekking through the wood in a skirt."

Leer grinned. "Can't say I'd like the challenge." He looked over at her, studying the profile of her face. "So, what of your family?"

Her tone shifted. "What do you mean?"

"Tell me about them."

"Why should I?" she asked, her tone shifting.

"I just figured it would pass the time."

Astrid stopped in place, Leer pausing with her. "I don't wish to be the topic of your conversation," she said, peering up at him.

"Look, lass—there's no need to be cross."

"*Astrid.* And there's no need for me to answer your endless questions."

Leer watched as Astrid continued ahead, her hand tightly gripped around her walking stick, her strides long and purposeful.

"Well, that went well, eh?" the Lieutenant smirked, passing Leer on the left.

Astrid's abrupt answer didn't sit well with Leer. "Wait," he called, jogging past Lieutenant Doyle to catch up to Astrid's side. When he reached her, he took her upper arm to stop her.

"I also don't wish to be handled," Astrid noted, eyeing his hand.

Leer released Astrid's upper arm. "Aye, my apologies." He cleared his throat. "You resent this arrangement, is that it?"

"No, I think it's just lovely," she replied, eyes narrowing.

"Well, it's better than the box, aye?"

"Do you forget I'm carrying a knife?"

"I mean you no harm," Leer assured, his voice soft.

Her nostrils flared a little as she studied his face. "Sure."

"I…" Leer sighed. "Look, if it was up to me, you'd be off doing…whatever it is you do. But I've orders to keep. There's more at stake than just me."

Leer watched Astrid's expression change. "Your princess," she murmured.

"She's...not mine."

Astrid laughed under her breath, looking away. "So that's why you're sore."

"Come again?"

"The Lieutenant. You're fitbloached over his relationship."

"Surely not," Leer scoffed.

"And I'm the Queen of the Forest." She sighed. "I can see a man smitten from miles away. I'll help you both get back your princess, but don't think of me as a midway opportunity to warm your bones."

"I...hadn't thought that," Leer stammered, a simultaneous cool and hot rush flowing through him at the statement.

She examined him for a prolonged moment. He stared back at her delicate face, admiring the freckles dotting her cheeks, and her ice-toned eyes, which seemed to spark an unwanted flame inside him. From the moment he saw them, they intrigued him. They seemed mystical, like carefully cut gemstones inlaid in the king's crown.

Unnatural.

Leer looked away, keeping his eyes on the snow, listening to her footfalls as she continued ahead alone.

"Well," Lieutenant Doyle remarked, coming to his side, "I suppose your charms extend only toward women of the paid variety."

Glaring at Lieutenant Doyle, Leer followed behind Astrid, keeping distance between them. He watched the swirl of her cloak hem against the snow, the pit growing in his stomach. He caught a glimpse of how a lock of her hair escaped from under her hood and danced in the growing winds.

He blinked, scanning the area as he tried to shake away his curiosity. He took in the profile of her face, relishing the curve of her nose. He knew his appreciation of her was foolish, disgusting even, in his current situation. Still, it was as if the lithe woman in front of him gave him little choice.

Alright, then. Blame the thief for it like a dirty javit.

It sickened him; he clenched his fist inside his mitten in an attempt to deflect his attention, but it merely dulled it.

Leer pushed forward, remaining resolute despite his exhaustion.

Why does she intrigue me so?

The air turned more bitter with each passing hour as the three trekked north toward the Eyne Wood. Leer grew worried as the darkening skies grew grey with the still brewing storm.

"We can't risk being caught unprepared when this storm begins," he warned, turning toward the others as the growing winds assaulted his back. "We need to seek shelter. This storm is going to be far too great to weather outside."

"Do you know how far Prijar is from here?" Lieutenant Doyle asked Astrid, who was struggling to keep her hood pulled over her head.

"It's about five miles over the ridge," Astrid shouted over the surging gusts of air sweeping between them.

Leer shook his head. "It's too far. We'll be caught in it. We need to find something now."

"There might be cottages on the outskirts," Astrid suggested, wrestling to keep her hair out of her face. "We might be able to rest in a barn until it passes."

"A barn?" Lieutenant Doyle asked, shaking his head. "Oh no, I'm not sleeping in a barn."

"Look, we haven't got a choice," Astrid snapped. "Either you sleep in a barn for the eve or freeze. I don't particularly care either way."

With a snarl, Lieutenant Doyle turned away, stomping ahead through the snow.

"Pansy," Astrid muttered.

"Do you know any of the peasants living in this region?" Leer asked, watching Astrid clutch at her hood to keep it over her.

"No," she admitted. "But I imagine all of the animals are already sheltered away from the storm, so we shouldn't encounter anyone if we're subtle."

Leer looked up at Lieutenant Doyle, who cursed to himself as he forged ahead. "Subtlety isn't his best trait."

Warmth rose from deep within as he caught how the corners of Astrid's mouth turned up in a genuine grin. "I should say not."

Smoke wafting from a chimney drew the three to a cottage at the edge of Prijar. By the time they reached the small barn on a plot of hilled land, Leer was chilled to the bone, and the bitter cold intensified the pain in his foot.

Leer quietly lifted the latch, opening the weathered door. Inside, two black driving celks pawed the ground, a few anxious reews bleated, each with a single short, knobby horn and thick, ashy winter coats, and a honey brown-eyed milking stotseen chewed cud.

"I suppose this will do," Astrid murmured with a nod.

The Lieutenant's forehead creased as he examined the space. "It smells like the trenches," he scowled.

"Don't worry," Leer assured, shutting the door against the wind and moving past him. He slid his pack off his shoulders and tossed it near a pile of golden straw. "They only relieve themselves in their pens."

"Had we not become sidetracked earlier," the Lieutenant reminded, "we wouldn't have to sleep in this filth."

"Aren't you an army man?" Astrid asked, her hands on her hips. "Surely you've camped somewhere before."

"Of course I have." The Lieutenant froze, lifting his boot with a grimace. "But not with waste lying about."

"We'd all do best to get some rest," Leer interrupted, trying to contain his amused expression. "I'm rather pooped myself." His smile spread when he heard Astrid's muffled giggle.

"Yes, yes," Lieutenant Doyle answered, rubbing the sole of his boot clean on some straw. "Enjoy your laugh."

Leer watched as Lieutenant Doyle made himself comfortable in a far corner. With a sigh, Leer found a seat along the wall of the barn, propping his back up as he covered himself with the blanket from his pack, watching as Astrid gathered loose straw around her in the darkened back corner. The wind grew in strength outside of the barn, whistling as it swirled against it, bringing bitter gusts that seeped between the cracks.

Leer took off his right mitten and withdrew Finnigan's journal from his pack, thumbing through the pages to find where he had left off. The last of daylight was fading fast, but there was just enough for him to make out a few lines.

Earlier pages only bore little snippets of information, none of which connected together to form a coherent thought. As if Finnigan blatantly avoided divulging information on purpose, and instead created a mosaic that wasn't yet assembled.

Perhaps to protect what he knew.

It seemed to make no logical sense otherwise.

Two divided
Maloden—suppression
Conditional transformation, subject to intent
Enter the gates, but do not fall
Eyes of stone
Gems within, power inherently possessed

Some incomplete sketches filled the spaces in between the fragmented lines; a set of claws in particular grabbed Leer's attention. The claws' splay wasn't like the padded foot of a tragurn or a willet. Instead, it was a hand, nearly the same as his own, except for the peculiar digits.

Leer breathed a sigh of relief when he happened upon a section containing an almost complete sentence, but once again disappointed with the results:

Luke Foreman, dillyburt farmer, Junivar
Accounts of Vei influence seen; quite possibly a tainted source,
as he is fond of nursing the bottle each eve.

"Well?"

Leer looked up, meeting Lieutenant Doyle's eyes. "Well what?" he responded.

"What does it say? Anything of importance?"

With a shake of his head, Leer turned back to the pages he held. "None that I can ascertain. Only a mention of a farmer residing in Junivar who might have information. The rest isn't clear."

"Perhaps I can help deduce it."

Leer's brow arched as he looked up, meeting the Lieutenant's gaze. "You?"

"Don't look so shocked," Lieutenant Doyle smirked, straightening up and leaning forward. "I was promoted to Lieutenant for reasons other than my devilishly good looks."

They heard Astrid's groan over the winds, which made Leer smile a little to himself. "Alright," he said, taking a deep breath. "What do you make of this: 'Two divided?'"

"Two divided?" The Lieutenant's eyes narrowed as he concentrated on some straw near his feet. "Hmm...Could it have something to do with insurgents?"

Leer nodded. "Aye, maybe. Hiline, and insurgents."

"Yes, that's what I'm thinking."

"But what relevance would that have?"

"History, perhaps?"

"Perhaps." Leer paused. "What do you make of, 'maloden—suppression?'"

The straw rustled as Astrid leaned forward toward them. "Maloden, did you say?" she asked. Even in the dim light, Leer couldn't help but notice the brightness of her eyes.

"Aye," he replied. "Maloden."

"Why does it bloody matter to you?" Lieutenant Doyle interrupted, turning toward Astrid. "You should mind your own affairs, thief."

"Excuse me?" Astrid replied, mouth agape.

"Come off it," Leer objected, glaring at the Lieutenant. "She's a right to speak."

"She's a liar by trade," Lieutenant Doyle argued. "You wish to trust her with intimate knowledge? For all we know, she could lead us into another trap with whatever she says."

Astrid scoffed. "Fine," she replied, leaning back in the straw. "I'll keep it to myself. If you wish to act like a child, so be it."

"I'd like to hear what you have to say," Leer interjected.

"No." She folded her arms over her chest. "I've nothing to say on the matter."

"And *I'm* acting like a child," the Lieutenant muttered.

With a growl, Leer snapped the journal closed, pushing to his feet and taking a few paces away. He inhaled deeply through his nostrils in an attempt to lower his racing heart, but it seemed to fail.

Silence washed over them, while only an occasional shift in the straw, a muffled bleat, or a snort from the animals permeated the swirling gusts of winds. It was too quiet for Leer. He craned his neck to stretch the muscles in it as he tried to make sense of the information Finnigan had left him.

An ache built above his temples; Leer kneaded at the skin under his curls with his fingertips, wincing as his fingers found the fresh gash from earlier.

As he massaged the area, tiny painful bolts of light flared through his closed eyes. Sharp strings of stinging energy made him nauseous.

I have hit my head quite a bit in the last week.

Still, the suddenness of the pain made only a little more sense than Finnigan's rambling.

Stress, perhaps?

Hunger?

He sighed, opening his eyes as he tried to take account of where the others were. Lieutenant Doyle was fast asleep in a rather unsightly manner, while Astrid was missing.

Leer scanned the darkness, attempting to spot her. The barn wasn't large, and had one entrance. Soon he saw her, standing next to a celk and scratching its ears as the beast munched on hay.

Swiping up his blanket, Leer approached her. "I apologize for the Lieutenant's behavior," he said when he came alongside her. "I suppose he's under a great deal of stress."

"And we're not?" Astrid countered, still petting the celk.

"Of course we are as well."

"Then why would I pardon him?"

"Pardon him or not, it's your choice. I just wish you to know that I don't share his sentiments."

She turned, looking into his eyes for a few beats as she lowered her hand from the celk's head, and reached toward Leer's. He closed his eyes, feeling her soft, warm fingertips as she investigated the cut in silence. He opened them again after she withdrew her hand. "It needs some herbs," she stated.

"I've yeran bark ointment," Leer offered.

She nodded. "That's good."

"I would still care to hear what you've to say about maloden," he whispered.

Astrid blinked, then spoke. "It's a stone."

"Aye, I'm aware."

"It's mined where I grew up," she continued. "It was said to have healing properties."

His brow wrinkled. "Healing?"

She shrugged. "I don't know. But I thought it might help for you to know that for your journey."

He nodded. "It does."

Astrid remained silent, staring at him. He cleared his increasingly parched throat. "…You're cold."

"I beg your pardon?"

He winced. *Wonderful.* "No, I meant, are you cold?" He offered up the blanket.

"I'll be fine without it," Astrid replied.

"Please, I insist."

With hesitance, Astrid took it, her fingers swirling over the wool. Her eyes turned toward Lieutenant Doyle for a brief moment. "I'm surprised either of you would consider sleeping in my presence."

"We haven't anything to worry about," Leer replied.

"You're the one who suggested I might deem it necessary to kill you in your sleep," she admonished with a shy smile. "What makes you so sure you aren't right?" She looked up at him, the shadows failing to dull her brilliant eyes.

"You would've left by now if you didn't have a taste for adventure."

Astrid cocked her head to the side. "So that's your game, is it? Is that why your bonny king pays you so well? Because you're a snoop?"

Leer laughed. "Who said I was paid well?"

"Well, it is your game, isn't it?"

"What is?"

"Knowing a person."

"I suppose, aye."

Astrid's lips pursed as she eyed Leer. "And what would you conclude about me, then?"

"That you don't care for games."

She smirked. "Is that all?"

He paused thoughtfully. "That, and you're missing something…or someone. It's why you live the way you do."

Astrid's face changed; she lowered her eyes. "Good night, Private Boxwell."

Leer became pensive, watching Astrid take her corner opposite of Lieutenant Doyle, cocooning herself in his blanket among the straw. Even with his vagueness, he had obviously struck a nerve.

Don't, he told himself as he considered approaching her. *Let it be.*

With a sigh, he turned and returned to his now cold spot near his pack.

Propping his head against a bale of hay, Leer fiddled with his position, becoming irritated as he found it increasingly difficult to settle in. He sat awake for quite a while, staring into the darkness and listening to the wind hiss through the slats.

Rest wouldn't come easily; there were too many questions, too much to consider. The cryptic journal entries and events of the recent days swirled around in his mind more violently than the storm outside the barn.

He sighed in defeat. It was going to be a long journey.

-9-

"Private, get up."

Leer stirred, blinking his sleep-crusted eyes open to find Astrid expectantly crouched down in front of him. The barn was still dark, and he swore he just fallen asleep moments before. "It can't be time yet," he mumbled, still trying to focus.

"It is, if we don't wish to get caught."

With a groan, Leer stood, Astrid rising to her feet beside him. "Where's the Lieutenant?" he asked, rubbing his jaw as he yawned.

"Attending to business," was her response. She folded the blanket, and gave it back to him in a neat pile. "Thank you," she added softly.

Leer nodded, taking the blanket. "My pleasure."

"Well," Astrid adjusted her cloak, pulling up her hood, "now that you're awake, I'll be off."

"To where?" Leer asked, brows wrinkled.

"Does it matter?" she countered, appearing confused. "I don't believe that's your business, Private. Only mine."

A few beats passed before it registered with Leer. "Oh," he said with an awkward nod. "My apologies. Go…Go right ahead."

She nodded. "We're meeting on the ridge. I'd be gone within a few minutes, if I were you. Dawn is approaching and you don't want to risk anyone seeing you." She turned and left through the door, not bothering to close it. True to her nature, she soon slipped out of sight. Darkness still covered the land outside, but the sun was beginning to rise beyond the ridge.

She's like a little willet, he mused to himself.

Was she inherently sly and deceptive like one too?

Leer stuffed the blanket into his pack. He drew the satchel over his shoulders and tightened the straps before leaving the barn, latching the door behind him as inconspicuously as he could.

A few minutes later, he stood at the top of the ridge, the small barn appearing even smaller with the distance. He moved a few paces closer to Lieutenant Doyle, who wore an impatient scowl.

"Well?" He looked to Leer expectantly. "Where is she?"

"How should I know?" Leer asked.

"You mean you didn't accompany her?"

Leer scoffed. "Certainly not."

The Lieutenant threw his hands up in the air. "Oh, that's rich. Wonderful. That's great."

"She has no thoughts about running," Leer insisted.

"Are you joking? A thief with no intention to deceive?"

Leer sighed. "You really should stop doubting her, or else she might live up to your expectations."

"I've no reason to trust her." Lieutenant Doyle put his hands on his hips. "And neither do you."

"She won't run."

"So say you."

"She won't."

In a huff, the Lieutenant turned away from Leer, releasing a long breath with a hint of dramatic flair. "Fine," he muttered. "But if she's not here within five minutes, I'll—"

"You'll what?" a voice behind them asked

Both men turned, finding Astrid with a small smirk on her face. Lieutenant Doyle's mouth opened, then he rolled his eyes. "Whatever. Let's be off."

"How do you do that?" Leer asked her as they all began to head north.

Astrid shrugged. "It's not hard to sneak up on two men bickering like feanets."

She passed by Leer, who laughed to himself as he fell in step with Lieutenant Doyle.

"You're just fortunate she came back," the Lieutenant muttered, a sour expression on his face.

"I knew she wouldn't run," Leer countered. Lieutenant Doyle gave an unintelligible reply. "After all, she's a thief, and there's a reward once we're through."

"*Might* be." Lieutenant Doyle sighed.

"Surely you have faith in us rescuing the princess?"

"I want to. It's not easy to."

Leer looked at Lieutenant Doyle, a new window of perspective opened about him. "We will find her," he assured; the Lieutenant didn't reply. "You care for her a great deal."

"I care for the wellbeing of an innocent woman taken against her will."

Leer drew a deep breath as he thought about Princess Maegan's expression just before he fell in the crack of the earth:

She looked eerily calm, peaceful.

Willing.

What would make her as willing such as she was?

Perhaps the light the beast emanated?

It must have been. After all, the guard had fallen under a similar spell.

But unlike the guard, why didn't she catch flame?

He sighed as Astrid's revelation regarding maloden came to mind. It was laced with unexpected power. The stone was nothing extraordinary, in and of itself. Why would anyone think it had healing powers when it was never used by brewstresses?

The mere thought of maloden sent a surge of pain through Leer's temples and deep into his skull. He held back a groan, stopping sudden as a tremor shocked him. He shut his eyes, but flecks of light filtered through his lids, and his mittened hand tightened around his walking stick as he braced himself on it.

"Are you alright?"

Although he couldn't see the expression her face, he heard Astrid's concern in her tone.

"I'm fine," he forced out, eyes still tight closed.

"What is it?"

"I..."

"Bloody hell." Leer heard the Lieutenant flop his arm against his side. "We haven't got all day, Boy."

"Come off it," Astrid snapped; Leer heard her gentle footsteps through the snow as she approached. "Private, what is it?"

He couldn't respond. The pain refused to lessen as it had before, and instead kept building pressure inside of his head. Leer moaned, his words to Astrid indecipherable.

He heard her asking him something, but he couldn't comprehend it. Vivid images that flashed in and out of his mind's eye replaced coherent thought and speech.

A gruesome battle had already been fought—heads severed from bodies, strings and chunks of innards strewn across valleys of blood that stained the grass. The stench was revolting, the putrid scent of decaying flesh emphasized by the summer sun.

He was walking among them, his stomach roiling with sickness as he observed the barbaric display. His boots sank into the streams of crimson blood, nearly disappearing from view with each step. There were women among the men, there were children. No one was spared from whatever horrific evil had come upon him or her.

The sun glinted off two small objects on the ground. He walked toward them, picked them up, and inspected them as blood dripped from his fingertips.

They were somehow still brilliant, but out of place.

Unnatural.

Leer collapsed to his knees, crying out in pain as he released the walking stick. He opened his eyes, panting as he kneeled in the snow. His breath came in short bursts, his heart racing.

What the bloody hell was that? he thought.

"Private, speak to me."

Astrid's voice was strained, but it sounded close. Leer slowly lifted his head, finding her eyes on his as she knelt in front of him in the snow.

He closed his eyes again, the images still lingering. He could still see insects landing on their lifeless faces.

"Are you alright?" she asked again.

Leer opened his eyes, unable to speak. How could he convey what had he just seen? And why did he keep seeing it?

Was this the awakening Bennett had spoken of?

Astrid's eyes widened as she yanked off a mitten and rested her small hand on his cheek. At her touch, warmth surged through Leer as an internal flood of calm washed over him.

He blinked, and felt relieved but confused.

The images vanished.

"Private," Astrid whispered. "Please, say something."

Leer swallowed. "What do you wish me to say?" he replied, equally as soft.

"Perhaps an explanation would do."

"I have none," he answered.

He rose to his feet, finding Lieutenant Doyle evaluating him with a piercing stare.

"Are you ill, Boxwell?" he asked.

"Nay," Leer replied, hearing Astrid stand behind him. He swept his walking stick up from the ground, giving the Lieutenant a small nod. "Let's be off."

He walked ahead, not waiting for a response.

Leer's odd behavior created an awkward silence, which lasted most of the day until Astrid exclaimed, "Look!" As the sunset flared in the distance, Leer paused to search for the spot over the ridge where Astrid pointed.

"Junivar," Leer said with a small nod as he spotted the distant torchlight.

"Never heard of it," Lieutenant Doyle shrugged.

"It's rather small," Leer explained, readjusting his grip on his walking stick. "My father took me here quite a few times to peddle furs for grain."

"Dare I say we're close to a normal place to rest?"

"I've been here too," Astrid chimed in. "There's an inn there that shouldn't cost us many pence."

"We haven't any money for an inn," Lieutenant Doyle reminded her.

"Right," Astrid groaned.

"Have they got a tafl board?" Leer asked.

"A tafl board?" she scoffed. "Why would you need it?"

"I've my reason."

"Yes, they do. But what about it?"

"And men who play?"

"A few. But they're—"

"What in the blazes would you need a tafl board for, Boxwell?" Lieutenant Doyle asked with impatience.

Leer grinned. "If they've got a board, then we've got all the money we need."

The warm, inviting atmosphere of the inn was a welcome change from what they'd endured so far. Lively fiddle music accompanied gregarious laughter and chatter. The Lieutenant disregarded any sort of manners and pushed through the door, sighing with relief. Leer gestured for Astrid to go ahead of him, which she did with hesitance.

The three weary travelers stomped the loose snow off their boots as they entered, shivering as the chill slowly left their bodies. The smell of fresh baked bread, hearty stew, and dark spirits drew Leer, his stomach growling in anticipation of nourishment beyond meager jerky rations.

"I would keep your statuses as army men to yourselves," Astrid quietly warned as she pushed her hood from her head. "People around these parts don't exactly have the best rapport with men of your profession."

"Well, the blundering fools should have respect for us," the Lieutenant testily replied, yanking a nearby chair away from a table and sitting in it.

"And that's exactly why they don't," Astrid mumbled, remaining alongside Leer.

"Ah, well," said a middle-aged barmaid, who glanced at the trio from across the room, "seems as though we've got visitors. Bit nippy out, ain't it?" The small group of local men laughed, most hunched over large, steaming mugs. "You three obviously aren't familiar with the weather of these parts."

"Three pints of ale," the Lieutenant demanded without a hint of manners. "And make it quick."

"Please," Leer added with sheepish smile, seeing the way a large man behind the bar counter began to approach. "Sorry."

The barmaid examined Leer with an appreciative smile. "Of course, Blondie," she said, sashaying away to retrieve three glasses. "By the way, I'm Ettie and this is Jon-Jon, the innkeeper," she purred, gesturing to the large man behind the bar.

"Six pence," Jon-Jon barked to Leer in a harsh baritone, his fat palm smacking against the grain of the wood counter. He paused as his eyes examined Astrid. "Unless you're planning on bartering the wench. I need another barmaid."

"Excuse me?" Astrid asked, glaring at the innkeeper as she stepped past Leer's side in challenge. "How dare you, you—"

"Easy, feisty," Leer whispered to Astrid, pulling her back toward him.

"I'm not property to be sold."

"Darlin'," Ettie said with a laugh, "for the right price, everything's for sale." She waggled her eyebrows. "Even me."

"Well, I'm not," Astrid replied.

"Fine then. Six pence," Jon-Jon repeated, crossing his arms over his chest.

Lieutenant Doyle looked at Leer, to which Leer sighed. "Have you got a tafl board?" Leer asked Jon-Jon.

"Yeah," Jon-Jon said gruffly. "So? It'll still cost you six pence."

"Aye," Leer said with a patient nod. "However, I wish to propose an exchange of goods through a challenge against the current champion."

A hush fell over the inn; the lone fiddle player abruptly dropped his bow as he listened. A single belch echoed in the small space. Heads turned, taking in the scene with awe and shock at Leer's bold proposition.

"My brother is the reigning champion, though his prize will come to me, since he owes a tab." Jon-Jon crossed his arms. "What would you want to be exchanging?"

Leer replied, his voice even and confident, "Should I win, me and my lot are fed tonight and tomorrow morn, as well as put up for tonight for free."

The room broke out in fits of laughter, the large men more than amused at the suggestion of anyone besides Jon-Jon's brother winning.

Jon-Jon raised his hairy hand, silencing the group. "And should you lose?" he demanded, waiting for the response.

"Then you keep the girl as your new barmaid," Leer replied, nodding toward Astrid.

"What?" Astrid gasped, shocked at Leer's bargain. "How dare you!"

The men laughed again. "Oh, 'tis were me, I would like that prize very much," one cackled.

"Yeah, yeah," another chimed in. "She's a fine young thing. She looks so…soft."

Astrid stood and tried to move away from the table, but Leer pinned her against it, his palms flat on the table behind her.

"Move, you dog, or I'll gut you," she cautioned under her breath.

"You're in safe hands," Leer whispered into her ear. "You've got to trust me."

"Trust you?" she asked, stunned as she laughed. "I don't even *know* you, and you hardly take direction well. Besides, aren't you the man who told me to never make a deal with someone you don't know?"

"Yes, but you're not that someone in this case," Leer explained patiently, his lips close to her ear as he spoke in a hushed tone. "I've given you my word to protect you, and protect you I shall. Now, you've got to trust me. Do you?"

Leer waited for her answer, feeling how Astrid's breath swept over his neck as he blocked her.

"I don't know," she admitted.

"At least you're honest." Leer sighed. "Alright. Well, do you trust me more than them?"

She mulled over his words, glancing behind her at the men snickering around her. "Yeah, but not much, and you shouldn't fail to remember that."

"Aye," Leer said with a small grin, "I shan't."

"And also so you know, Private Boxwell," Astrid whispered, "you may have managed to twice inhabit such an intimate space without me killing you, but don't get used to it."

"'Tis a shame, really," Leer flirted. "I thought you rather enjoyed it."

"Make no mistake, Private—you're not to confuse me with an easy Vale woman," Astrid corrected sternly.

"Nay," he responded, his voice turning serious as he looked at her, "I hadn't ever thought you were."

He felt his chest tighten as her soft breath continued to coast across his skin through her parted lips. He lost awareness of what was happening around him beyond her eyes.

A stout man with a wiry salt and pepper beard rose from a far table, his crook nose flaring as he smirked with unmistakable pride. "'Tis me you seek, Boy," the man said, interrupting the tense moment between Leer and Astrid. "Gorton McNeil, Jon-Jon's brother."

His tablemates cheered him on, heartily clinking their glasses together to salute their victor.

Leer's concentration shifted up from Astrid, remaining in front of her. "Have you got a yen for a game then, Sir?" he asked the man.

The man laughed. "Gort will do just fine," he corrected. "Perhaps when we're finished, you'll be more inclined to call me 'master of the board.'" He shifted his attention to Astrid as she glanced at him over her shoulder. "I look forward to getting to know you better too, dear," he goaded.

"Private," Astrid whispered to Leer, irritated at Gort's insinuation, "I can imagine these men won't stand for a cheat. I'm sure they won't hesitate to drive a blade through your chest should they figure you tricked them."

Leer glanced back at Astrid's soft features. His lips curled up at the sides. "Who said anything about a cheat?" He peered up above her. "So it's settled then?" he called out to Gort, hushing the other chattering patrons once more. "Will there be a challenge?"

After a pause, Jon-Jon nodded in approval toward Gort. "If you'd like to call it as such," Gort laughed.

Some of the patrons began laying out the board at a far table near the fireplace; Leer slid around Astrid, stripping his heavy brown coat with relief as he mentally prepared himself. He snatched a hot mug of ale from the bar and stretched his neck, his steps confident as he sauntered toward Gort and the game.

He looked at the board as he took his seat across from his opponent. "So Boy," Gort said with a grin, "which would you be liking? The white or the black?"

"As reigning champion of this inn, I say you should have first choice," Leer replied, taking a drink from his mug. He caught Gort's toothy smile out of the corner of his eye.

"White," Gort chose; the men behind and around him cheered in support of his selection.

"Aye," Leer agreed, drawing his black pawns toward him, setting each one thoughtfully in place. "To be the king is always a good choice."

"Feeling lucky, Boy?" Gort taunted as he arranged his own pawns.

"I'll let you know when this game is through," Leer replied with a smile.

As he adjusted himself in his seat, he caught a glimpse of Lieutenant Doyle standing in front of Astrid.

He was surprised to see her so close to him. The Lieutenant spoke softly to Astrid, his mouth mere inches away from hers. Leer couldn't hear what the Lieutenant said, nor what Astrid replied in an equally light tone.

Leer grimaced as he noticed the Lieutenant's hand resting over Astrid's hip. The man's long fingers flexed against her curves, and she looked down in response.

Leer shut his eyes momentarily, distraction flowing through his mind like a current, tearing his attention from the important task he had at hand. He couldn't stop looking, though, and despite his better sense urging him not to, he resumed watching the intimate exchange between his two travel companions.

Lieutenant Doyle's hand reached up from Astrid's hip and stroked her cheek, his fingers languidly tracing up her jaw as he moved her dark hair from her face, tucking it behind her ear. His hand coasted downward across her neck and clavicle before departing slowly as he whispered something to her that made her full lips part.

In a flash, Leer saw the searing fire, the heat the Grimbarror had made as the castle guard writhed and died before his eyes.

He heard screams of sheer terror, he saw Princess Maegan's vacant eyes just before she fell into the earth's opening.

He saw the bodies in the war-torn field.

He saw blood drip from his own hands.

Leer swallowed, suddenly parched. He internally panicked, the unexpected impact of it all on him not making any logical sense.

"Boy," he heard from Gort across him, the round man snickering as he slurped his ale. "Aren't you playing me a game this eve?"

With a deep breath, Leer tore his eyes from the scene, facing Gort once again. "Aye," he said, flicking a glance back to Astrid once more, seeing her eyes locked on the Lieutenant's. "Let's be on with it."

-10-

If there was one thing in life that Leer knew beyond absolute certainty, it was that he was an astute tafl player.

Yet, like the unforgiving snow that fell last night, negativity swirled through Leer's mind. Doubt upon doubt compounded together with no apparent end. Still, he kept his faux exterior of poise and calm; it was all he had to cling to, a security blanket of familiarity to counter the unexplainable sensations of distraction he was experiencing.

"Now Leer," Finnigan had once whispered as he crouched over a battered tafl board in the same seat as Gort now sat, "why are you so angry?"

"You have all of my pawns," an adolescent Leer exclaimed in defeat, blonde curls falling onto his forehead as he sulked.

"You still have your ones over there," Finnigan reminded, pointing out a few black pegs left.

"They won't make it. It's too far."

"Have you looked to make sure?"

"It's too far."

The weathered man smiled. "Alright, 'tis how you wish to play, then. Giving up, are you?"

Leer sighed, his small arms crossing over his chest. "There isn't a point."

"Nay, Boy," Finnigan corrected. "There will always be a point to everything—it's up to you to make it, though."

"Your move," Gort said, taking a long sip from his freshly refilled ale mug. Ettie then looked to Leer's with silent questioning as she held the pitcher.

"Nay," Leer mumbled as he came back to the present, waving her off as he stared at the board.

He knew he had initially been far too lax in his offense, resulting in the gap between his black pawns and Gort's white ones. He lost many strategic moves early on. It wasn't like him—he wasn't as sloppy as he showed tonight. A dark brew of hate and vengeance created an evil creature of distraction inside of him.

Leer squeezed his eyes shut. He couldn't afford such dawdling. He had to be aggressive, to employ a diversion strategy. The game mattered most, the outcome providing much needed shelter and nourishment to help him continue forward to save the princess and ultimately bring justice to Finnigan.

Count, count, then once more, Leer recited in his mind, the adage his mentor gave him steering his hands through a few turns. Leer didn't respond to Gort's chuckle, watching him remove the pawns he'd purposely sacrificed. *Never quit a moment before.* Leer flexed his fingers and kept his dark eyes focused as he shifted his back pawn, ignoring the surprised response from the crowd.

"Yours," he said, looking at Gort.

"Bit of a risk, isn't it?" Gort challenged with a grin.

"What's life without risk?"

"Ah, you say that because you're young."

"And now you're too old?"

Gort's face changed at the implication. "If a lesson is what you insist upon, then that's what you shall receive."

Leer leaned back, sipping the last of his ale. "By all means." He closed his eyes for a brief prayer for luck. It was grasping at straws, really. He needed a miracle.

When he opened his eyes, he watched as Gort's irritated expression revealed hints of internal panic. On his turns, Leer made a precise move, then another after that, slowly gaining back the advantage.

Thank you, he breathed in relief, though part of him wondered what divine intervention he had just accessed to achieve the help he got.

The men around Gort had become quiet, taking in the turning of the tides with fascination.

"You can always surrender," Leer whispered a while later, seeing the way Gort clutched at the underside edge of the table with his free hand.

"I'll do no such thing," Gort snapped.

"Aye, well…s'long as you're certain."

Gort made his move, infuriated. "Blast," Gort growled, seeing the last move he was forced to make, the only choice he had left—one that would cost him the game. "What kinds of tricks be up your sleeve, Boy?" the stout man asked, bursting from his seat. Another man passed Gort a sword, and Gort pointed the tip at Leer's throat.

Out of the corner of his eye, Leer saw how the sudden ruckus got Astrid's attention; he heard her gasp as she stood from the seat she had taken in the corner.

"No tricks," Leer replied, a bit offended, his hands up at his sides in surrender. "Search me if you'd like. I've played nothing but fair."

"That he has," one of the men murmured, receiving unsure throaty agreements from the others.

"Never have seen a victory like it in all my days," a second man commented.

"The boy's a natural," another by him agreed.

Furiously, Gort shifted his attention and the blade of his sword. "It's that blasted woman," he continued, shaking his free hand toward Astrid. "She's a brewstress. She's cursed me!"

"A brewstress?" some of the others asked with anger, horrified at the possibility.

"Don't be ridiculous, I'm not a brewstress," Astrid protested.

"You be wearing the cloak of one," Gort argued.

"This is a typical cloak of Hiline."

"For a man." Gort shifted his weight toward her. "Tell us, did you bewitch and kill him to steal his cloak, whoever he was?"

She scoffed, her mouth agape. "This is madness. You're a bunch of drunken beasts who haven't a bit of sense left in you."

"Oh, I've got enough sense to know a brewstress when I've seen one," Gort yelled, charging forward. "There's evil about you, wench."

"Stand down," Leer growled, coming between Gort's blade and Astrid with his own drawn sword, his blade crossing stiffly against the other. He kept his eyes locked on Gort. "Lay down your sword," he warned.

"You shan't tell me what to do, Boy," Gort snapped.

A loud clatter on the counter next to them startled Gort and Leer from their face-off.

"Enough," Jon-Jon yelled as he folded his large arms across his chest. "Now, put your blades away, lest I toss you both out into the snow for a desperate tragurn to eat." Jon-Jon's brow wrinkled when he saw Gort's hesitation. "Gort, the boy won fair, however arrogant of an arse he might be. There be no sorcery here tonight."

The room remained quiet as Gort tucked his sword away first, the anger still quite visible on his face as he eyed Leer, who shifted his weight as he followed suit and put his sword back in its sheath.

"So, the people here believe in sorcery, then?" Leer asked, intrigued by the development.

"We've seen a few things," Jon-Jon replied.

"Such as what?"

The surrounding group shared unsure glances as their eyes shifted. "Strange things have been witnessed in the northernmost Eyne Wood near Cabryog by hunters," Jon-Jon said after a pause. "White hot fires burning despite sheets of rain, men with good heads losing all sense and killing each other over nothing. A groaning from deep within the belly of the earth. Darkness."

Leer watched Gort return to his table, the other patrons peeling off to follow.

"You've got the last three rooms on the far right wing. Now," Jon-Jon said, his tone cool, "I suggest you three eat and be off before you wear out your welcome." He draped a cloth over his large shoulder and walked away, leaving Leer standing in the middle of the room, Astrid and Lieutenant Doyle behind on either side of him.

Eventually, the fiddler resurrected the music, the first few songs he played more solemn than those previously. Ettie skirted around, depositing bowls of stew in front of the Lieutenant and Astrid, who had returned to their previous locations.

Leer groaned. His ribs ached with pain and hunger. The burns on his foot, arm, and face desperately needed the yeran bark ointment from his pack near the Lieutenant's table, but he didn't have the strength to move. With a sigh, he sank onto a stool in front of the abandoned counter, staring ahead at the numerous colorful carved dalecarlians, textured pots, and painted crocks on the shelves across from it.

Ettie set a bowl of steaming stew down, seeing Leer's preoccupied look. "Well, you did win fair," she noted. She came a bit closer. "Tell me, how did you do it?"

"I just know how to play," Leer wearily responded, grateful for the bland stew.

"No," Ettie insisted, "I've seen many a men fail to beat Gort. He's good." She smiled. "But you...you're something else."

"If you only knew," he replied cheekily, sipping his ale. "Tell me more about the dark magic witnessed in the north."

"Why would a solid man like you care about such tales?" Ettie asked, pouring more golden brew into his mug after he set it back down.

"I've a curious side, I suppose."

"Well, if you ask me, those tales are nothing more than campfire stories about the Vei spun together by frightened and drunken men."

"So no one has ever actually produced evidence?"

Ettie paused. "There's been a few things," she replied, eying Leer.

"Please, do tell," Leer said with a charming smile.

She exhaled in defeat. "There were a few deaths, but it isn't unusual for men of these parts to get a bit hotheaded, as you now know. And there was the talk of spotting Emelda."

Leer's eyes met Ettie's. "Emelda?"

"Yes." She paused. "You do know who Emelda is, don't you?"

"I'm afraid not."

Ettie laughed. "'Course you don't, strapping man like you not one for mixing with such nonsense."

"Please," Leer urged, "do go on. Who is Emelda?"

"She's the daughter of Balane," Ettie explained. "Any one of these dimwits in here will tell you she's real, but the sensible folks know better, don't we?"

Leer forced a soft laugh. "Right, of course." He leaned in a little. "But, say I was curious about her. Where might I find information?"

Ettie cackled. "The village crier says he saw her once, so who knows if it's true." She leaned in with a hushed voice, "Let's say that Looney Luke's word has never been of a reliable nature."

"I can hear ya from over here, Ettie," croaked an old man tucked in a nearby corner. Leer shifted his focus onto him, observing his wrinkled skin and beady eyes with curiosity. He watched as the man tipped back his mug, somehow never breaking the gaze he held on Leer.

"Oh hush, Luke," Ettie scolded, her hands finding her plump hips. "You know no one believes the waste you spew."

"Luke?" Leer asked, eyes widening. "Luke Foreman, aye?"

The old man's eyes narrowed as he lowered his mug. His crooked finger scratched his predominant nose, his gaping mouth exposing the holes of his missing teeth. "What's it to ya?" he asked.

"Sir, if you're the man I've read of, then surely you remember the name Finnigan Lance."

Looney Luke stared Leer down. "I may know the name."

Leer's pulse quickened. "Sir, I would like to ask you some questions."

"'Bout what?"

"The Vei."

Luke rose from his seat with an unhurried stretch. "You'd leak your breeches, Boy."

Leer matched Luke's visible smirk with his own. "I'll consider myself forewarned."

"You can't be serious," Ettie challenged Leer in shock.

"It's imperative to heed the advice of our elders, aye?" Leer asked her back with a smile.

As he watched Ettie leave with a groan of disgust, Leer stirred his stew, listening to the clopping of Looney Luke's gait intermixed with the crooning of the fiddle across from him as the old man approached and filled the stool next to his with little grace.

"I would think you know of the Grimbarror then, yeah?" the old man asked with a thin smile.

"Aye. I've heard the tales from Finnigan."

With dirt-caked fingernails, the old man scratched his stubbled face. He leaned in with a grin; as a result of their new proximity, Leer caught the sudden infiltration of unpleasant odors from him. "So," Luke said, "what have you heard about the Grimbarror?"

"It's a vile beast made from dark Vei magic for the purpose of killing."

"And that's all?"

"Aye," Leer replied in truth.

Luke's grin widened significantly. "You poor reew," he said with pity. "You shan't be any wiser than anyone else in Hiline."

Leer tilted his head back as he examined the man next to him. "Perhaps you could enlighten me, then," he offered. He watched as Luke grasped his mug's handle, bringing it to his lips.

As he finished drinking, the old man wiped his mouth with the back of his hand. "Before you were born, Sortaria was a far more fruitful land than it is today," he began. Leer saw a distinct sparkle in Luke's eyes. "All was well for both countries, the trade bounty plentiful."

"Yes, I know this," Leer sighed.

Luke continued with a huff, "For centuries, people of divine Sortarian birthright, known as the Keepers, were charged by the Vei Master with keeping rule over the Amulet of Orr."

"What—"

"Shush," the old man interrupted with narrowed eyes. "Just listen, Boy." He shifted in his seat, a slight scowl threatening to dull the excitement in him. "Every twenty years on the Eve of Listra, those who possess Vei magic in their blood are tested under the Keepers before them. If a person is determined to be of divine right, they sequester themselves to live in the underground caverns of the Fell. There, they learn the ways of the Keepers before them to ensure the continuation of proper Vei usage, as well as to ensure safety of the Vei from darkness."

"How do they ensure it?" Leer asked.

"By protecting the amulet," Luke replied, wetting his lips. "See, those who are found to possess the Vei magic, but have darkness of heart instead of light, they are…" He paused. "They are sacrificed."

Leer's eyes widened. "Killed, you mean?"

Luke gave a heavy sigh. "It's for the greater good."

"How can that possibly be for good?" Leer scoffed. "They are killed in cold blood, aye? What would be fair about that?"

The old man's wiry brow raised. "Suppose, then, that you had livestock, and you saw in the wood a sick willet. Probably a boney, scraggly thing that hadn't yet done the evil, but you could see the foam on its lips. Should you leave it to poison your reews or your celks with a bite of its jaws?"

Leer's jaw flexed. "Sick willets shan't be any comparison to human life."

Luke clucked his tongue. "You daft boy, that's a child's reasoning. It must be nice to afford such a luxury as your thoughts."

"But—"

"Hush," Luke warned, waving Ettie over to pour him more ale, to which she obliged. "I need to find some patience for the likes of you. 'Tweren't for Finnigan, I might not even try."

The older man sipped his drink, the lines on his face taut as he stared ahead at the wall, muttering unintelligibly to himself. For a moment, Leer turned back to his stew, now thicker from growing cold as he listened to Luke. He pushed his spoon around in it, nostrils flared as he considered the grim reality of Vei preservation. Was undue death truly necessary? Was the life of one less important than the lives of many, even if the one was innocent?

Finnigan believed in the sovereignty of the Vei.

He realized that his boyhood idol believed in murder.

Nay. Finnigan wouldn't have supported it. I know he mustn't.

"The amulet," Luke finally murmured a bit later.

"Aye, as you said," Leer replied.

"The Keepers guard of the Amulet of Orr, because it has vast power. Only those pure of heart should have possession of such a thing because of the magic it holds."

"Such as what?"

"Strength, foresight. Infinite wisdom."

Leer swallowed. "So the amulet can be used for darkness as well as good?" Luke nodded. "Who is Emelda, then?"

Leer caught the subtle shift in Luke's demeanor. "In the time before Finnigan was birthed, no doubt, Emelda was a very powerful wielder of Vei magic. She was the daughter of Balane, the Vei Master of that time. However, she was far from pure."

"What do you mean?"

"Balane had two children, twins: Ishma, a son, and Emelda, a daughter. Each were gifted with the Vei, and while they were both favored to be masters, only Ishma was granted the right before their father died.

"On the Eve of Listra's birth, when they both competed for their birthright, Ishma succeeded, but Emelda failed her test. She became jealous, darkness entering her and tainting the Vei within. Knowing her envy would mean her death, she fled, hiding for years in the mountains, disguised as a simple brewstress, waiting for the right opportunity to exact her revenge.

"For several years, Emelda was alone, until she took a lover and became pregnant with her daughter, Lana. Lana was born with the Vei in her blood, as were Ishma's sons, Tyne and Naetan. Still, Lana did not share the same darkness of heart as her mother, and when Lana reached the age of maturity, she fled her mother's home before her mother could convert her.

"Lana sought out her cousin, Tyne, for protection, to which he obliged. See, Tyne was next in line to be Master after Ishma, and because of this, Naetan was jealous. So, Naetan sought out his aunt so he could be granted power. Thus, the first Son of Night was created."

"The first Grimbarror," Leer concluded.

Luke nodded. "Naetan's anger helped him to grow more powerfully evil each day, the darkness turning even his body into a monster. He wanted his father's and brother's deaths, so he could possess the amulet. Naetan soon returned to the Fell with Emelda, where he slayed his father, and she, her daughter. However, Tyne's Vei was greater, and he killed his brother."

"So, then how could there be another Grimbarror now?"

"That is a mystery only Emelda could reveal. She hasn't been seen since Tyne slayed his brother."

"But you saw her, aye?"

Luke nodded. "That I did. One night at the edge of the Vale, not far from the castle. I had traveled south to trade Finnigan some fur."

"How do you know it was her?"

"I just did."

Leer pursed his lips. "You can't possibly know in the dark of night unless given reason."

"Reason," Luke muttered. "So that's what you need, eh? Reason? Proof?" He shook his head. "Nary a thing like your mentor, you are. Everything you require is all Finnigan despised."

The familiar heat of anger tinged the skin of Leer's neck. "You know nothing of Finnigan," he growled.

Luke pushed to his feet with a huff and a slight unsteadiness. "You know much," he sneered, "but you know nothing at all." His face twisted with a grimace he tried to conceal the downward curve of his bent spine. "My eyes may be fading, but it is you who cannot see."

Leer felt panic mix with his rage as he watched. Out of the corner of his eye, he saw Ettie approach the counter. "I've more questions," he stammered.

"And I've no more answers to give, Boy."

He turned away, swiping his cloak and knotted wood walking stick from where they rested against the counter. Leer watched Luke pull the cloak over himself, the old man never once looking back in his direction before he left through a side door.

Leer was quiet as he thought, his heavy gaze shifting back to the wall behind the counter. He silently absorbed the story he'd just heard.

"So tell me," Ettie began sweetly as she leaned in, her fingers trailing up Leer's arms, "why isn't there a pretty thing on each of these arms of yours?"

"Perhaps because I haven't the sense to maintain such things at the moment," Leer replied, still distracted.

Her fingers began to descend down his sleeves. "Sounds like you need a woman who can understand the troubles of a man, not a girl who needs maintenance."

Leer smirked, shaking his head. "Won't waste time beating around the bush, aye?"

"Why be subtle?" Ettie countered, her fingers coasting over his knuckles. "Life is short."

"Terribly so," Leer said, moving gently away from her reach.

"Hmm," she pondered with a grin, watching him, "alright then, Blondie—what is it you do care about then?"

Leer shook his head. "I would doubt you'd care to hear the topic of my fascination."

"Wouldn't I?"

"There is no joy in it."

Ettie smirked, shimmying closer. "Try me."

The sound of the front door banging shut distracted Leer, while a gust of cool air whipped across the room. He caught sight of Astrid slipping out of the door, the Lieutenant already missing from his seat.

"Thank you for the stew," Leer said to Ettie, glancing back at her. "Though I think it best if I retire for the eve."

She pulled away from the counter with a knowing look of disappointment. "G'night then, Blondie." She leaned back as he shrugged his thick coat over his back and shoulders once more. "Perhaps you need to let go of whatever it is that troubles you so," she added.

He paused for a moment to contemplate what she suggested. "I can't," he decided as he walked away.

The candlelight didn't offer much guidance for Leer's fingers as he scooped the yeran bark ointment from the small jar. He applied it to the still sore wound on his foot before pulling back on his thick sock. He shivered in the cold room; the firewood was too saturated with fresh snow to be very effective at completely catching fire.

He sat on the edge of the straw mattress, resting the candle down on the small bedside table. The ambitious trek and other events thus far had irritated his aching body. He peeled his evergreen sweater off and tossed it across from himself in the pile of other discarded clothes near the tiny fire. The air from the flying shirt made the fire dance, the light of the flames glinting off of the blade of the sword propped up next to the bed. Leer watched the flickering choreography and lost himself in thought.

An unexpected knock on his door startled him. Leer stood, creeping curiously toward the room's entrance with the candle in hand. "Aye? Who might it be?" he asked, his voice gruff from the long period of silence.

"Open the door, Private."

Leer slid the bolt of the door open. His right hand gripped the candle as he held it up and examined his visitor.

Blue eyes stared back at him, the owner of them clutching a large hunting knife.

-11-

"Astrid," Leer breathed, seeing the knife she wielded.

"Back in your room," Astrid ordered, looking over her shoulder. Leer hesitated, confused. She turned back to him. "Back inside," she whispered, shoving him backward.

She ducked into the chilly room and shut the door behind herself. Pressing her back against the door, she raised the knife toward Leer. "Don't approach me," she warned, her hand shaking, "or I'll gut you like a poncher."

"Steady, Astrid," Leer whispered, glancing briefly at the out-of-reach sword leaning near the cot. He met her wild, unpredictable eyes. "Just tell me what is wrong."

"I need you to answer me two questions with truth," Astrid snapped, grabbing the candle from Leer's hand and setting it down on a surface adjacent to her without concern.

"Aye," Leer agreed gently, "I shall. Just be at ease." He watched her heavy breathing, her cloak hanging on her narrow shoulders, as if it had been thrown on in haste.

She narrowed her eyes. "First question: Why did you offer me as a prize to be had for the game?"

Leer shook his head, exhaling with a bit of relief. "You were never at risk. I knew they wouldn't be able to resist the possibility of winning you, but believe me when I say that you were never in any danger."

"Should you have lost, what then? Part ways with me and never look back, is that it?"

"Astrid, it was impossible for me to lose," Leer argued.

"Impossible?" she repeated. "It's never impossible to lose, Private."

"Listen, lass, you don't know what I'm capable of."

"And neither do you," Astrid snapped, stepping forward as she raised her knife. "I'm not a 'thing' that you own or that you can just freely give like that. And if you were that stupidly sure of yourself, you could've offered the sword."

"Aye," Leer agreed with gentle reluctance. "'Twas a poor decision. I apologize."

Astrid was silent for a moment, then took another step toward him. "Second question: Why do you seek the heart of the Fell?"

"To save the Princess of—"

She stepped forward again, raising the knife. "The truth, Private," she warned.

Leer held his hands up, exhorting her to be still. "Alright," he surrendered. "I haven't lied to you regarding my intentions, but I do confess that I haven't told you everything." He saw how she waited for his answer. Silently, he tried to figure out the reason for her sudden skepticism and anger while simultaneously preparing himself for her reaction. "I seek the Grimbarror in the heart of the Fell," he explained,

She began to move forward, and then froze. The thick cloak she wore fell from her shoulders with the sudden pause. It pooled around her ankles, the cool air flowing through her tunic and vest.

"What did you say?" she asked, her voice hesitant.

"I said," Leer repeated, not moving, "it is the Grimbarror that I seek in the heart of the Fell."

Astrid's lips tightened into a thin line. "I asked you to tell me the truth," she growled.

Before he could respond, she lunged at him with her knife, swift and agile in her attack as she knocked Leer to his back in front of the fire. With her blade pressed against his throat, she panted, pinning him to the ground with her body weight.

"I did," Leer insisted, knowing he might need to hurt her in order to protect himself. "It has taken the princess. I seek its evil face for justice for Hiline."

She remained on top of him, their proximity close as the silence surrounded them. With the light of the small fire, Leer could see her nim-like cornflower eyes in detail, noting their truly strange the hue.

He couldn't ignore the softness and warmth of her body, the weight of it stirring heat inside of him. Not merely the familiar heat of desire, but another, one he couldn't explain. It enveloped him, if only for a moment, with the sincerest comfort. Then, it tried to destroy him.

The rapid-fire lights struck his eyes, and he squeezed them shut, groaning as he cowered within himself against the pain. He felt Astrid move to his side, faintly hearing the clatter of her knife as it dropped to the ground. Her echoed call was shrouded in fog, a swamp like thickness choking his sight and hearing.

Pockets of time slipped in and out of his internal view, his pulse pounding against his temples. Each beat was a slice, a burn, each image an assault.

He heard voices, indistinguishable tongues.

He felt the surge of his bloodstream in his veins.

Just when he was ready to scream, it stopped.

Leer swallowed back the painful dryness of his throat as his eyes flickered open, resting on Astrid's craned neck. Her skin glowed in the firelight.

Her hand rested on his stubbled left cheek, her palm concealing the scar as her fingertips brushed across his lower lashline. A few small callouses roughened her cool skin.

Leer blinked heavily, looking up toward her face. Her lips parted in wait.

"Private, speak to me," she whispered. "Are you alright?"

He stared at her for a moment. "I don't know," he whispered back.

"What…What has been happening to you?"

He chose not to answer, only because he was unsure himself. Instead, he sat up with a grimace, his ribs still quite sore. He took Astrid's hand and pulled her up with him as he stood.

"But what—"

"I can't answer that," Leer snarled, letting go of her hand. He shut his eyes. "I haven't the slightest."

"You speak the truth," Astrid remarked after a moment of silence.

"I take it you expected something else."

"You mean to tell me that you believe in the Grimbarror?"

Leer chuckled. "Not only do I believe in it, but I know it to be true."

Astrid's mouth fell open. "I don't believe this."

"I'm sorry I've disappointed you."

"It's just...the Grimbarror?"

"Aye."

Leer stooped to pick up Astrid's knife, keeping it out of her reach as she tried to take it from him. "Nay, lass," he corrected, tossing it onto the mattress beside them. "I've answered your questions." He snatched her wrists. "Now you answer mine." He kept her close, feeling both the heat of her body and of the fire next to them radiating over him. "What has you frightened like this?"

"Let me be," she screeched, yanking at the restraint.

"Nay, not until you tell me."

"I owe you no explanations."

"And neither did I."

"I disagree, Private," Astrid argued. "It is *you* that has forced me on this suicide mission of yours for a belief in a creature of fairytales and legends."

"Nothing was forced on you," Leer argued back, not flinching in his grip. "You had a choice."

"A choice? You honestly believe yourself and your Lieutenant to be noble in your actions, then?"

"Don't speak to me of nobility. After all, you're the thief."

She glared at him. "I wouldn't have need to steal if it weren't for your bonny king."

"Blaming the royalty for your troubles now?" Leer asked, pulling her a bit closer. "As I recall, since you're living here in Hiline, he's your bonny king too, lass."

"You know nothing of me," she reminded through a harsh tone.

"And you know nothing of me," Leer agreed.

They faced each other for an instant, the silence ringing in their ears as they stood in front of one another. Leer's Adam's apple bobbed as he swallowed hard, his pulse racing.

"I don't wish to handle you in this manner, so please," he said with an angry sigh, "tell me what has you troubled so I might be able to help you."

"I don't need your help," Astrid retorted. "I can handle myself. I have for all my life."

"Please," Leer whispered, keeping his grip firm. "Allow me to help you as I know you shall continue to help me."

Leer waited through Astrid's silence, continuing to study her face in the stillness between them.

How old was she? She appeared as young and as fresh as a nimling, but was shouldered with burdens of a person far beyond her years. A flurry of unfounded lust swirled within him as he watched her inhale slowly through her opened mouth. She drew her bottom lip inward and as she released it, he found himself examining it, taking note of the moisture on it.

"You'll think me mad," she objected, shaking her head.

"I know a bit about people thinking me mad," he reminded gently, his hands adjusting over her wrists. "I can assure you that I'm the least of your worries."

He watched her draw another deep, contemplative breath. "I'm not sure what it was," Astrid whispered, looking away from him to the fire. "I...I was in my room and it was as if it came to me all of a sudden. I..." She glanced back up, seeing Leer watching her with patience. "I heard a voice."

"A voice?" Leer asked.

She nodded. "Inside my mind. Telling me to..."

He leaned in a bit when she stopped. "To what?"

"To fear you...because you are evil," Astrid whispered, swallowing. "I-I had no such thoughts before, but it was as if in that moment that...that I couldn't *not* fear you. As if my life depended on it." She peered up at him with wide eyes. "It all sounds mad, I know. I fought the suggestions with every bit I had in me. I swore it was the ale or the stew or—"

Leer released one of Astrid's hands, his fingertips sliding down her wrist as he kept his eyes fixed on hers. The back of one of his hands found the skin of her forehead, pressing against it gingerly.

"You're warm," he said, his dark eyes flicking over her facial features. "Do you feel ill?"

"No," she replied, motionless under his examination.

"And you said it was as if..."

"As if every negative thought I had was somehow so much larger and more powerful. So much more...frightening. It was as if I wasn't in control of my own self."

In silence, Leer withdrew his hand from her forehead, lowering it. He slowly released her other wrist, thoughts racing through his mind.

He, too, had heard the voices, the ones that had tried to tell him things. But would she think him mad, or perhaps a liar, if he admitted it? The coincidence was hard to ignore.

Could it be, then, that there was a force attempting to speak to him? And to her? A power trying to break through?

"And now how do you feel?" he breathed, peering down at her. His hands had found her waist, hovering across the sides with careful curiosity.

The fire hissed beside them, the wood popping as it burned. They remained still, his hands on her unchanged with the passing time despite the growing sear he felt within.

Astrid inhaled, hesitantly releasing it. "Fine," she said, her brow furrowed. "I've felt better since the moment you touched me."

He glanced away, his eyes coming to rest on the shine of her dark curls. Bits of Looney Luke's story of the Vei filtered through his mind, dissipating as he searched the depths of Astrid's eyes. He examined her, his grip tightening around her.

Let go of her, he warned himself.

Still, he couldn't. The pads of his fingers dug a tiny bit deeper into their grip around her; he drew her closer to himself, engrossed. He saw her, but didn't see, felt her but couldn't feel anything as black smoke rose around his vision, fogging his awareness.

This is madness, his consciousness rang in his mind. *You've a sickness.*

His right hand crept to the small of Astrid's back as he held her, tracing the dip of her spine. He felt the contact of her hand brush across his pants on his upper thigh with the adjustment. The wind howled against the wall of the room, but was still not as deafening as his pulse in his ears.

"...Private!"

Leer blinked, the haze descending to reveal Astrid's frightened expression. He moved his mouth to speak, wordless as he saw he had been holding Astrid the entire time.

"I said, let me go," Astrid demanded, a shakiness to her voice.

With a sudden awareness, he rejected her like a hot pot handle, taking a step away from her. "I—I'm sorry. I—"

"Save it," Astrid interrupted, giving him an icy wave of her hand. "I should've known a madman like you would be inclined to abuse herbs at leisure."

Leer's pulse was thready, his throat painfully dry. Not even his saliva could relieve the ache of it. Mouth gaping, he watched in perplexed silence as Astrid swept her cloak from the floor and draped it over herself as she scurried toward the door. With realization, he moved from his place, snatching the hunting knife from the mattress. He strode to the doorway with purpose, meeting her.

"Astrid," he said, gaining her attention. "Your knife."

He pressed the knife's grip into her bare hand, gritting his teeth as he felt the scorching heat of her flesh briefly make contact with his own. She wordlessly took it and slipped out of the room, shutting the door as she left Leer to feel his own hand in stunned confusion.

A fire surged in his mind and body; the room was almost too warm, the heat compressing around him. He, too, now had a flurry of voices ringing through his head, as if somehow the problem Astrid had felt had transferred through her simple touch.

Only, Leer knew his voices told him different things than hers had. Much different things—things he wished had never entered his already clouded mind.

Breakfast at dawn consisted of stale, dark rye bread. Still, the trio welcomed the food without complaint. Leer knew the odds were against them for securing another such meal in the near future.

"Anything else I can get for you?" Leer heard Ettie ask, his head bent downward as he kept to himself. Sleep had eluded him, the countless whispers he heard the night before still echoing in the walls of his mind.

"A bit more ale to drink, yeah?" the Lieutenant asked, holding up his mug.

"Sorry," Ettie said, "but that's about all the ale we can give away."

Lieutenant Doyle sighed in disgust. "Water, then."

"Would it kill you to say please?" Ettie asked as she walked away, the grumble from the Lieutenant under his breath following in her wake.

"I've had about enough of our outstanding accommodations," Lieutenant Doyle said to Leer. "Are you quite finished with your bread yet? Because I certainly would appreciate moving on."

"Inns don't suit a man like you, I take it?" Leer asked without looking up, leisurely tearing another chunk of bread off of the loaf.

The Lieutenant frowned. "You're not the one that was in the room nearest to the privy." Leer caught in his peripheral how Astrid couldn't help but smirk. "It's not funny," the Lieutenant argued.

"Actually, it is," Astrid replied. Leer's hand collided with Astrid's upon blindly reaching for the loaf of bread at the center of the table. His eyes met hers; they each urgently recoiled from the contact.

"Sorry. Please," Leer mumbled, nodding toward the bread as he tucked his hand behind his mug, his long finger drawing a line down the side as he busied himself with an easygoing outward air.

He shut his eyes, a small groan resonating in his throat. He could feel the Lieutenant's curiosity boring into him without even looking. He knew his reaction to touching Astrid was brief, but still enough to trigger questions—questions he didn't care to answer at the moment, and possibly not ever.

"What's got you, Boxwell?" the Lieutenant asked.

"Nothing," Leer insisted, tossing back the last of his ale.

Through the tense silence that followed, Ettie set down a mug of water on the table in front of the Lieutenant. "It's up to your knees in some spots out there from the drifts," she warned, nodding toward the frosted window. "I would think you three will want to have driving celks for traveling in this weather?"

"What a wonderful question. You'd think we would," Lieutenant Doyle agreed, taking the mug.

"They'd break their legs losing their footing on ice, even with spiked shoes," Leer argued, resting his head on his hand. "Besides, without peddlers traveling from Cabryog to clear the way, there are probably too many downed branches along the northern road to navigate a celk through."

"The northern road?" Ettie asked with surprise. "Why on earth would you be going up there this time of year?"

The Lieutenant stood, tossing down his rag on the table. "If you'll kindly excuse us, we'll be on our way." He looked down to Astrid, who stood. Leer, however, remained seated, continually massaging his temples, trying to relieve the perpetual ache that didn't seem to fade.

"The Fell," Leer answered, his head lifting so he could look Ettie in the eye. Everything about him conveyed the utmost seriousness. "We're traveling to the Fell by way of Cabryog."

"The Fell?" Ettie croaked.

What little background noise in the inn ceased, quiet conversations halted at Leer's firm response. Leer caught a glimpse of Jon-Jon gawking at him from behind the counter, his stomach sinking in anticipation as he felt the onslaught of ridicule coming.

"Are you three out of your minds?" Ettie asked with a surprised laugh, her hands resting on her full hips.

"We needn't answer to the likes of you," Lieutenant Doyle sneered,

"We've business there," Leer replied, sparking an eye roll from Lieutenant Doyle.

"Business?" chuckled a man in the far corner. "So then your business is to die?" His question elicited a hearty laugh from the others around him. "Only fools would go to the Fell. Extraordinary fools go to the Fell in the middle of winter."

"Extraordinarily daft fools at that," Jon-Jon added, slinging a rag over his shoulder. "Not even Looney Luke would be dense enough to claim such a thing," another chorus of laughter erupted from the other patrons.

"Wonderful," Lieutenant Doyle muttered. "We're a notch below a man named 'Looney Luke.'"

Before Leer could speak again, Astrid cut in. "Let it go," she advised him under her breath, catching his eyes. "They haven't anything but more mockery for you. Spare yourself. Tell them what you said was in jest."

Leer shook his head. "I won't do that," he whispered, hearing the snickering of the voices across from them.

"Who are they but men you'll probably never meet again?" Astrid argued. "They needn't hear any details from you. Telling them the truth will hurt you more than a simple misdirection will hurt them."

He narrowed his eyes. "I do suppose you know the benefits of misdirection, don't you?"

The choice of words wasn't considered and his tone was far harsher than he intended, but Leer was caught on the downward spiral of the moment and he couldn't escape it. He burst from his seat, shoving his chair away from the table and running through his thick blond hair as he scanned over the on-lookers.

"So, what is your business at the Fell?" asked the man who had previously mocked Leer.

"To retrieve the Princess of Hiline," Leer replied.

"The princess?" the man asked, stunned. The others around him tittered with shaking heads. "I should figure you'd know it was insurgents who took the princess."

"You're wrong," Leer lashed, capturing everyone's attention. "It's not insurgents who claimed her."

Whispers of confusion rose within the inn among the patrons. Another man said with a wrinkled brow, "Surely even if you doubt insurgent involvement, you'd agree that no town other than Cabryog is to be found that far north. Are you saying skimmermen took the princess?"

Leer straightened up a bit, eying the man. "Nay. I don't believe a man to be responsible."

His elusive statement caused another rise of hushed conversations among the patrons.

"What *are* you are saying then, Boy?" Jon-Jon asked, his deep voice silencing the room.

"Oh great," the Lieutenant mumbled next to Leer.

"What I'm saying is," Leer answered, ignoring him, "it is the Grimbarror we seek."

Silence permeated the room, not a sound made as the people stared at Leer dumbfounded. Jon-Jon's thunderous laugh rose out of the quiet, others joining him as they mocked Leer with abandon.

"The Grimbarror, you say?" one man said through his own laughing. "My, what a marvelously stupid boy you are."

"They believe in the Vei and the beast like ol' Looney Luke," another cackled.

"Didn't know people with power that doesn't exist could summon a dead creature," a burly man in the corner giggled.

"Oh, come off it," Astrid snapped. "Just last eve, you believed me to be a brewstress."

"Aye, and we still don't know you aren't one," Gorton replied, a threatening tone to his voice. "Besides, a brewstress only uses maddening herbs. We don't believe in tales told by uncivilized people."

"I'd hardly call you lot civilized. You're nothing but a group of buffoons."

Despite her protest, the voices grew in volume; snickers, chuckles and guffawing pierced the air and stung Leer's ears. The patrons seemed nearly uncontrollable in their amusement, each throwing a comment regarding Leer's sanity out to the others with glee.

"Might any of you cease cackling like a bunch of feanet hens for long enough to point us in the direction of the Eyne Wood?" Leer finally shouted in a darkened timbre.

All activity ceased in the wake of his sudden outburst. The room became awkwardly silent, no one daring to respond to his request.

"Fine then," Leer said. "We will do just as well without your help."

He snatched his coat he had slung over the chair next to him, breezing around behind Astrid as he left the inn, the iron handle of the door rattling as it slammed behind him.

-12-

None of them spoke to each other after breakfast, each keeping his distance in silence over the next few hours as they continued their journey. The afternoon sun shone brightly overhead, beams of light glinting off of the snowy ground as the northern wind chapped the little bit of exposed skin on their faces. Another thick layer of snow burdened the ground from the previous storm, leaving in its wake several cracked evergreen branches along the seldom traveled village road that cut to the north. The excessive climbing up, over, and under the burdensome and hazardous debris forced them to slow their pace. The weight of his encounter with Astrid the night before laid heavily on Leer as he trekked through the Eyne Wood. Over the last day, he too, had experienced similar oddities, and the recollection of each of them continued to fill his mind since the moment she left him the night before.

Tension, he concluded to himself as he toyed with a small branch, twisting it in his mittened hand as he walked. He concluded that the tension was nothing more than stress from their demanding and quite unusual circumstances.

That was the answer. It had to be.

"Can we stop for a moment?" Leer asked, exasperated. *Maybe another look at the journal would help,* he considered.

Lieutenant Doyle merely responded with an exaggerated sigh, which Leer ignored as he found a thick branch to sit on. Retrieving Finnigan's journal, he thumbed through the pages to the section that seemed to be the most cryptic:

Two divided
Maloden—suppression
Conditional transformation, subject to intent
Enter the gates, but do not fall
Eyes of stone
Gems within, power inherently possessed

Just the portions regarding, "two divided," and the, "eyes of stone" seemed clearer.

Ishma and Emelda, and the amulet.

Aside from that epiphany, Leer was at a standstill.

"Any revelations you care to share?"

Leer looked up, finding the Lieutenant a few paces in front of him, seated on a partially snow-dusted tree trunk. "I've only more of what you call fairytales," he replied to him.

The Lieutenant gnawed on a piece of jerky. "I don't suppose I'm otherwise occupied at the moment."

"Alright, then." Leer pursed his lips as he flipped back a page. "I do believe I've two pieces explained. Remember the part about two divided?"

"Yes?"

"Well, that is likely referring to Ishma and Emelda of twenty years ago."

Lieutenant Doyle's brow furrowed. "Come again?"

"The two children of the Vei Master, Balane."

"So they divided, I gather?"

"Aye. Ishma took his father's place, and it made Emelda angry. After he was chosen on the Eve of Listra, she fled, plotting her revenge."

"The, 'Eve of Listra?'"

"Listra, one of the first wielders of Vei magic," Astrid chimed in, coming to stand between them to Leer's left. She looked between them. "The eve refers to her birth."

"Right," Leer looked up at Astrid. "Thank you."

"Sure." She gave a small shrug. "Not that it's based in any truth. The olden myths were just stories, really."

"So was the Vei, until nary a week past," Leer challenged, holding her gaze.

"I'm fairly certain it still is," she replied, unfazed. "After all, you were the lone surviving witness."

Leer smirked. "It's quite incredible that you should refuse belief."

Astrid's eyes narrowed. "I've no reason not to."

"Anyway," Lieutenant Doyle interrupted, "so what of these two, Ishma and Emelda? Do they remain divided?"

"Aye," Leer answered. "Emelda turned her one of her nephews into the first Grimbarror, who then killed his own father."

"Well that doesn't make for a happy family, does it?"

"I would think not."

"And what of the other part you figured out?"

"Aye, the, 'eyes of stone.'" Leer posited. "I believe it refers to the Amulet of Orr."

"The amulet?" Lieutenant Doyle asked, leaning forward a little.

"Aye. Luke said it was vastly powerful, protected by the Keepers."

"What can it do?"

"It contains both light and dark magic. It was believed that if the amulet fell into the wrong hands, it could destroy the world."

"Hmm." Lieutenant Doyle leaned back. "So…If the Grimbarror exists, that means that this Emelda person is likely still alive." He paused. "So why wouldn't she just take possession of it herself?"

"Perhaps she can't. Perhaps she needs the power of a Grimbarror to take the amulet," Astrid suggested.

Lieutenant Doyle looked over to Astrid, his eyes roaming from her body up to her face. "Very clever," he commended. "So, then we can assume she has possession of it in the Fell, yes?"

"I would think," she replied. She looked over at Leer. "Then the Grimbarror you seek now is the same son who was turned?" Astrid asked.

"Nay," Leer said. "It must be a different one. Tyne slayed Naetan."

"Then why wouldn't the Grimbarror kill Emelda to keep it, then?"

Leer sighed. "I don't know it hasn't. I also don't know why if the Grimbarror possesses the amulet, what purpose it would have to take the princess."

The Lieutenant stood, eyes tracking toward the north. "Well, I do know we need to keep moving if we wish to retrieve her."

Leer nodded, rising to his feet as he stowed the journal in his pack.

Despite the midday sun above them, the veil of the hewens in the Eyne Wood shrouded them in dim light. An eerie collection of shadows darkened their surroundings. As they trekked north, each step was met with cooler air than the last. The wind made a shrill hiss as it wove between the trees. The oddity of it permeated Leer, an involuntary chill coasting through his body.

Over and over in his mind, he tried to make sense of the puzzle Finnigan left, regret sinking in as he wished he had asked more questions while Finnigan was still alive. His thoughts kept him quiet; for the most part, he ignored his travel companions.

"You know," Lieutenant Doyle remarked a while later as he scrambled over a thick fallen tree limb, "I find it surprising that the way to such a wonderful destination as the Fell is so untraveled this time of year."

Leer ignored the comment so the Lieutenant wouldn't receive his expected response.

"Awfully quiet today, Private," the Lieutenant continued, Astrid a few paces behind them both as they walked together single file, Leer in the lead. "I would've figured you to be a bit jollier and conceited considering your tafl win."

"I prefer to keep my elation to myself at the moment," Leer replied, lost in thought. He was too tense, too consumed to engage in a battle of wits with the Lieutenant. Still, the Lieutenant kept egging him on.

"The play you utilized—it's an unexpected one, I'll give you that," the Lieutenant noted matter-of-factly. "But it's nothing more than a diversionary tactic coupled with elementary mental manipulation." Leer resisted the urge to look back at him, sensing the trap the Lieutenant set for him. "All child's play, really. It impresses the common man, but admit it, Private— you'd be lost in a grander arena that didn't merely contain simpletons."

"As I recall, the king was quite confident with my abilities."

"The king is currently a very desperate man. Surely you know your being here is nothing more than him grasping at straws."

Leer ground his molars together, twisting the stick in his hands.

Steady and balanced.

He tried to even out his breath, but anger's invisible grip only squeezed tighter.

Nay. The sack has it coming.

"Hmm. Interesting. Then that must mean he hasn't much faith in your abilities either, I suppose?"

His reward was a moment of silence.

"I'm with you, Boxwell, to be sure your lunacy isn't meant for Hiline itself rather than the non-existent mythical beast you seek," Lieutenant Doyle said, his tone thickened with irritation.

"Then why ask questions regarding the journal?" Leer challenged, his contempt building.

"For the most part, I'm bored." Lieutenant Doyle shrugged. "Insight, perhaps. You've a bit of a reputation for instability, and I'm curious where it came from," he added as he kicked a branch away with the toe of his boot. "Which now I see undoubtedly comes from your deceased mentor's lifestyle."

Leer's rage exploded; he whirled around to face Lieutenant Doyle, who stopped in front of him. "And your specialty seems to be having a keen eye for the obvious." He snapped the stick he held and tossed the halves deep into the woods running parallel to the road they traveled. "I'm impressed by your expertise on what is already so blatantly clear. Tell me, did you receive special training for that? Or are you just naturally so average?"

The Lieutenant grabbed Leer's arm, pulling him toward himself. "You listen to me, contract boy," he warned, "the moment we set foot back in the Vale, you'll wish you had stayed in these wretched woods."

Leer tore his arm away from Lieutenant Doyle, his nostrils flaring as he stared him down. "Why wait?" he growled. "You're the one who started it. I'm not opposed to a challenge, if that's what you wish for."

"You're no challenge, Boxwell," Lieutenant Doyle barked, grabbing Leer's coat and shoving him down into a bank of snow. Leer hit the ground, groaning as his ribs collided with the thick mossy rocks hidden underneath the powder. Lieutenant Doyle stripped his mittens from his hands, casually tossing them aside. "You're nothing more than an arrogant, gullible runt pretending to be something you're not."

"Hey, enough!" Astrid yelled behind them. Leer saw her rushing toward the scene as he stood, tossing off his own mittens, the wool flying through the air to his right.

He didn't pause for even a moment before springing forward and snatching a fistful of the Lieutenant's coat. "At least I'm not a flea-ridden pet of the king's, whipped and trained like a dumb beast." He swung his right arm and delivered a solid blow to Lieutenant Doyle's jaw.

The Lieutenant fell to the ground; Leer jumped on top of him like a wild animal, readying himself to take another shot.

"Stop!" Astrid yelled, pulling against Leer's arm as hard as she could.

The distraction threw Leer off balance and Lieutenant Doyle rolled out from under him, both jumping to their feet. The two men exchanged savage looks, standing paces apart when Lieutenant Doyle, growing angrier, lunged at Leer.

Astrid stepped in between him and his enemy, her hands out as she faced Lieutenant Doyle and screamed at him to stop. Leer could clearly see over her tiny shoulders. His chest tightened; time moved slowly as he saw the back of the Lieutenant's hand viciously collide with Astrid's face.

"Don't you dare challenge me," Lieutenant Doyle warned her while his other hand pushed her down out of his way.

As her body fell despite his efforts to defend her, Leer pounced on the Lieutenant with a snarl of pure, unadulterated rage.

"You churlis scoundrel," he raged, as Lieutenant Doyle gained an advantage over Leer.

"You're nothing but a meaningless, cheating piece of common scum," the Lieutenant growled, throwing a punch into Leer's still tender cheek. Leer groaned, ducking another swing from the man above him. He braced himself with Lieutenant Doyle's body and shoved his knee into the Lieutenant's stomach, knocking the wind out of the larger man.

Leer freed himself from the pin, standing more quickly than the Lieutenant, who crouched over as he held his abdomen. Snow cascaded from Leer's clothes and hair as he caught his breath for a brief moment.

Leer's dark eyes grew wide as he saw Astrid stand, wiping blood from her lip. A rush of cold dread lined his stomach. His palms grew sweaty; his pulse rose as his mind reeled with memories of his father.

His drunken father, stumbling in the door late at night as Leer watched from his hiding place behind a large basket. His mother, snapping to attention and trying to serve his every need, despite how cold and useless of a husband he was. His father, a man who never cared about anything more than himself, beating his mother as she begged for him to spare her. His mother, bruised and torn by a man who would later abandon her, leaving her to raise Leer alone.

He then began to smell the same stench of death that had once tainted the sweet floral notes of a past spring day, the one in which he found his mother in bed—still in her dressing gown, although nearly noon. Her stiffened hand clutched a small vial, a sad smile fixed on her colorless lips.

Just as quickly, his mind refocused on the present. "Are you alright?" Leer asked Astrid mere moments later, his voice strained.

"I'm fine," Astrid insisted, squaring her shoulders, as if to ward off any show of weakness. She glared at Lieutenant Doyle, who met her look with equal disdain.

"You listen to me, you whoreson," Leer fumed, his pulse racing and his face tightening as he stared at Lieutenant Doyle, who resolutely took to his feet. "If you so much as look at her the wrong way, I swear I'll end your worthless life."

Lieutenant Doyle leaned to his left, spitting at the ground. He wiped his mouth with the back of his hand as he smiled at Leer. "Got a weak spot for the thieving little wench, have you?" Leer watched Lieutenant Doyle fix his eyes on Astrid. "As a Lieutenant, I'll be generous despite your insubordination and give you a piece of advice. You might think you've got it all figured out, all squared away just like on your tafl board. It seems as cut and dried as any calculation you can make. But hear this—be wary of who you turn your back on." He paused; Leer saw his eyes narrow a bit as he smiled at Astrid. "And be even more wary of who you don't."

Lieutenant Doyle swiped his mittens from the ground and walked away, continuing to cut a path north. Leer remained still, watching him as he tasted his own blood on his tongue.

"It's not far, now," Astrid said. "Perhaps the two of you can stand each other long enough to reach there?"

"Perhaps," Leer muttered.

The tension had swirled into an undeniable thickness around them, choking out any interaction between the three. Leer was far too lost in his own head to be aware of the others. Despite the overall ache that ran through his bones, the flares of light that ebbed and flowed in his mind seemed more tolerable with each occurrence.

With a heavy sigh, he craned his neck to the side, stretching out the tight muscles. He needed to find both the princess and the Grimbarror, saving one and proving the existence of the other. It was all that mattered now.

"Private," Astrid murmured.

"Not Private," he quickly corrected, raising his head and looking at her. "Leer. Just Leer will do."

Astrid nodded. "Alright, Leer…I'm sorry."

He peered down at her. "You needn't be sorry."

"I do," she insisted, pulling her cloak around herself against the chill of the air. "I needn't make you feel responsible for me."

"I gave you my word to protect you," Leer corrected.

"I don't wish for that burden for you."

"'Twas mine I gave myself, lass."

He heard her grumble. "Astrid."

"You know," Leer said, a small smile threatening the corners of his mouth, "being called 'lass' isn't a bad thing."

"It is if you're not fond of it," Astrid snipped.

"If I meant you any harm, I certainly wouldn't have stuck my neck out back there for you."

"I suppose you can just ignore my wishes, then, because you're noble?"

Leer scoffed. "It didn't stop you from letting the Lieutenant 'handle' you last night."

She stopped, her mouth opened. "You child. Surely you're not trying to imply that you think I favored him before."

"Didn't you?" Leer asked back, pausing in front of her.

"Of course not."

"Not even a mite?"

"No!" Astrid exclaimed, her hands on her hips. "Not that it's any concern of yours even if I did."

Leer looked into her eyes. "It isn't. I just noticed the looks you exchanged with him since the moment we first met."

"You mean since all of days ago?" Astrid asked, rolling her eyes.

"Then you deny what I'm referring to?" Leer challenged.

She shook her head in disbelief. "Perhaps you should redirect your aggression, Private. You're growing petty over things not concerning you."

He then turned and continued down the northern road toward the Fell. He could hear Astrid's shorter strides nearing him from behind, trying to catch up to him.

"You should go, you know," Leer reminded when she came alongside him. "I doubt the Lieutenant will be willing to share any potential reward with either of us."

"I'm no longer motivated by money," Astrid replied quietly.

He glanced over at her. "What's your drive, then?"

"Seeing that you don't die before you get there."

Leer grinned. "You think me that fool-born when it concerns the woods, Astrid Browne?"

Astrid shook her head. "No—I know the woods aren't your enemy, Leer Boxwell."

"Oh really? Who is my enemy, then?"

She looked somewhere between hopeful and solemn, meeting his gaze.

"You," she replied, continuing ahead of him as he paused, taken aback by her answer.

-13-

Dusk settled over the Eyne Wood as the towering mountainous landscape concealed the day's final rays of sun.

"It's getting dark," Astrid noted to Leer; Lieutenant Doyle was a bit ahead of them, his form a silhouette against the setting sun.

Leer read between the lines of her suggestion. "Aye. We might be making a house of hewen branches soon."

"We'll waste too much energy wrestling with hewens," she argued.

"Perhaps you'd like to wrestle with frostbite instead?"

"Don't be facetious."

"Not that I particularly care," the Lieutenant interrupted, shouting from up ahead, "but are either of you coming this eve, or should I keep the cave I spotted to myself?"

Despite his desire to not share close quarters with the Lieutenant, Leer was relieved to hear they had a shelter to rest in. "Aye, we're nearly there," Leer called back.

"I do hope it's abandoned," Astrid murmured to Leer.

"We'll just have to have faith that it is."

"And what if it's not?"

"Then I'll fight whatever's in it. After all, what's another fight when you've already been in two in a day?"

"It's a risk for you to assume that I have that much belief in your capabilities," Astrid said with a smirk.

Leer smiled at her, then turned back toward the cave. "What's life without risk?"

The small fire that Leer fed in the rear of the shallow cave flickered its light over the surrounding stone, shadows cast high above their heads as he and Astrid sat quietly beside the flame. Lieutenant Doyle opted to collect more wood, leaving them alone.

Leer stole a lingering glance at Astrid, noticing that the cool tone hadn't yet fully left her lips despite the newfound heat source and consuming a serving of rations.

"You alright?" he asked, catching her subtle shiver. She merely nodded, her attention on the fire. In silence, Leer shook open the blanket from his pack, draping it around her shoulders.

"Thank you," she murmured, gratefully accepting the layer.

"Tell me a bit about yourself," Leer said, hoping to keep her mind distracted.

"There's not much to tell," Astrid replied, still fixated on the fire before her as she pushed back a section of dark hair behind her ear.

"Where are you from?"

"I don't know."

Leer's brow wrinkled. "How is that possible?"

"I was abandoned as a child," Astrid shared. "I don't know who my birth parents are, or where my blood hails from. I lived most of my life in the eastern region, in Lindone."

"Lindone? I'm not familiar with it."

"It's quite a small place guarded by the Hammerfall Keep. Not much there other than laborers to work the mines."

"For iron?"

"And maloden."

Leer nodded. "Aye, that's how you knew." He leaned in with interest. "Anyway, if your parents abandoned you, then who raised you?"

"A widow at the edge of the village. She told me I was placed on her doorstep in a basket, with nothing but a blanket one eve when I was but days old. She never knew who left me there. She told me she never tried to find out where I came from because she considered me an answer to her prayers for a daughter."

"Doesn't she still consider you that valuable?" Leer questioned.

"She's gone," Astrid explained.

"I'm sorry."

"She died when I was fifteen. I left Lindone shortly after."

"For where?"

She shrugged. "Anywhere I pleased. I lived like a kulipe, flitting from tree to tree without any need to call one or the other home."

Leer added another branch to the fire, carefully rearranging the already flame-consumed wood to help welcome it. "And now where might you call home?"

Their eyes met. "Why?" she asked with a coy smile, drawing her knees to her chest. "Are you planning a visit?"

"I might," he replied with his own half grin.

"And what's to say I'd allow it?"

"Perhaps if I brought something other than jerky you'd welcome me."

Astrid smiled. "I haven't a real home at the moment," she admitted, "so you won't have to worry about that."

His eyes narrowed in confusion. "Then where do you sleep?"

Her head sunk down. "For a while, I was living in the barn of a tavern owner on the borderlands of the Cursed Waste. Then I came west because I heard how easy the pickings were there with the gamblers, especially for a woman."

"'The pickings?'"

"What I could steal," she explained.

Leer nodded. "Ah, I see."

"You think less of me because I'm a thief by trade," Astrid stated, her head rising as she analyzed him.

"Nay, not true," he objected.

"You're a man contracted to keep order and law. Surely it bothers you, whether you're willing to admit it or not."

"Nay, and I shall tell you why." Leer leaned in a little. "Because you're not a thief by choice."

"Of course I am."

"You're a thief by necessity," he corrected. "Stealing is the means by which you not only survive physically, but mentally as well. The thrill of it draws you. The unknown outcome excites you. Perhaps having started life with a vast number of questions yet to be answered still, the unknown comforts you. It's familiar. Yet—" Leer stopped, scanning her eyes for a moment in silence. "Yet, you detest believing in the extraordinary. Perhaps because all you've ever wanted was stability and to be grounded, but all you ever received was uncertainty, and you can't bear to take on any more questions."

Astrid quietly shifted her body, wrapping her arms tighter around her knees. "Well, what about you? Where does Leer Boxwell hail from?"

"The base of the Kibundush Mountains," Leer replied, suddenly interested in the material of his pants.

Her soft laugh was melodic. "That would explain your arrogantly prideful nature—you're a Vale boy."

"Not by standard definitions," Leer argued, relaxing when he saw her knowing smile. "My parents weren't wealthy, like one might think based on where I was raised." He sighed. "In fact, it was just the opposite. My father worked as a furrier to the king and army men who lived there. He was quite skilled at his craft and drew business, so we lived in a home at the edge of town due to the demand. Though, my father was never a very savvy man with money."

"Then I assume being raised around Vale boys led you to your training in tafl?"

"It did help to pique my interest," Leer admitted. "My mentor was the one who taught me how to play."

"Your father didn't care for the game?" Astrid asked.

Leer moistened his lips, shaking his head with the memories that flooded him. "Outside of furs, my father never cared much for anything besides the drink. He was a rather troubled person," he explained. "Both my parents were, I suppose. I was too young to know why they chose the paths they did."

"Are they…?"

"Aye, at least my mother is." His dark eyes skimmed over to the fire. "My mother poisoned herself shortly after my father abandoned us. I was a boy at the time."

"I'm sorry," Astrid whispered; Leer saw the genuine emotion in her face as he glanced over at her.

"You've nothing to be sorry for," he assured, his smile warm. Leer was distracted as he watched Astrid comb a thick section of her hair behind her ear. "So," he teased, "I've an arrogantly prideful nature, do I?"

"You are a bit thick-headed when it comes to the possibility of failure," she agreed with amusement.

"I'm confident," he corrected. "There's a stark difference."

"Well, your prideful confidence is nothing more than foolishness."

"Really?" Leer moved closer to her, snagging a twig from the pile to his left. He held it out in front of them. "Suppose I bet that if we broke this branch at its bough together that I would surely retain the larger half." He held the branch at the base, offering her a side of the V-shaped stick. "Care to test me?"

"An observation of your size in comparison to mine would suggest that your strength would offer you more leverage," Astrid countered, resting her chin on her knee. "So of course you'd end up with the stronger side of the branch."

Leer didn't remember the last time he genuinely smiled last like he did in response to her at that moment. "You're certainly observant."

"It's just simple odds."

Leer reached over the few inches that separated them, taking Astrid's mittened hand while keeping his eyes locked on hers. "It's strategy," he uttered, moving her hand to the same placement as his on the opposite side of the branch. "Take the branch here." His hand lingered on top of hers for a moment, pressing her fingers tightly around the stick. "Now, when I pull, you remain still and true to your grip," he instructed.

Astrid frowned despite keeping her hand in place. "Then you'll end up with the entire thing."

He studied her eyes, golden flecks appearing throughout the blue from the glow of the fire beside them. "Do you trust me?"

He saw her swallow, her lips moving a little further apart from each other. "I'm not sure," she whispered.

"At least you're honest," Leer smirked. He moved his hand to his own side of the branch. "Would you like the honor?"

"On three, then?"

"On three."

"One...Two..."

He knew she chose to trust him when he felt her resistance, the branch splitting shorter on his side when he pulled. "See?" he said. "If you had pulled up and out like expected, then your assumption regarding my advantage would've been correct."

Astrid held the larger portion of the stick, examining it in thought. "So you are a master at manipulation," she concluded. "Had you not been trying to prove a point to me, you surely first would've led me to believe that I actually had a chance at winning when I, in fact, never did. Then this one would've been yours because of my eagerness to succeed against you." Astrid's eyes darkened, her head tilting slightly as she studied him. "You use people's innermost desires against them."

"Nay," Leer corrected, finding urgent need to clarify his skills. "I don't use it against them. I just make sure that I understand what they are in full detail."

"So you can exploit a weakness?"

"So I can know what to expect from whomever I face."

Astrid tossed the stick into the fire, studying the darkened entrance of the cave. Leer couldn't help but watch her.

"You enjoy retaining control," she observed. "You grew up surrounded by men who embodied control. Your own father was controlling, wasn't he? Vicious, perhaps? He never let you be the child you should have gotten a chance to be." She paused, glancing over at him. "That's why you reacted as you did to Lieutenant Doyle's actions toward me. It reminded you of him…and perhaps the relationship he had with your mother." Leer swallowed hard as he listened. "Control makes you feel safe, but pursuing the fantastic is all that keeps you away from the memories."

Leer chewed on the scab on his bottom lip for a moment before speaking. "As a boy, I thought for a while that I'd surely succeed my father in his trade when I was older, then be married perhaps. Maybe even with some luck produce a son of my own." He watched the dancing flames in front of them. "Then, when I was about nine years of age, my father began to nurse the drink from sunrise to sunset. It was an impossibly fast change, and I never knew what sparked it in him. All I know is he would take nary a step without a jug."

Leer paused, drawing a deep breath as he picked up a twig from the ground beside him. "He spoke very little to me and mostly screamed at my mother. I recall my mother begging to understand what vexed my father so, but he refused to speak of his secrets. I was but a boy, yet I could plainly see the war within him. Soon after that, he began beating her over nothing." Leer squeezed his eyes shut. "I never stopped him," he whispered. "I…I was too frightened. He somehow seemed larger than he was before, more capable. Like he could destroy us with a single glance. I failed my mother. I hid."

Though he didn't look to verify it, Leer felt Astrid studying the profile of his face.

"You didn't fail her," she reassured sincerely. "You were a boy."

"A boy who could've done something," Leer interjected, tossing the small stick into the flames. "But what was there to do?" Gritting his teeth, he kept his eyes forward. "When my father abandoned us a short time later, then my mother drank poison days after that, I felt horrible. Not because I just lost both of my parents, but rather, I felt horrible because of the relief I felt from their absence." With narrowed eyes, he looked over at Astrid. "Tell me what kind of a man that makes me."

"A human," Astrid whispered with empathy. "Very much human."

Leer kept his eyes on Astrid's for a while before speaking again. "Finnigan took me in to live with him and I did for many years—very happily so. His death is still a fresh wound."

"How did he pass?" Astrid asked.

Leer ran a hand over his stubbled jaw, his fingers tracing the burn scar forming on his left cheek. "I found Finnigan's body when I returned to the Vale, after scouting for insurgents. It was mauled, but still warm." Leer looked into the fire. "And then, in the wood near him, I saw the beast's yellow-rimmed eyes. I could feel the beast's presence, see its grotesque shape. It just stared straight at me."

He looked back over at Astrid, his eyes following the gentle curve of her nose. "I've no understanding why the beast would have slain him in cold blood as it did, but that was the night I realized Finnigan had been telling the truth all along. I had ignored his superstitions of the Vei...and now I wish I hadn't."

Leer paused as his eyes wandered over Astrid's face. "The people of the Vale now mock me for my obsession. They call me mad. Crazy. They say my mind is gone. No one keeps company with me for fear of how people will judge them. I can hear their laughter; they barely wait until I've turned the corner anymore before they begin. But I know it's out there, Astrid. I've heard it speak, seen its power. Soon, I shall return to the Vale with the proof in my hands. And on that day, I will be the only man left who even cares to know what that truth is."

"Then why come all this way?" Astrid countered, glancing back over at Leer. "Why risk so much for men who mock you?"

He shrugged. "What's life without risk?"

"You say that," Astrid argued, "but is the risk worth your life?"

"The truth is."

Astrid sighed, shaking her head. "What is the truth, Leer, but words from men who lie?"

"The Grimbarror exists," Leer insisted, his voice raising.

"Listen to me," Astrid pleaded scanning his eyes, "your heart is in the right place, wanting truth to prevail and be known. But what if no matter what the truth is, they don't wish to hear it?" Leer sighed, his head dropping down toward his lap as he rubbed small circles against his temples. "Leer, should you produce a claw or even its head, those who refuse to believe might not even care. If this beast is as dangerous as you say it is, then is it worth it? Is it worth your life to prove its existence to ignorant fools in power who would sooner do away with you than to admit their own mistake? Why does proving it matter?"

He looked up into her eyes. "Because the truth never ceases to matter." Leer ran a hand through his hair, breath escaping through his lips in resignation. "Tomorrow morn, you need to leave," he uttered. "From here on out, it's far too dangerous."

"I can handle myself. Besides, you clearly need me as a buffer so you and the Lieutenant don't kill each other."

"Go back to your life," Leer urged. "Just because I'm willing to pay whatever price it is for the truth doesn't mean you should as well."

"What life shall I return to, Leer?" she asked quietly. "The one where I have nothing but what I take from the hands of others?"

Leer sighed, the weight of everything pinning him to the ground in silence. He knew Astrid was right, that unveiling the truth didn't guarantee belief in those who doubted it. Still, he couldn't ignore his desperate desire for the truth to be known. Perhaps he was so determined to see his quest through to the end because he needed to complete it for his own sake. Perhaps he was the only one who really needed to know the truth.

Leer drew a deep breath, shutting his eyes against the discomfort it caused. "What about your health?" Astrid asked him. "I know you've physically been through more than you've shared as of late."

His ribs ached, but he didn't want to worry her. "I'll be alright," Leer replied.

"I can see your pain that you conceal. What happened?"

He swallowed. "I tried to stop the Grimbarror from taking Princess Gresham. I fell into a split in the earth and was hit by collapsing stone. My muscles suffered a bit from it."

"What happened to your face?"

Leer felt his left cheek, running his mittened hand along the length of it into his forming beard. "Burned it on the iron bar of a prison cell while trying to escape."

Her brow arched. "A man of the law in prison, then breaking out?"

"Aye, well, no one thought me right in my head when I said it was the Grimbarror that eve. They locked me in a cell thinking I was a daft fool. I did what I could to protect the king and princess."

"How did the iron become so hot?" she asked as she toyed with some small stones on the ground beside her, rather than looking at him.

"The guard was burnt to death in white hot fire," Leer replied, bits and pieces of the night coming into his mind's eye. "He was trapped by the light that came through the window. It consumed him." Leer examined the material of his coat. "Fire from the light engulfed the guard, and the light's fire grew so hot, that when the guard grabbed the iron bars of the cell door…" When he looked up at her, he saw Astrid watching him intently. "I kicked the bars apart. Not enough, I suppose. I just I didn't want to die like the other two."

"The other two?"

"The roach in the cell next to me died after debris impaled him. Then the guard."

Her head shot up. "The 'roach' next to you?"

"Aye. A filthy roach. He wore the colors of the insurgence, but it's still a shame the way he died."

"What was his name?" Astrid asked. Leer's eyes rose to meet hers.

"Why would you have interest in his name?" he asked, brow arching.

Her mouth opened; she was silent as she looked down. "I was just curious is all."

He squinted a bit as he examined her. "I can't remember," he replied. "I can see his face, but with how my head was shaken, his name seems to have left me."

"It's alright," she assured, offering him a thin smile. "I suppose I'm too curious for my own good sometimes."

Leer nodded. "Aye, I can understand that myself."

Leer noticed the falling darkness outside of the shallow cave. As a scout, watching the darkness fed him, comforted him, and satisfied his restless mind.

"Do you always watch the skies this way?" he heard Astrid ask.

"Usually," Leer replied. "I am a scout."

"But now instead of rebels, you're searching for the truth," she concluded.

"Aye."

"What about other truths? The truths of life—do you search for those as well?"

He grit his teeth, biting back the surge of bitterness. "The beast *is* a truth of life."

"For you."

"Then if it's not for you, why do you remain?"

Lieutenant Doyle crawled back into the cave, his arms full of timber. "That ought to do it for the eve," he said, tossing the wood onto the diminished supply they already had. He looked at both of them. "What did I miss?"

"Nothing," Leer growled, moving toward the opposite side of the fire, propping his head against the cave's wall.

The light of dawn splayed through the opening of the cave, a beam of the rising sun bright against Leer's still shut eyes as he roused from his sleep. He lifted his head, feeling the ache in his muscles of the last week's compounded emotions.

With a heavy blink, Leer surveyed his surroundings. Lieutenant Doyle was still sleeping, but it didn't stop him from expressing his rage.

"Dammit," he growled, rising to his feet. He scanned the area, a sinking feeling lacing his stomach.

Finnigan's journal.

It was in his pack.

With a snarl, Leer kicked the dead fire, ash and rock scattering across the cave. Lieutenant Doyle had been right, loathe he was to admit it. He sided with a thief, and it got him nowhere. In fact, it had made him lose the one thing left he had of the person he was closest to.

In the midst of his rampage, Leer caught glimpse of the shimmering blade of his sword, still where he placed it the night before.

It doesn't make sense. Why leave the sword?

Leer stooped and took hold of the weapon, examining it as he straightened.

"Lieutenant," he barked. "Wake up." His tone reflected his stress.

"What?" the Lieutenant grumbled, sitting up with a grimace.

"Astrid's gone," Leer growled, scanning the woods that lay outside the cave. "And she took our packs."

-14-

The northern skimming town of Cabryog nestled into the nooks and crannies of the mountains and along the powerful and plentiful Ellys River. It was a welcomed sight for Leer and the Lieutenant. Leer's stomach groaned; with no rations, he had settled for a small palm full of finnel berries and melted snow, and that was hours ago. He hoped the people of Cabryog were as pleasant as Finnigan once claimed, and that they'd take interest in bartering his sword for a lesser weapon and some more rations. It was his last option left, aside from quitting.

A weight settled on Leer's shoulders, burdening his steps.

Finnigan wouldn't approve of his resignation.

But Finnigan was the reason he came here in the first place.

Sure, blame it on the dead. Coward. 'Twas your choice, Boxwell. Nary another's.

Still, the doubt called out to him, taunting him with its vice-like grip. It took residence with the growing rage he couldn't seem to shake.

"I do suppose, if I were in the mood, that this is where I could gloat a bit," the Lieutenant interrupted, a couple steps behind Leer.

Leer shook his head. "It doesn't make sense," he replied. "Why would she leave the sword? The sword is far more valuable than the tools and packs."

"Who the hell knows. All I know is, Cabryog had better have someone willing to barter that weapon of yours."

Leer caught a glimpse of the hilt of his sword strapped to his hip, the milkwood bright in the slices of sunlight that filtered through the trees.

Jarle.

Jarle was the only other constant Leer had in his life, aside from Finnigan. Leer met him when he took his sword in for repairs, befriending Jarle the moment he told him his sword was embarrassing garbage.

The idea of giving up the sword Jarle crafted made him ill. Whether Jarle would admit it or not, he made a significant sacrifice to give him the weapon he now would have to trade to survive his journey.

A fool's journey.

The closer they got to the border, the less confidence Leer had in his quest.

What if Astrid is right? What if I am fighting a losing battle? What if this is all for naught?

Leer froze, the hairs on the back of his neck standing up at the sound of a voice he heard distinctly nearby:

"Stay the course."

He turned back to look at the Lieutenant, who had his head down. "What did you say?" he asked.

Lieutenant Doyle looked up, his brows lifting. "Me? I didn't say a word, Boxwell."

Leer turned away, taking a deep breath as he continued forward.

"You've almost got him surrounded."

"Alright," Leer snapped, stopping in his tracks, his breath building into short, angry puffs. "What's your angle?" He whirled around to Lieutenant Doyle, jaw set. "What, you like to knock a man down, then try to pep him up? Is that how you get your jollies?"

"What in the blazes are you talking about, Private?" Lieutenant Doyle asked, defenses rising. "I haven't spoken a word to you." He took a step closer. "Trust me, you'd know if I had something to say to the likes of you."

"I *heard* you," Leer retorted.

"It *wasn't* me," the Lieutenant insisted with a hiss.

"Then who was it?" Leer shouted, raising his hands in askance. "Who might have told me to, 'stay the course?'"

"I don't know, and I don't care."

The Lieutenant brushed by Leer's shoulder as he passed him, the force greater than necessary.

Breathe, Leer coached himself, staring down at the snow. *Breathe.*

After a moment, Leer began walking again, following a few paces behind the Lieutenant, the distance between them growing larger. His heart clenched when he heard the voice a third time:

"Steady and balanced. The truth awaits you."

With a surge of rage, Leer growled and kicked the snow repeatedly. Fractals and leaves he unearthed flew in the air, small twigs and rocks scattering with his fit.

Everything in his way became a target, nothing was safe from his angry tantrum. His sword slapped against his hip as he destroyed the landscape around him; kulipes fluttered out of the tree branches with the commotion.

Shortly thereafter, Leer stopped, panting as he caught his breath. He could feel the Lieutenant's judgmental observation, confirming it as he looked toward him. Seeing Lieutenant Doyle's unsuppressed smirk sparked the flame again. With a swallowed snarl, he stormed past him in heated silence, fists clenched at his sides.

As they trekked downhill toward the valley, Leer caught a glimpse of something on the trunk of a nearby tree. He squinted, approaching it with curiosity as he withdrew one mitten. He ran his fingertips over the aged grooves in the wood with realization.

Insurgents.

Leer froze, pausing at the distant sound of branches snapping underfoot. He instinctively reached for his sword, his hand hovering over the hilt as he scanned the perimeter. He saw Lieutenant Doyle in nearly the same position.

"I've a sure arrow aimed for the towhead, and two more bowmen readied," a stranger's voice boomed.

Leer drew his sword, holding it defensively, though he couldn't see anyone besides the Lieutenant.

"Your weapons won't stave off our aim. Now, throw the swords on the ground to your right and press your hands behind your heads."

"Show yourself," Leer challenged, keeping his grip tight on his sword.

"Filthy rebels," the Lieutenant snapped. "Don't hide like children behind skirts."

"Do as I say," the voice replied, "or else meet your fate for your ignorance."

Wonderful. Perhaps we can outwit them if we lead them on. As Leer reluctantly bent over to lay his sword on the ground, the Lieutenant interrupted him.

"Keep your weapon, Private," he hissed.

"We're outnumbered," Leer replied.

"Says the coward hiding from us."

Leer rolled his eyes. "Oh, so now you're able to believe in what you can't see?"

The Lieutenant wasn't amused. "Shut up, you twit."

"Your choice will get us killed for certain."

"Well, yours is not leaving us at any more of an advantage."

"You wish to fight them, then?"

"Don't you?"

Leer didn't know. He was drained, exhausted. All sense of purpose had left him. It was almost easier at this point to be robbed than to pretend like he could succeed.

"Bloody twits," the hidden voice growled, "you're like two milkmaids with this. Just throw down your swords."

Without a word, Leer tossed his sword to the ground, still hunting for the hiding men. He heard the Lieutenant groan at his choice, then the thud of the Lieutenant's sword dropping against the snow.

The two bowmen the man had mentioned rose from the snow-covered brush in the distance, draped in light-hued furs.

"We wish the people of Cabryog no harm," Leer insisted, licking his lips.

"No harm?" Taking Leer by surprise, the man crashed through the trees and landed next to the Lieutenant. The lanky stranger's messy, dark ponytailed hair framed his bronzed skin as it draped over his shoulder. His clothes and winter accessories bathed in the same tones as the woods around them showed his skill as an outdoorsman.

The man smirked, swiping Leer's sword from the ground, evaluating both the Lieutenant's purple hued blade and Leer's milkwood grip. "It's difficult to believe a statement like that when you're both bearing such unusual weapons." The man looked up from Leer's sword. "Tell me, who was your intended target?"

"That doesn't concern you at present."

"Actually, it does. See, we here in the north prefer to keep the riff-raff out. We also don't do well with scouts on missions for our eastern neighbors."

Leer laughed. "You believe me to be a roach, is that it?"

The man raised a brow. "I wouldn't think any man coming from any sort of distance would be daft enough to travel alone without supplies, and in the winter, no less."

"They were stolen, you imbecile," the Lieutenant growled.

The man was unfazed. "Stolen, eh? By whom?"

"A woman," Leer sighed.

The man hooted, his voice booming through the wood. "Oh, that's rich." He paused when he saw Leer's unchanged face. "Oh. From the looks of it, you're not kidding."

"I'm afraid not," Leer replied stiffly.

Pursing his lips, the man looked back down to the sword. "Well, was she at least skilled?"

Leer sighed. "Not that I believe it's any of your business, but I didn't sleep with her."

"Why in the hell not?"

"I—" Leer paused. "Look, can you decide whether you'd like to trust us or kill us? I've no patience right now for games, and I'd like to attend to our business if you'll pardon us."

The man tilted his head back. "What is your business in Cabryog?"

"To barter the sword for another weapon and some rations for the remainder of our journey."

"To where?"

Leer cleared his throat. "The Fell." He winced when the man erupted in laughter again. "Aye, it's all a laugh, isn't it? Will you let us pass or not?"

"What in bloody hell could you possibly want in Sortaria?"

Leer drew a deep breath through his flared nostrils. "The Grimbarror." Silence followed, each ounce of it fueling Leer's inner fire.

"Are you mad?"

"Give me my sword."

The man examined Leer's sword with a twist of his wrist. "I'm afraid I can't do that. This would bring a nice purse in these parts."

Leer rolled his eyes. "Fine," he growled, moving past him. "I'll go on without it."

"Get back here, Boxwell," Lieutenant Doyle snapped. "That's an order."

"I'm under no one's orders any longer."

"Dammit, you fitbloached habbersnitch. Return at once!"

Leer waved him off, continuing. He made it a few more paces before he heard a thud behind him in the snow. Turning, he saw his sword on the ground, the man from the trees standing behind him with his arms crossed.

"If you'd venture on to the Fell without a weapon, then you are mad," the man stated, brow raised.

"There is no question of his madness," Lieutenant Doyle agreed.

"Well, I'll not have his blood on my hands." The man nodded toward Leer. "So take the sword and at least be an armed madman."

Leer analyzed him. "Aren't you afraid I'll rob and pillage Cabryog?" he spat.

"Nay. I'm afraid more of the guilt my mother left me than that."

Leer straightened after retrieving his sword and tucking it in its sheath. "Leer Boxwell." The man's brow raised, and he chuckled to himself. The reaction confused Leer. "Something amusing?"

"Only if you believe in fate. Garren," the man replied, shaking his head. "Garren Esel. This here is Beval." Garren nodded to the shorter of the two bowmen, a stout, sharp-eyed man with rich brown skin. "And next to him stands Edgar," he added, gesturing to the skinny young man with unkempt hair. He turned back to Leer. "They're my right hand men, the finest of the village." He bragged. "Welcome to Cabryog, Leer Boxwell."

Salvia filled Leer's mouth as the scent of skimmers roasting on spits wafted toward him. The town bustled with activity. The people of Cabryog proved to be far different than those of Enton, not only physically, but also socially. Instead of the usual washing of pale skin and fairer features, they boasted rich skin tones in varying shades of clay and umber, and hair of all shades. And they were friendly.

"I must confess, I feel out of place," Leer noted as he walked beside Garren, the Lieutenant on Garren's other side.

"It's because you are," Garren explained with a shrug.

"They won't question our arrival?" Lieutenant Doyle asked.

"Unlike the Vale, we believe in hospitality."

"As does the Vale," the Lieutenant replied with an edge to his voice. "Except we prefer to be a bit more selective."

"As in, you'd rather have guards and clergy?" Garren countered.

Leer's hand flexed beside him, feeling the weight of his sword as he walked. "I suppose those outside the Vale regard it with a bit of disdain?"

"Disdain is a rather harsh word. We prefer to see the Vale and those in it as…crotchety."

Leer gave a small nod. "You wouldn't be wrong."

"Garren!"

All three men stopped, looking ahead at the sound of the feminine voice calling his name.

"Tana," Garren acknowledged with a nod, her smile bright. He waved her over with his bare hand.

Tana was taller than average for a woman with faint lines around her hazel eyes and robust curves that showed even under the furs she wore. "You've taken up more company now, have ya?" she asked when she stopped in front of them.

"Nay. They're travelers. Mother's guilt made me see them to town," Garren replied with a grin.

"May her soul rest in peace," Tana replied, eying her brother. "So you've been gone for over a fortnight, yet ya refuse to greet me with an embrace? Ya remind me of your nephews."

Garren laughed, stepping forward and wrapping Tana in a hug. "Ah, dear sister. I just wanted to save you from the stench."

Tana laughed, wrinkling her nose. "Did ya wrestle tragurns all the way to the Cursed Waste, then?"

"Something like that," Garren replied with a wink. He sighed. "But where are my manners?" He looked back to Lieutenant Doyle. "Meet..." Garren's lips pursed. "Funny. I never got your name."

"Lieutenant James Shelton Doyle," the Lieutenant replied with annoyance.

"Man of the Vale, eh?" Tana asked.

"Yes I am."

"With no sense to pack for a trip this far north?"

Lieutenant Doyle scoffed. "Have you no sense of propriety?"

Tana shrugged. "Only for those who earn it."

Leer couldn't help but smile at Lieutenant Doyle's expression. "Madame, I can arrange to have you arrested."

She scrutinized both of them. "Doesn't look like you're in much of a position to arrange anything at the moment."

"And," Garren said, loudly interrupting his sister with a hinting glare, "this here is Leer Boxwell."

Tana paused, but recovered with a quick smile. "It's a mighty fine sword you've got, Leer Boxwell," Tana acknowledged, eying Leer's weapon. "Double weighted steel, the hilt inset with polished caratrim of milkwood, yes?"

Leer's brow furrowed. "Aye, it is. You're well versed with weapons, ma'am."

Tana laughed; it mimicked her brother's laugh Leer heard earlier. "Tana, please. And I should be. I'm the local blacksmith in these parts."

Leer spluttered. "My apologies, I—"

"Ah, save it," Tana interrupted, giving him a wink. "My guess is you're used to your women in silk and slippers, yes?" She shrugged, not giving him a moment to respond. "We here up north divide labor a bit differently."

"Doesn't mean she won't fix a rather delicious skimmer roast, though," Garren smirked.

Tana put her hands on her hips. She looked first to Lieutenant Doyle, then to Leer. "Maybe for him," she said as she looked at Leer, "but certainly not for you. Not until ya wash."

Leer shook his head. "We certainly couldn't impose."

"What, and leave ya in the cold?" Tana asked, shaking her head. "I doubt your Vale bones could take such a thing."

"Skimmer roast would be lovely," the Lieutenant said, flashing Tana a brief smile.

"I agreed to seeing them to town," Garren corrected, his expression sobering. "Not to bringing them to the house with my nephews."

"They're harmless travelers," Tana interrupted. "Ya needn't puff your chest out like a surly grupe, Garren."

Garren scoffed in response. "You don't even know what they're after. This one," he gestured to Leer, "fancies himself a trip to The Fell. He's as drunk as your loon of a father in law."

"Aldred Lance has earned his right to believe in fae and merfolk if he'd like to," Tana said, eying her brother. "Ya know right well of that."

"Being old doesn't justify fantasy, Tana."

"Being there to see it, does," she snapped. She turned, flashing Leer a quick smile that faded as she glanced at the Lieutenant. "Well, come on, then. You'll need some food to keep your bones warm, wherever you two might go."

Leer's lips parted. "You...your surname is Lance, aye?" he asked her.

"Indeed it 'tis. But my husband is gone now. Caught a dirty roach arrow too deep."

"I'm sorry for your loss." Leer cleared his throat. "Would 'Lance' be a relation to Finnigan Lance?"

Tana's face changed. "Where do ya know that name from, Boy?"

Leer's pulse quickened, his palms growing clammy. "Finnigan was my mentor. He...he was a father to me."

Tana glanced at Garren, then back to Leer, giving him a small nod as she tucked a wayward strand of black hair behind her ear. "Come," she commanded, drawing a deep breath. "I can imagine Aldred will have much to discuss with you."

-15-

Garren slid the bolt of the cottage door in place as Leer and the Lieutenant watched Beval and Edgar strip their coats and move toward the fire, slinging them over the backs of nearby chairs before disappearing into the back of the cottage.

"Well, well," a man's gravelly voice came from the opposite corner of the main room.

Leer saw a weathered man, who he assumed was Aldred Lance, seated in an equally weathered chair. His wiry silver hair was drawn to the side, much the same as Garren's. Aldred's eyes could have been Finnigan's with their resemblance, small green pebbles surrounded by wrinkles. Only, they held a film of white over them, clouding the grassy hue.

"Decided to finally come back, have ya?" Aldred sneered, standing with the aid of a notched walking stick.

"Senseless grupe. You make it sound like I've been eating tarts in a spring meadow," Garren said, hanging his coat on a nearby hook with more force than necessary.

Aldred huffed. "Might as well have been, with how long you were gone."

"Father, please," Tana soothed, unlacing her fur vest with a small sigh.

"He left you and his nephews for over a fortnight!"

"And I'm right capable of taking care of myself." Tana eyed him. "Garren was kind enough to take us in. Ya needn't test his generosity with your tongue."

Aldred grumbled, shuffling toward the table Leer stood on the other side of. He paused, sniffing the air. "Who be that with you, Boy?" he asked; Leer was amazed at how Aldred looked right at him despite his obvious blindness.

"Travelers in need of food," Garren replied.

"And you brought them to your sister and nephews without knowing them?"

"I was hoping one of them would run you through with his sword."

Tana glared at Garren, then turned to Aldred. "They're my guests as well, Father. There is no need for rudeness. Now, if ya men can attempt to be more civil than jeet-stung tragurns, I'll get to making the roast."

"I don't suppose you have a wash bucket, yeah?" Lieutenant Doyle asked.

Tana nodded. "Garren'll take ya."

As she disappeared into the adjacent section of the cottage, Garren sighed and left, the Lieutenant following behind him with an equally displeased look. When Leer heard Tana fussing with a pot, his stomach growled. The idea of a skimmer roast made him realize just how hungry he was.

Aldred took another step, keeping his clouded eyes on Leer. "Name?"

"Leer Boxwell," Leer responded, with trembling hands. "Sir, are you—"

"Boxwell..." Aldred's lips curved a bit. "Ah, yes. The towhead tafl boy. Well, no longer a boy from the sound of it." He chuckled. "No wonder they brought you here."

Leer's throat felt dry. "Are you Finnigan's brother?"

"Yes, yes." Aldred rapped his walking stick against the bench in front of him. "Sit. We've much to discuss."

Sitting with hesitation, Leer kept his eyes on Aldred, who shuffled toward the bench and took a seat with surprising fluidity.

"Well," Aldred said, exhaling, "I suppose you're as full of questions, as am I."

"I am," Leer replied. "Finnigan never mentioned he had a brother."

Aldred nodded. "I see. More than likely because I was less than good to him in our younger years."

"How so?"

"Ah, well...I nary believed the things he claimed. Surely he taught you of his ways, yes?"

"Aye," Leer nodded. "'Tis the reason for my travels now."

"As I thought," Aldred muttered as he lifted a shaking hand. "Pour me some ale."

Leer spied a jug and a few mugs at the end of the table. He retrieved them, pouring two out, placing one in front of Aldred.

"I'll keep a lengthy tale short," Aldred said after taking a sip. "Finnigan and I were nearly inseparable as boys, but later became insufferable to each other as men. Much to my embarrassment, he believed quite longer than I did. We stopped speaking after he made his claims of the beast's existence. And later, I could never admit my fault."

"So you know of his passing?" Leer asked. Coldness churned in his stomach as he saw Aldred's lips part in shock. "I—"

"When?"

"...Just a few weeks ago."

"Where?" Aldred demanded.

Goose flesh prickled Leer's arms under his coat. "The Vale."

"How?"

"...The beast, Sir."

Aldred set his mug down and leaned back. "It must have sought him for some reason."

"Nay," Leer murmured. "He gave it no reason for its madness."

The following silence killed Leer, the icy chill in his gut spreading through his veins. "I've not given up my path," he assured. "I've vowed to see the beast to its end. For Finnigan."

Aldred's hand curled into a white knuckled fist. His vacant eyes told Leer more than a sighted man's could. "Alas, I'm too late," he whispered.

"Surely your bond wasn't broken."

"The damage is done."

"But—"

Aldred pounded his fist on the table with a growl. Leer fell silent. "Your eyes..." Aldred shook his head, his jaw tightening. "You see much through tunnels, through narrow paths, but you ignore the abundant fields that surround you. And when you finally do see them, you'll be as helpless as I am."

Before Leer could respond, Beval and Edgar reappeared from the rear of the cottage, taking seats at the table as Tana brought out a slab of hewen with a dark loaf of bread on it. Beval and Edgar didn't hesitate, unwilling to wait for the others to begin eating.

"Eat, Leer," Tana encouraged with a small smile. "You must be famished."

"Thank you," Leer replied, taking a piece. He held it, distracted in thought, running his fingers over the nutty texture of it.

The cottage door flew open, two nearly identical sinewy boys stampeded in, slamming the door behind them.

"Maw," one yelled, his small bronze hand gripping a feanet upside down by its feet. "Loo' at wha' I caught."

"I caugh' it," the other insisted, shaking out a mass of black curls after taking off his cap.

The first boy used his free hand to swipe under his nose. "No, ya didn't."

"Did too!"

"Ya couldn't catch a bebbet with broken legs."

"And you couldn't sling a stone withou' a bough to steady yer arm."

"Boys!" Tana hollered; both children stopped, rolling their plump bottom lips between their teeth. "If I hear nary another word against each other, I'll give your uncle permission to whoop you both." The boys stopped, and one boldly stared at Leer. "You hear?" Tana asked, her eyes narrowing. They nodded, giving the feanet to her. "Now, you did good finding the bird. Take yourselves to the basin to clean up."

They scurried off, Tana watching them as they disappeared in the same direction as Garren and Lieutenant Doyle had. "The one still with the cap is Malin. His twin is Ricker. They've been feisty ever since they came from my womb ten years ago." She smirked, looking down at Leer as she set out more mugs and another jug of ale. "Ya haven't touched your bread. If you're not fast in this house, you'll lose your meal."

Leer glanced down at the uneaten chunk of bread in his hand, then back up at Aldred, who ate quietly across from him. He took a bite, chewing it as he watched Aldred through the turmoil in his mind. He hadn't noticed when Tana left, too consumed by Aldred's words.

"What did you mean when you said I haven't yet seen?" Leer asked, swallowing his bite.

Aldred's body shook as he continued eating. "There is much to know," he said.

"What?"

"Do you want me to serve you like Tana?" Aldred snapped, looking up at Leer, blinking. "If the truth is what you're looking for, then seek it, Boy."

"I am, Sir," Leer replied stiffly, squeezing the bread between his fingers. He sighed. "Yet every time I seek it, it leaves me with more questions."

"Some truths are not answered simply. Some truths require more than a sacrifice of time."

Leer bit his lip, finding the scab with the tip of his tongue. He shut his eyes, taking a deep breath. Garren's and the Lieutenant's footfalls made him open his eyes, his blood pressure still racing from the lack of answers.

"So northeast of here is Sortarian territory, aye?" he said to Garren.

"It is," Garren replied hesitantly as he took a seat across from him to Aldred's right.

Leer nodded. "Right. Has there been any unexplainable phenomena as of late?"

Garren shifted in his seat. "Such as?"

"White hot fires in the middle of rain storms, unidentifiable sounds deep within the wood. Irrational behavior. The people of Junivar claimed to have seen such things in the woods in this area. Any insight as to what might be happening?"

"Perhaps it's nothing more than their own misinterpretation," Garren suggested. "Woods catch fire, the weather is nature's business, and more often than not, men behave irrationally without any magical influence."

Leer leaned back in his seat. "Perhaps its significance is tied to the Vei," he challenged.

"Oh, please," Lieutenant Doyle groaned.

Garren met Leer's eyes and laughed. "The Vei died a long time ago, if it ever even existed," he argued.

The Lieutenant gave Garren a small nod. "As would any sensible man know."

"Vei magic might explain the things we witnessed," Leer argued; silence followed. "Was the wood where you found us Sortarian territory once?"

"I wouldn't classify it as territory, really. Anyway, might we discuss something else? I've just returned from weeks of scouting Roach Country. I'd rather be spared of the history lesson."

"And that's why you're a fool," Aldred sighed.

"Because I'd rather not give into the idea of Sortarian witchcraft willy nilly?" Garren retorted, eying

Aldred. "The fools are those who store the entirety of their goods in one basket."

Aldred waved him off. "The remains of some of the Sortarians killed in the Junich War were buried in the woods below Cabryog," he said to Leer.

The Junich War.

It was before Leer's time. King Gresham was a Lieutenant, much like James Doyle, who led a raid against the infiltration of Babrystians from across the Sea of Zita into Sortaria. It was the war that sealed Hiline's superior power in the region of the trinations, and the victory that made Calvin eligible for king.

"That might explain it," Leer noted.

"Explain what?" Tana questioned as she entered with a hewen board full of roasted skimmers.

"The voices," Leer replied with growing realization.

Were the ghosts crying out?

Tana sighed as she set down the board. Malin and Ricker rushed in, eagerly taking seats at the far end of the table near Beval and Edgar, who helped themselves to food.

"Enough talk of magic," Garren warned, his eyes narrowed at Leer. "I'll not have you speak of such madness in front of my nephews."

"It's what makes sense, whether or not it is what you wish to believe," Leer argued.

"I believe in real things," Garren replied. "I believe in things I can see."

"Men have seen, but you deny their experiences."

"Men only see what they wish to, mostly."

"You're wrong," Leer snapped in a dark tone, his hand balling into a fist on the tabletop. "The kidnapping of the Princess, the fires, the insensible deaths—all of it is in response to the power of the Vei."

Malin and Ricker stopped chewing, their round dark brown eyes shifting to Garren as their mouths hung open. Leer felt everyone staring at him, the silence choking the room.

Garren licked his lips, nostrils flared. "Tread carefully, Boxwell. Tossing out possibilities of Vei influence is a sure way to put yourself in a scrape."

Leer ignored the advice. "The Grimbarror is an embodiment of Sortarian magic. It is a vessel, purposefully created both in the past, and now again."

"And the source of the Grimbarror's power lies in the beast itself," Aldred finished, leaning back and staring in Leer's direction. A small sad smile curved his lips. "The blood in its veins is dark magic, crafted by those with the power of the Vei."

Garren pushed away from the table, slamming down his mug. "I won't stand for this any longer," he snapped. "You've overstayed your welcome, Boxwell. I won't have you or your friend here poisoning my nephews with your filth."

"I'd just like to take this moment to say, I don't believe him either," the Lieutenant noted with a raised finger.

"Garren!" Tana exclaimed. "You're—"

"No, woman," Garren snapped, glaring at her; Tana became quiet. "So long as this is my roof, I'll say who enters." He looked back to Leer. "And who leaves."

Leer stood, his eyes on Garren. His fingers flexed beside him. *Steady and balanced,* he tried to remind himself as a familiar warmth bloomed behind his ears. *Stay steady and balanced.*

His gaze shifted to Aldred, drinking in the familiar face that brought to mind images of Finnigan. "I still fight for Finnigan. You have my word," he pledged, silent for a moment before turning away, moving toward the door.

Leer heard the Lieutenant's reluctant grumble and approaching footsteps as he gripped the handle, his back to the others. He paused, turning to Tana. "Thank you for the bread," he mumbled, giving her a small nod. "I wish blessings on your family."

Despite the sun that shone on him as he left the cottage with Lieutenant Doyle, Leer could feel the invisible grip of darkness tighten around him, pulling him further into its depths.

-16-

The bustle of the Cabryog market became white noise, the cold air a familiar blanket as Leer wove his way through the dirt walk to the large inn he was promised was at the south end of the town. He barely checked whether the Lieutenant kept up with him. His company was the furthest thing from Leer's mind in that moment, the passageways instead clogged up with Aldred's words:

"Your eyes...You see much through tunnels, through narrow paths, but you ignore the abundant fields that surround you. And when you finally do see them, you'll be as helpless as I am."

"Must have been nice to have stayed long enough to get some bread," Leer heard the Lieutenant say near him. "Unfortunately, I didn't have the pleasure."

"You'll get your bread soon enough," Leer grumbled, rolling his eyes.

The sight of the thick stone building relieved Leer. A small wooden plaque flapped above the entryway, its name burned into the face of the hewen.

Kicking off the snow from their boots, they ducked inside. Leer breathed in the heady scent of ale and roasted meat as he prepared himself.

This is what you need to do. Do it, and be done.

Still, the idea of letting Jarle's sword go made his stomach knot.

With a quick prayer, he crossed to the counter, nipping at his lip as the keeper approached.

"Good day," Leer said with a friendly smile. In his peripheral sight, he saw the Lieutenant come to stand alongside him. "Might I interest you in a barter?"

The innkeeper, a stout man with thin rimmed glasses, eyed Leer. "What would you like to offer?"

"My sword, in exchange for a hunting knife, and rations and board for tonight for both of us."

"Hmm. Must be a fine weapon to assume it carries that much value."

Leer unsheathed his sword, laying it down on the counter. "Double weight steel, crafted in the Vale with milkwood."

The innkeeper's brow rose as he examined it, the blade glinting in the boonwax candlelight. "It is a nice piece," he confirmed, a smile spreading on his face. "Deal." He held out his hand, waiting for Leer to grip it.

"No deal!"

Leer and Lieutenant Doyle spun around, matching the voice with a familiar face.

Astrid.

Astrid strode through the threshold, the door slamming behind her. "No deal," she repeated, watching Leer as she stepped to his side. He noticed two packs slung over her narrow shoulder. She drew her hood down, looking at the innkeeper. "I've enough pence here for three rooms, three meals, and three washings." She fished in her waist belt and retrieved a satchel, tossing it with a nod to the innkeeper, who let go of Leer's sword and snatched it. "Count it."

Leer's nostrils flared, his pulse rising as he watched the innkeeper dump the coins on the counter. "I don't want your dirty money," he argued.

Her eyes met his. "I came by it honestly." Before he could object, she looked to the innkeeper. "Are we settled, then?"

The innkeeper shook her head. "No, lass. Only enough for two of everything."

"Impossible," Astrid scoffed. "I made sure of it."

"Price increase."

"Since when?"

"Since you spoiled the deal on the sword."

Astrid's eyes narrowed. "Why you—"

"Easy, feisty," Leer whispered, taking hold of her shoulder.

"We'll make do with it," the Lieutenant announced as he noticed Leer's disapproving look. "What? You need the sword, and the wench owes us." Astrid narrowed her eyes at him as he snatched his pack from her shoulder.

"Very well, then," the innkeeper nodded, scraping the coins into his palm. "Two rooms, two meals, two washings. I'll have the maid bring you each a plate. The washtub is up the stairs to the left."

As the innkeeper left, Leer snatched up his sword and stalked away, squeezing his eyes shut. "We don't need your help," he argued.

"Then what were you planning on doing with a hunting knife? Nicking the beast?"

He turned, facing her. "You don't even believe in it."

Astrid nodded toward Lieutenant Doyle, who made himself comfortable at a nearby table. "And neither does he. But I believe that you do," Astrid countered, taking a step closer to him. "And I can't rightfully let you go into it all without the proper weapon."

"So you thought I could do without the last of my rations, aye? Or that taking the only thing I care about was a good course of action?"

Astrid sighed, handing him his pack. Leer took it, grateful to feel the familiar weight of Finnigan's journal in it. "I forgot the journal was in there until it was too late. I just meant to delay you. I hoped you'd come to your senses."

"Losing a bit of jerky isn't enough to change my mind."

"Which I realized. Hence why I'm here."

He swallowed, watching how her long dark hair glinted in the low light as she removed her cloak. Sighing, he took a seat at the table with Lieutenant Doyle, shrugging off his coat. "You needn't waste your pence on me, nor your breath trying to redirect me."

Astrid took a few small steps toward the table. "I won't be. And it isn't a waste if it means you're sheltered and fed this eve."

Leer paused and looked into Astrid's eyes. "Then I'm in your debt," he concluded before gesturing to the empty chair across from him.

She took a seat, shaking her head. "No, you're not."

"Aye," Leer argued. "I am."

"Please," the Lieutenant mumbled. "She stole our supplies from us twice. If there's any debt outstanding, it's hers."

"Perhaps for you," Leer corrected, taking a seat. "But not for me."

The Lieutenant rolled his eyes. "Of course not. I forgot ol' Private Undue Nobility's station in life."

The bar maid approached the table, placing two plates in front of them, and filling two glasses with ale, slipping Leer an extra fork before she left. Leer pushed the plate toward Astrid.

"Take your fill," he said with a nod.

"There's plenty to share," she said, sliding it back to the middle between them.

The aroma of roasted skimmer filled Leer's nose, reminding him of his tense meeting with Garren, Tana, and Aldred.

Aldred.

Why hadn't Finnigan ever told him of his brother? And how could his belief have separated them so?

Leer drove his two tined fork into the skimmer, slicing off a section. The meat nearly melted in his mouth; his stomach groaned and churned, happily accepting the much needed fuel after all of the miles his body accumulated on the journey thus far.

He almost finished his half of the meal before he resurfaced from his thoughts, aware once again of Lieutenant Doyle and Astrid's presences.

"Well, I'm stuffed like a springtime tragurn," the Lieutenant mused, leaning back a bit with a contented sigh.

"Have you no shame?" Leer asked, tilting his head toward Astrid.

"Regarding?"

"Perhaps not having enough decency to share with a lady?"

"Lady?" The Lieutenant chuckled, looking over at Astrid. "That's an awfully generous title you've bestowed on her."

Leer tensed in his seat, palms flat on the table as he readied to stand, but Astrid's gentle touch on his forearm halted him. He paused, nostrils flared as he tried to swallow back his bitterness. He watched Lieutenant Doyle stand, tossing his rag on the table.

"I'll be taking a room for myself. Enjoy your evening together," he smirked, winking at Astrid. "Perhaps your generosity will reward you, Private."

Leer remained silent despite his desire to reply. Astrid's gentle touch lingered as he watched the Lieutenant climb the stairs to his room. Leer blew out a breath, shutting his eyes.

'Tisn't worth it.

Quietly, he turned back to face Astrid, who withdrew her hand from his arm, looking down at the plate. Leer watched, examining her. She seemed burdened, worried.

"What troubles you so?" he asked.

Her gaze rose to meet his, her crystalline eyes round. "Nothing."

"Surely something must. I can see it."

She swallowed, pushing away the plate. "If you must know, I'm still worried for you, for your insistence on this quest."

Leer picked up the last crust of his bread, taking a bite as he continued to look at Astrid. "Nay. 'Tis not what plagues you."

"So you claim to know my thoughts now?"

"I know a thing or two about the look on a person's face."

Her eyes narrowed. "Then tell me—what does my face say now, Private?"

He smirked, observing her for a moment. "I'm not sure you'd like me to say it aloud, Miss Browne."

"You're an imbecile."

"I've been called worse."

She rolled her eyes, putting her napkin on the table as she rose from her seat. "Take the mattress. Your ribs will appreciate it more than mine, I'm sure. We leave at dawn."

Leer's brow arched. "We?" He shook his head. "No, lass. If I'm indebted to you, then I choose to repay it through sparing you the trip."

Astrid scoffed. "First of all, you owe me no such debt. Secondly, I do right well as I please—I've no patience for you to tell me where I can go. Or for you calling me, 'lass.'"

Leer sighed, standing and tossing his napkin on the table. "As I've told you before, this is far too dangerous."

"Do you consider me delicate as a lowe, then?"

"Nay. I'd just rather not have your blood on my hands."

"You won't," she stated, stepping away from the table toward the stairs that led up to the rooms level.

Leer inhaled deeply, watching her as she walked up the stairs and out of view. With a grumble, he turned and eyed one of the buckets of water near the fire that burned in the center pit of the tavern. One should at least somewhat cut the chill of the wash water in the barrel, he imagined.

He crossed toward the fire, relishing the brief, sharp warmth of the open flames as he lifted the bucket and carried it toward the stairs. He assumed Astrid's failure to take one meant she'd likely bathe later, and he wanted nothing more at the moment than to clean up and rest.

The water in the large tub behind the fabric curtain was mild, even after the addition of his hot bucket. Still, Leer stripped and sank into its depths with relief, the harbored chill of his skin eased into remission as it flooded over his body.

He sat motionless for quite some time, unmotivated to begin the task of scrubbing off the layers of soot and dirt that clung to him. The wall in front of him was decorated with an oval looking glass, his reflection examining him in return as he stared. Leer squinted, analyzing the way his blond locks drooped over his forehead, a subtle curl playing at the ends of them. It had been quite some time since he had apprised himself with such scrutiny. It was an uncomfortable task that he now couldn't seem to refrain from.

Why does Aldred believe I've been blind? he wondered, looking at his reflection. His dark eyes narrowed in on the cut on his left cheek; it was healing nicely, though sure to become a permanent reminder of his jail escape. He looked down at his hands where they rested on his thighs, the water lapping over him in gentle strokes.

He had always viewed himself as smarter, wiser, one step ahead at all times. His nearly flawless ability to appraise the validity of people and their motives was a constant—he relied on it both professionally and personally. Had it finally failed him?

Have I failed myself?

He washed his skin and hair without concern for the passage of time. His body moved with independence from his mind, sinking deeper into his own thoughts, including Astrid. The gentle carving of her face and toned thighs flitted through his mind as the water tickled his skin.

A different kind of heat stirred within his loins. He groaned and shifted, trying to block out the reaction, but it seemed nearly impossible. A cold wave of guilt fought the deep warmth, becoming unbearable.

Stop, he inwardly pleaded. *Stop thinking about her.*

Instead of total absence, though, his thoughts shifted to her words. Was Astrid right? Was his insistence on finding the truth a lost cause by now?

Was he, himself, a lost cause?

Dunking his head, Leer rinsed his hair and re-emerged above the lukewarm water with a small gasp. The water dripped from his brow against his eyelashes, sliding down the length of his nose and across his cheeks, falling away as it reached his strong jawline. He stood, stepping over the tub onto the cool floor. Droplets of water coasted down his chest, puddling at his feet.

Absentmindedly, he yanked the dry fabric from the nearby table and ran it over himself, drying off as he tried to shake away the conflicting thoughts from his mind. He dressed at an unhurried pace, pulling on a pair of extra trousers from his pack, gingerly buttoning them. He grimaced, the fabric far too confining for his current situation. With a groan, he slipped on his woolen socks, and his boots.

The curtain drew away sharply, and Leer turned to find Astrid wide-eyed behind him, clutching a small pile of clothing to her chest.

"Leer," she gasped, taking a step back.

He found himself staring, his breath heavy. The dim boonwax lighting enhanced her full pink lips, which parted as her gaze hovered in the area of his stomach.

Leer cleared his throat, turning away, his bare chest prickling with gooseflesh as he realized his appearance both above and below his waist. His trousers suddenly became even more unbearably tight. "I'm nearly finished," he murmured, snatching up his things as heat rose through his cheeks.

"I-I assumed you were done by the…length of…the amount of time that's passed," she stammered.

After gathering his tunic and pack, he turned, looking over her in silence. Her hands squeezed her clothing as she shifted her weight, her eyes downcast. His gaze drifted to the neckline of her partially unlaced tunic, trailing down the milky curve of her clavicle and cleavage that was visible in the absence of her willet vest.

He bit the side of his cheek as the fire ignited again, sparked by the scent of her hair—hewen needles and something else he still couldn't place, even after the days he had spent with her. Whatever it was, it was oddly sweet and smoky all at once. His throat dried up as he drank in how her chest rose and fell, her thick lashes batting against her cheeks as she kept her eyes down.

Leer's heart drummed against his chest with each blink.

Leave, Boxwell, he ordered himself, his mind becoming clouded rapidly. *Go, now.*

He swallowed, more incapable of moving with each passing second. His palms became coated with sweat.

"I'm terribly sorry. I shall leave," he mumbled, breaking away for the exit.

"Leer, wait," Astrid said. He paused, his back still toward her. "We need to talk."

"Aye," he agreed with a hard swallow, "and we can once you're settled."

"It can't wait," he heard her argue.

"It must," he insisted, squeezing his eyes shut, beginning to feel powerless.

"But—"

"Astrid—" Leer drew a breath, moistening his lips.

He heard her step closer to him, her steps as light as they had been when she first led him through the woods away from the insurgents.

Her voice was pained. "I...I can imagine how you'll take this, but—"

He reached the curtain, his hand on the fabric when he felt her small hand grip his forearm.

"Please look at me," he heard her plea gently. His fingers tightened around the cloth against the searing heat of her touch. "Leer, please...please look at me. I can't speak to someone's back comfortably."

With reservation, he turned, her hand falling from his arm. The candlelight that flickered behind them illuminated her, a glow surrounding her features like a mystical aura. Leer struggled to ignore her bare skin, his eyes squeezing shut in embarrassment at the temptation to gaze.

Go. Go now. Steady and balanced. Focus—focus! She's but a pawn on the board. Move around her. Stay on course.

The pain and flares of light that haunted him nearly the entire duration of the journey struck him. Leer winced, a prickle of gooseflesh raising over his skin despite the growing warmth surrounding him.

"Stay the course," the familiar voice whispered.

"What?" Leer snapped, bringing his fingertips to his temples.

"The truth awaits you."

"I didn't say anything," Astrid breathed, gripping his forearm. "Leer, what's wrong?"

"Protect the power."

Leer gasped when the pain subsided, lowering his arms to the side. He looked up at Astrid when he felt her grip release and he heard her shift in front of him, the floorboards creaking in response.

"Leer," Astrid whispered, taking a deep breath, her face wrought with emotion.

The room swelled around him, his heart slamming against his chest as smoky trails of black tinted the surrounding frame of his conscious, indiscernible whispers trickling through his mind. He held back a quiver as he tried to fight the dark heat that seemed to want to consume him.

"Leer, I can't..." Astrid paused, suppressing a tremble. "I can't, in good faith, allow you to continue. You're...You're not right in your mind. You know not what you do."

"I—"

"No. No, Leer." She stared at the left side of his chest. "You're not well. You're ill."

His fingers flexed by his sides. "I'm fine. I just…For a moment, I—"

"Please," Astrid interrupted, looking into his eyes. "For a moment, you heard imaginary voices speak." She shook her head. "And then a moment from now, what—you'll think me to be this horrid beast you've created in your mind?" She held up her hand as he opened his mouth to speak. "You can do what you must for your sake, to destroy yourself, if that's what you desire. But first, you need to listen to me."

Leer clenched his molars together, his hands tightening by his sides as he fought his embarrassment and rage.

"Leer," Astrid began, her gaze wavering for a moment. "Leer, all of this…All of this is not what you believe it to be."

"I—"

"Hear me first," she snapped, silencing him. "Leer, my true surname is Falstad. Astrid Falstad."

Leer blinked, wetting his lips as he looked down at her. "Falstad."

Vivid images of the night of the averil flooded his mind—the bright light, the sourceless flames, the blood pouring from the mouth of the man in the red tunic.

Bennett. The insurgent.

-17-

"Bennett Falstad," he breathed. "He was...in the cell when..."

Astrid nodded, chewing on her lip. "Yes," she whispered. She tried to conceal her shudder. "He's my adopted brother."

Leer lifted his chin. "An insurgent."

Astrid's face twisted with her anger. "Perhaps for a moment, you'd like to forgive the idea of my dead brother being an insurgent," she whispered hoarsely.

"I...I'm sorry," Leer murmured. She set her jaw; Leer wasn't sure if she would continue. "Please. Forgive me."

She eyed him for a moment, then sighed, looking away. "Six months ago, his brothers from the eastern camp said that some men were captured during a raid. I assumed it included Bennett, too, since he never met me at our post. I kept coming back, every two weeks, as we swore we would. But he never came." She paused, in evident pain. "Then, I'd heard there was a sighting of him in Junivar. I crossed the eastern wood to scout the area when I happened upon the likes of you two. I knew you both were guards—that wasn't hard to see. I didn't have a plan, really. But I..." She looked into his eyes. "I felt drawn to you." Leer's lips parted. "Not in that sense," she clarified quickly, the apples of her cheeks tinting pink. "Just that…there was something about you. Something I couldn't place."

"So you helped us," Leer finished.

Astrid nodded. "Though I often later questioned myself why. Anyway, after I learned the Lieutenant's name, I knew I had to stay with you."

"Why?"

"Because he's the one the men spoke of at the camps. I knew he might have some information. And he did, as I found out two nights ago at the inn while you played tafl."

Leer recalled the interaction between her and Lieutenant Doyle that nearly cost him the game that night. "Aye, I see that now."

"As you played, I managed to learn that he had Bennett locked away. He…offered me a deal. Bennett's and my own freedom."

"For what?"

Astrid looked at him, hesitating. "For seeing you to the Fell."

Leer stepped closer to her. "Me?"

"Yes."

"But…I don't understand—"

"Listen to me," she interrupted, her voice soft. "That man is not on your side."

Leer shook his head. "I know he's a bit of an arse, but—"

"No, listen," she snapped. "He's *not* who you believe he is."

"He's the king's highest ranking guard."

"And that doesn't concern you?"

"Why would it?"

"The man outright lied to me since the moment I met him," Astrid said, exasperated. "You told me the imprisoned insurgent died the night of the averil. He knew all along Bennett was dead, yet continued to try to deceive me."

Silence hung between them while Leer mulled over Astrid's information. After all, Lieutenant Doyle's motive already seemed pretty clear—save the princess, and ensure him the crown.

"He's motivated by politics, Astrid," Leer said quietly.

What else could it be?

"Leer," Astrid pleaded. "You've no understanding of what it is you're involved in. You're nothing more than a pawn on a board."

The searing dark heat that had previously left him began to seep back into his consciousness. It teased at his conscious, flowed over his skin and around his chest like an expensive fabric trap.

Then the flares of light split into his mind's eye, as if trying to slice through and reach him.

The truth awaits you.

With a growl against the voice he heard, he snapped at Astrid: "In whose game? Yours?"

Her mouth dropped open. "I'm not—"

"Who are you?" Leer demanded, grabbing her wrists and clamping down on her as she winced in pain.

"You must listen—"

"Why should I? Everything you've ever said and done is a lie."

"No," she argued, remaining still under his grip. "No, it isn't."

"At the inn that night, when you came to me with a knife...You intended to kill me."

"I didn't want to. I—"

"And where did you take off to with Finnigan's journal?"

"I didn't remember I had it," she hissed. "And I left last eve to see if I could meet with Bennett's brothers on the western borders. For help against Doyle. For *you*."

"Tell me what the truth is, Astrid."

"It is the truth," she pleaded. "I made a terrible mistake, one which I have tried to correct without success." She shuddered. "Leer, I made a deal with a man I didn't know." The pain filled her eyes. "You must understand that—"

"A deal to kill me," Leer continued. "My life for what, Astrid? Money?"

"No," she insisted. "Never to kill you. I *never* agreed to that. Just to seeing you to the Fell."

"All lies, only to make me weak," Leer spat.

"He was all the family I had left," she snarled, "and I was ready to do what I needed to in order to save him."

Leer stared vacantly at Astrid, releasing her wrists with the tiniest bit of sympathy. He knew the feeling all too well.

"He tricked us both, Leer," she whispered.

Leer shut his eyes, trying to control his anger. *Steady and balanced.* "What do you mean?" he asked, his voice rigid.

"He surely is keeping secret his real reason for going to the Fell," Astrid explained as she rubbed her sore wrists. "He somehow knew you'd be useful and made it his business to be with you. I know you don't know whether to believe me or not, but I vow on my brother's life that all I have said to you is the entirety of truth that I know." There was a terrible hurt in her eyes as he stared at them, one that made his heart soften. "Doyle hasn't told me as such, but it's all that makes sense for why he should care to bring you to the Fell."

"What would he need there?" Leer asked in a low growl.

"I don't know," Astrid replied firmly. She paused for a moment, her eyes locked on Leer's. "Whatever his reason, it's for certainly no one's benefit but his own. And he won't be concerned about what happens to you after he gets what he wants."

The journal, Leer realized. *Finnigan's knowledge. Does he actually believe?*

Leer felt his pulse rising; he shut his eyes as he tried to calm himself. "How do you expect me to trust you?" he asked, strained.

"Leer—"

"You orchestrated a plan with that fobbing whoreson!" Leer snapped, peering down at Astrid. "You lied to me. And you pretended like everything was fine downstairs."

Astrid took Leer's hands into her own; he winced at the contact. She was pleasure and pain, heat and ice, energizing life and consuming death. "Nothing I said has been a lie," she insisted. "I may have not told you about my brother, but everything else I have is the truth." She swallowed. "I don't know anything of Doyle's motivations. I never meant to harm you, which is why I came to you in this manner. And whether you believe it to be true or not, whether or not you wish to accept what I have to give, I vow to do all I can for you because…I believe in you."

Leer withdrew his hands from Astrid's, his jaw clenched as he wrestled with what to do.

Walk away, Leer told himself. *Walk away and don't look back. You shan't be weak now.*

He quietly drank in the sight of Astrid in front of him, confused by her conviction. "What is it about me that you believe in, Astrid?" he asked, a thick brow arching.

"Your uniqueness," Astrid explained. "The part of you I'm drawn to but can't explain. As if by a power, or something."

The headaches, the visions, the voices.

Could it be…?

He shook his head to himself. "Even if I bore such power, why should you care about it?"

She seemed confused. "Why wouldn't I?"

"You abhorred the possibility of the Grimbarror last night in the cave, and at the table a short time ago," he scoffed.

"What I abhor is the way in which you continually seek the Fell with such zeal," Astrid corrected. "I was trying to deter you, hoping you'd come to your senses, but I quickly learned that you aren't a man easily persuaded."

"Aye," Leer said softly. "On that we both can agree."

His palm moved over his face, his fingers digging into his temples. He was convinced he might leave permanent indentations in his head from the harsh pressure he inflicted on himself.

What to do? he thought as he squeezed his eyes shut. *Believe in the liar, or lie regarding my desire to believe? Why must I wish to believe her so much?* His stomach knotted. *What if she speaks the truth? What if what she says about me is true?*

Withdrawing his hand from his face, Leer peered down at Astrid with a deep sigh, as her sparkling eyes seemed to pierce his hardened heart further. A twinge of remorse crept inside of him, rippling outward until it made him more vulnerable than he cared to admit. Astrid's face was illuminated, her skin still bared. Leer's eyes fell on it momentarily, noting how the tone reminded him of ivory parchment, delicate and pure. The sight of her reddened wrists from the twisted grip he'd held on them made Leer's stomach lurch.

What have I done?

He swallowed back his self hatred and shut his eyes in prayer.

Perhaps it's a trick of my mind. Perhaps when I look again, she will appear unharmed.

Yet, he was wrong—the marks remained after he opened his eyes.

He was no better than his parents were.

Selfish like my mother. And a monster like my father.

Convinced he would be sick, he swept his belongings up from the floor and ripped the curtain away, only to find Lieutenant Doyle pointing a sword at them.

-18-

Leer swallowed, his bare skin chilled with the cool air and the knowledge of Lieutenant Doyle's deceit. His own sword was tucked in the Lieutenant's sheath.

"You," he breathed, taking a step back toward Astrid.

"Fancy seeing you again, Miss Browne," Lieutenant Doyle said with a smile. "Oh, pardon me. Miss Falstad."

"Burn in the underworld, you olis," Astrid spat.

The Lieutenant ignored her. "Put your clothes on, Boxwell," he ordered, gesturing with the sword. "I was hoping we'd at least get some sleep before Miss Falstad tried to save the day, but no matter."

"I won't take another step with you," Leer said, grinding his teeth together.

"Oh, but you will." Lieutenant Doyle took a step toward Astrid; Leer moved backward in an attempt to shield her, one arm stretched behind him. "See, I won't hesitate to cut ties with her, so to speak. If you don't care about her life, then by all means, ignore my orders."

"Bloody scoundrel," Leer growled.

"We'll have plenty of time for name calling on our way to the Fell."

"You're insane, thinking you can travel at night," Astrid gasped.

The way Lieutenant Doyle smiled at Astrid made Leer's blood boil. "That's why there will be torch light, my dear."

Darkness shrouded the Eyne Wood, save from the bits of moonlight above and the torch Leer carried. He kept his pace steady slightly behind Astrid, putting himself between her and the Lieutenant, who took up the rear.

Despite every breath of the bitter, thick air, Leer was anything but cold. The blistering blanket of darkness had taken a firm hold on him from the moment they left the inn.

The light shone in his mind's eye with each blink, the breathy presence of the voice lingering over his shoulder. He had no other name to give it but darkness—the darkness Finnigan had always managed to avoid. It now seemed easier to accept it passively than to fight, especially since there seemed to be few reasons for him to fight anymore.

"You'd think all this walking would keep one warm," Astrid said, snow kicking up around her feet as she hiked in front of him.

Leer glanced over at her. "We'll stop. Take my coat."

Astrid laughed under her breath. "You surely didn't come all this way to reach the border and die of frostbite."

"No stopping. Keep moving," the Lieutenant barked. "We're nearly there."

"If you know the way, why make us come? Why not go yourself?" Leer snapped.

A tremble that vibrated the earth made the three stop, their focus immediately shifting to their feet. Leer's eyes widened, his heart stopping in his chest.

"What in the world was that?" Astrid breathed.

The earth continued to shake, seeming to grow stronger with each passing moment. Astrid screamed when a large cracking noise resonated through a tree trunk. Leer couldn't see beyond the light of the torch he held. The flame flickered, the wind that grew stronger around them threatened to douse its light.

"Give me my sword," Leer called back to Lieutenant Doyle.

"The hell I will," Lieutenant Doyle replied.

"What is happening?" Astrid asked, gripping Leer's coat sleeve to brace herself against another deep rumble.

"Stop right there," a voice shouted in the thick night as the rumble ceased.

Through the wavering torchlight, Leer saw the vague shadows of men in insurgent red pouring out from behind the trees, swords and bows trained on them.

"You set me up," Leer growled, glaring at Astrid.

"They're on your side," she insisted. Leer saw the truthfulness of her expression, the shock visible on her face.

"You filthy wench," Lieutenant Doyle sneered, trying to reach for Astrid. Leer blocked her, glaring at him. "So be it," the Lieutenant said to Leer, spitting to his side.

"You're surrounded," one of the insurgents barked. "Drop your weapons."

"He's with me," Astrid corrected, gesturing to Leer. "The other you can kill, for all I care."

The earth below began to grumble again, vibrating underfoot and shaking the trees. Snow started to rain down from overhead, dusting everyone under the branches. A groan emanated from deep within the ground as it shook.

The wind picked up, swirling around them at torrential speeds; its howl pierced their ears, mixing with the scurried voices of the insurgents around them. A loud crack of wood echoed in the distance. Leer saw thick trees splitting in two, toppling forward as their impact further shook the earth.

"What in the hell is doing that?" Astrid demanded, gasping as she shifted her stance to keep her balance.

Leer's throat dried up, his pulse rising as he furiously scanned the woods, spreading his arms a bit to steady himself.

"It can't be," he breathed.

"It can't be what?" Astrid asked, panicked.

Unable to keep her balance, Astrid fell, rolling down the incline of the road. Leer dropped his torch and ran after her, the darkness engulfing him. He swooped down, frantically grabbing around until he snatched her arm. He brought her to her feet, bracing her as more tree trunks collided with the frozen earth.

"Leer!" she gasped. "What is happening?"

A shrill, angry shriek filled the air, the tone eliciting familiar gooseflesh over Leer's arms. An invisible source pummeled them with forceful gusts of air.

Wings.

A stark light pierced the woods. Against his better judgment, Leer turned toward the source, still clinging to Astrid.

The Grimbarror.

The intense glow burned his eyes. He groaned, unable to see through it, and turned back toward Astrid. "Don't look at it," he warned, drawing her closer when he saw her dumbfounded expression. "Don't look at its light."

Screams of men mixed with the snarling winds, piercing the air. Leer's stomach sank as he scanned the area for any sort of weapon, relieved to find his sword on the ground a few paces away. He stepped toward it carefully as he tried to determine the location of the wings. "Take hold of my coat," Leer ordered Astrid.

"Leer—"

"Keep your eyes closed!"

Leer winced as he tried to take in his surroundings through the dense light. The uncontrollable tears that sprang from his eyes further blurred his vision.

His blood ran cold when he saw the silhouette of an arched figure ahead of himself, massive wings holding impressive span. They embodied as much grace as they did power, as much purity as they did evil. Its outstretched arms ended in terrifying claws that threw the insurgents like wet rags into a heap, fire consuming their flesh after just a glance from the creature. Leer held his breath, watching as one insurgent bravely tried to finish the beast with his sword, but failed.

"The Lieutenant is gone," he heard Astrid breathe as he took up his sword from the snow, unsure if she even meant to say it aloud.

"Close your eyes, Astrid. Do it now," Leer ordered, turning her away from the light.

Suddenly, a vice-like *something* clamped onto his shoulder. Claws dragged down the middle of his broad back, sinking into his flesh, drawing blood. Leer screamed; his arching body tearing him from Astrid's embrace. He clumsily slashed his sword at the body on top of him. The beast shrieked at the strike, but didn't falter as it again clamped down on Leer. Leer's sword fell to the ground like a child's toy under the Grimbarror's strength.

Leer never felt more vulnerable as he looked into the beast's golden-rimmed eyes. Sticky, hot blood trailed down his body—he wasn't sure if it was his own or the beast's. He gasped as another clawed hand latched around his neck, the pressure enough to make him instantly lightheaded.

As the Grimbarror began to twist its wrist, it took a deliberate pause.

"*Boxwell*," it exclaimed, recognition spreading over its face as it braced for the kill. The ground stopped shaking. Though they didn't move, Leer saw the color soften in the beast's eyes. "I suppose he failed to spare you after all. He was a fool. They all were such fools."

As its claws tightened around Leer's throat, throbs pierced Leer's temples with unforgiving strength. Leer's flesh burned, as if he could feel the raging current of his own blood. His every sense was lit on fire.

With suddenness, he heard multiple voices speaking in many different tongues. He understood some of them, while others he had never heard before in his life. The onslaught was nauseating, debilitating. The voices didn't leave despite his silent, fervent pleadings. They continued to speak, each one layering on top of the next, competing for his attention, fighting for his focus.

His fear and rage intersected, collided. Time slowed but urgency quickened. With a heavy groan, Leer squeezed his eyes shut and wrenched against the clawed grip that held him, power emanating through his arms as he shoved the beast off of himself and several yards away.

Once free, a shocked Leer sucked in deep breaths of air.

What had just happened?

"Leer!"

He opened his eyes, his focus flashing to Astrid, who screamed as the beast tossed her into the snow, her body skidding violently across the ground to the side of him. With grace and speed he never experienced, Leer sprinted toward her and wrapped both arms around her, lifting her limp, unconscious frame up and drawing her against himself. A twinge of relief struck him when he heard her shallow breathing.

"It is mine," the Grimbarror shrieked across from him. "You will never take it from me."

Leer felt the blast of cold air from the wings of the beast on his raw back wounds. He turned toward the beast, whose eyes honed in on him.

For the first time, Leer could see it clearly. Its body, dress and stance were mostly human, but it had two vast, dark green wings across its back, each detailed in several razor sharp pointed edges. A mass of fiery red hair, like Princess Gresham's, framed its haunting yellow-rimmed eyes. It wore an elegant deep purple cloak over its tunic and pants. It had a noticeably human face that bore dusty green scales in an irregular pattern. Leer saw the creature's thick hands constrict by its sides. It balled its fists concealing them. Still, Leer could still see the tips of bloodied claws that finished each of the Grimbarror's digits.

Leer pressed Astrid closer to his chest as the Grimbarror shifted its weight. Although the light was beyond brilliant, Leer's eyes were unaffected. He could see perfectly, better than he had ever before. He blinked. He wasn't sure he even needed to. The revelation made Leer's heart jump; he eyed the Grimbarror, lips parted.

The beast stared intently back at him. Leer swore there was a hint of a smile playing across its thin mouth. Its feet, concealed in tall, strapped boots, moved a confident step toward him.

"It is mine," it growled, the timbre jarring, beautiful.

"I won't let you harm her," Leer warned, drawing a wavering breath through his nose. He suppressed a shudder. *Am I arguing with a monster?*

"You will not take it from me."

Leer's jaw flexed. "She will not be harmed."

"It is mine." The Grimbarror flapped its wings as it took another step closer.

Leer's fingertips dug deeper into Astrid's arm. "I won't let you touch her."

He rocked backward on his heels, his right leg taking the first step away from the enemy. His left followed, his long stride placing distance between them. Leer's breath quickened, his chest constricting as he tried to find a weapon of any kind.

The Grimbarror was clearly angered by his defiance, its face resembling that of a scolding parent's. It straightened up, a rumbled snarl resonating in its throat. "The amulet is mine."

The amulet, Leer repeated to himself, recalling the reference from the night in Junivar. *The eyes of stone.*

Through the light that illuminated the wood, he tried to take stock of where Lieutenant Doyle was. *So that was his motive all along. The amulet. He's gone after the amulet, I'll bet.*

He kept slowly moving away, hoping he would happen upon his discarded sword.

"I'm fairly certain you acquired it in a rather unjust way," Leer replied, his brow arched.

The beast tilted its head back. "I am its Master," it murmured, a scowl visible on its face. "No one else shall ever be."

A foreign, sickening jolt of pain coursed through the crown of Leer's head to the soles of his feet without mercy or notice. The strange suddenness of it almost made him drop Astrid. He dug his heels into the ground, anchoring himself as he braced against it. His pulse climbed as he felt the searing heat tear through his body. He grimaced, a moan escaping in response to the brutal assault.

The beast flicked its yellow eyes down toward Astrid, then back up to Leer. "There's darkness growing in you."

"You see nothing," Leer spat.

"I see more than you ever will, because you are blind. Soon, though, you won't be," the Grimbarror noted, still smirking. "Soon, you'll see them all just as I do. And you'll hate them all as much as I do." It laughed. "The touch of their skin will singe more than the hottest fire, but you will crave the burn. You'll

224

embrace them before you slaughter them just to feel it. You'll lust for the satisfaction of their spilt blood."

"I'll never harm anyone," Leer spat, his fingers sinking tighter around Astrid. He trembled at the suggestion.

The beast tilted its head to the side. "Haven't you already?"

Leer's nostrils flared under his steely gaze. "I shall *never* kill to give any man or beast satisfaction," he spat.

The Grimbarror halted, its pause highlighted by its blossoming smile. "Never say never," it whispered.

Leer lifted Astrid higher against his chest, taking a fleeting glance at her before addressing the Grimbarror. His voice was thick, edged with fear laced under savage anger. "*Never.*"

On his simple word, the frozen ground began to tremble once more. Snow skittered as it shifted erratically under the soles of Leer's boots. Leer was motionless, but the earth moved around him, bending and swaying against his inner turmoil. Naked branches quivered, turbulent winds from an unknown source stirring them, swirling massive drifts of snow on the already covered forest floor.

Leer felt the ground split below him. He jumped backward in shock, watching the earth open. Astrid's eyes fluttered open, her expression confused as she witnessed the unfolding chaos—the sickeningly satisfying phenomena he made without explanation.

He continued to step away from the widening gap in the ground, his eyes flicking upward to the beast. The earth groaned; it resonated with a deep, feral ache. A swarming heat flooded through Leer's bloodstream. His veins pulsated with energy as he noted a thinly veiled emotion in the Grimbarror's eyes. Leer had seen it many times before, especially when seated across from a tafl opponent:

Shock. Anger. Confusion.

Fear.

He hadn't expected to see it in the golden-rimmed irises of his fearsome sworn enemy, though.

No sooner than it came, it changed. It flickered into one of praise and haughty approval.

"I knew I saw it in you," the Grimbarror confirmed, shifting its stance as the earth split apart between its legs.

"You see nothing," Leer growled.

The Grimbarror's smile made Leer's stomach sick. "I see the beginning of an army. I suppose I just hadn't expected it so…soon."

"Expected *what?*"

It smiled; its tongue flicked the air. "Your ascension, *Naetan.*"

Wooden limbs overhead snapped, bent under the unreasonable demand of the turbulence surrounding them. Leer ducked to his knees, sheltering Astrid with his own back and shoulders as a knotted bough of hewen whirled down from above. It crashed just left of them, evergreen needles colliding with fresh powder as it pulverized rocks hidden under the snow.

Leer felt the cold snow melt quickly against the rising heat of his neck as he hunched over Astrid, his nose buried in her hair. His chest constricted as his mouth sank against the tender flesh of her neck. As his lips inadvertently moved against her satiny skin, he felt himself becoming aroused, a physical and inner awakening stirring him.

Lust. Crave.

Push. Pull.

Kiss. Tear.

Kill.

It took every ounce of his strength to tear away from her. He pulled his face up, his eyes seeing through the thick darkness with no effort. It was as if it was dusk instead of the very early morning.

He searched for the Grimbarror, but it was gone.

Standing with Astrid in his arms, he scanned the empty road, accepting the silence he encountered. No creature made a sound. The trees halted, the ground stilled. Leer finally spotted his sword, along with several others, lying in the blood soaked, crimson colored snow. Erratic jagged lines tore through the earth. He picked up his sword, squelching the rumble in his stomach as he took in the gruesome collection of bodies.

Lieutenant Doyle's body wasn't among them.

The amulet.

He needed to find it first.

He had to get to the Fell.

-19-

Leer's senses assaulted him as he raced north on the path he imagined the beast had taken. The snapping of brush underfoot became like daggers to his ears, the brightness of the snow maximized in his heightened vision. He could taste the odd ash of the fire the Grimbarror made, even though they were long gone from where they encountered the beast.

Astrid's complex pheromones burned his nose. Aching heat rose through his body at an unbearable speed. He gripped her tighter in his arms, and a soft moan caught in his throat in response to how much more sensual she became to his touch.

He kept running, blind to any other course of action. He glided, soared, leaped. The pain he once felt had somehow vanished, a foreign thickness taking residence where the agony of torn skin and tissue once had.

Astrid's bloodcurdling scream stopped Leer in his tracks, his gait broken as he looked down into her eyes. Their hue reminded him of clear summer skies from the top of every mountain he ever climbed, of crystalline river waters glinting in the sun.

"Stop," Astrid begged, her voice strained. She was weightless in his arms, a feather cradled in his embrace. "Stop this instant!"

Leer swallowed against his raw, dry throat, clutching Astrid tightly. She locked her eyes on his, her bottom lip quivering ever so slightly.

"You're frightening me," she whispered.

It didn't make sense. "*I'm* frightening you?" Leer asked, stunned. "Shouldn't the large fire wielding beast with wings have given you more of a scare than me?"

She blinked a few times. With a raw, animalistic lust that struck him at his core, he noticed her dense lashes. He felt the inner current of her heart build, her doubt barely concealed.

"You broke the ground," she breathed, her expression unchanged as he tried to fight against himself.

"Aye," Leer breathed, watching her mouth move with fascination.

He wanted to touch it.

"You split the earth and…flung the beast like it was a bebbet."

"And that is more alarming than the Grimbarror you didn't believe in appearing within a few strides of yourself?"

Astrid moved stiffly in Leer's arms, pulling away from him. "Put me down," she stammered.

"Astrid—"

Leer hunched forward and groaned in pain as Astrid's well placed boot kick connected below his belt, debilitating him. His hands sprang open and she tumbled from his grasp, onto the snow.

After a moment of recovery, he straightened up and saw how she put distance between them. He kept his eyes on her, his fingers flexing at his sides as he observed her paleness, not missing the rose-hued flush of her cheeks from the crisp air around them.

Clear. His mind rapidly cleared after releasing her. His mouth opened gently, realizing the internal difference the absence of her touch made.

The beast was right, he realized with sickening guilt. *Her touch... 'Tis a poison to my mind.*

Leer refocused when he saw Astrid's silent decision in her body language. "Don't," he pleaded, taking a step closer as she froze. "Don't run."

"Don't come any closer to me," Astrid warned shakily, taking more small steps in the opposite direction.

"Astrid, please," Leer insisted, raising his hands in surrender. "Don't be afraid."

He took a soft step toward her. She stiffened in response as she stepped away; it was obvious she tried to suppress a shudder.

"For the love of Hiline," Leer grumbled. He sighed, dropping his head in defeat and shuddered, rolling his left shoulder against the new thickness in his back. He could still feel the Grimbarror's cold, rock hard claw digging into his flesh. He took a tentative half step toward Astrid. "I need you to trust me. Do you?" he asked, searching her eyes.

Astrid shook her head with a shiver. "You're a blasted fool if you think I'll—"

Leer rolled his eyes. "Stop being stubborn, Astrid." He took another step forward, extending his hand to her. "Look deep within yourself and answer me—do you trust me?"

Astrid stood still enough for Leer to notice her softening expression as she considered his question.

"I don't know," he heard her breathe with a tremble.

As he exhaled, warm, misty puffs of air appeared in front of his face. He took another step closer, his hand still outstretched as a sad smile curved his mouth. "At least you're honest."

She hesitantly stepped toward him. He met her more than halfway, understanding her lingering reservation.

"Speak to me," Leer begged, hating the silence. "Are you alright?" Astrid's lips moved in soundless motion in response. "Please," Leer whispered; his chest constricted with revived panic. "Please, say something. You hit your head back there. Are you alright?"

"Shit," Astrid breathed in shock, her eyes still wide as she looked at Leer with wonder.

Leer laughed with nervous release. "That's a start."

Astrid shook her head. "How…?"

"I haven't the faintest idea, Astrid."

"You…You broke the earth…"

"Aye."

"You…"

His eyes never left hers; he couldn't help himself from drowning in their blue depths. An inner flush overcame every inch of him, his stomach churning with unusual hunger. Leer's teeth dug into his lip and easily tore it, and he sucked the drips of sweet, metallic blood backward to his tongue.

"Don't be afraid," he pleaded. "Without your fear, I…it shan't harm you."

"What do you mean?" Astrid asked, her eyes narrowing.

Leer blinked a few times, silent as he put the pieces in place. "Just don't, Astrid," he pleaded. He clamped his teeth together against the darkness building in him, his thoughts becoming more sensual, as if on instinct. "The Grimbarror consumes it."

...I consume it.

"You're not making sense—"

"Listen to me," Leer interrupted, stacking his voice above Astrid's, his own fears mounting at terrifying speed as he looked north, "the Grimbarror has returned to the Fell to end the princess' life." He paused, looking back toward Astrid. "We need to go. Now."

"But—"

"We haven't the time for details." His breath deepened as he tried to control himself. *Steady and balanced. Dammit. Steady...Balanced.* He looked ahead toward the Fell. "Let's go."

"Leer, wait!"

Leer froze; he dug the toe of his boot into the snow with a grimace and a sigh. Some time had passed since he and Astrid started back out into the wood toward the Fell, though he didn't quite know how much. With his newfound power and speed, he was far more adept at the journey than before. The physical aches of his previous injuries disappeared, which, in turn, put distance between them.

The separation wasn't entirely unintentional; it was all Leer could do to keep sane.

When Leer was a child, Finnigan had once tried to explain to him the reason behind Leer's father's drinking habits. Leer hadn't understood it then, the concept of "uncontrollable urges" far too complex for him to absorb.

Yet now, as he trekked through the pure white powder at the base of the Fell, he understood what his uncle tried to say so many years ago.

He and his father suffered from unquenchable thirst, but while his father's thirst was for mead, Leer's was for blood.

It would never be the same. A simple touch or kiss, or even intimate possession of someone would never again be enough to quell the fire inside. He would always need more.

He would need blood.

"Leer," he heard Astrid call out again behind him.

"What do you want?" Leer growled, stealthily looking back at her.

"I want to know what in the world has you so twisted against me?" she asked when she drew closer. He winced as she took hold of his arm and turned him toward her.

Leer sighed, avoiding eye contact. "Nothing."

"Could've fooled me," she huffed.

"Not trying to."

"You haven't spoken a word to me."

"Sorry, but I didn't feel the need for a chat."

"Come off it, Leer," she snapped. "You mean to say that there's absolutely nothing you need to talk about?"

Leer kept examining the tree line above her hair. "Nothing that concerns you."

She was aghast. "I don't believe you. You're—"

He waited—waited for her to continue to yell at him, or perhaps even slap him. He deserved it; he knew he did. He didn't have a choice. He had to push her away. She couldn't be near him like this anymore, since he didn't know what he might do to her.

When she didn't say anything, Leer's eyes shifted from the forest down to Astrid, noticing the utter shock riddling her delicate face.

"What is it?" he asked.

"Your face," she whispered, her blue eyes scanning his left cheekbone intently, zeroed in on his forming burn scar.

His brow furrowed in offense. "What's the matter with my face?"

"It's…odd."

"Try not to be so sensitive, Astrid. It's rather confusing to know what you really mean when you are."

She rolled her eyes. "You're an imbecile."

He frowned. "Are you still wondering why I don't wish to talk to you?"

Leer tightened his jaw as Astrid's fingers grazed his skin, lingering over it. Her compassionate touch was more excruciating than the burn from the original fire.

"You've…You've an odd…growth on your skin, Leer," Astrid whispered, rising on tiptoe to get a closer look. Leer swallowed back a groan as he felt her balmy breath spread over his neck and cheek. "It's—"

She stopped short; he met her eyes upon her gasp.

"What?" Leer asked.

She fell silent.

"What is it, Astrid?" he repeated, this time a bit more frantic.

Her mouth opened, but words failed her.

"Dammit, Astrid—"

"It's scales, Leer," Astrid interrupted, an audible quiver in her voice. She paused, drawing a deep breath. "Scales. Like...Like..."

Neither of them spoke; neither moved.

He dove into her eyes, sinking into the rich tidal waves of clean azure and swam through the waters without a care, without concern. Without fear.

"Like the beast," Leer murmured. His heart stopped as he watched her brows knit together slowly, the confused realization evident through her widening eyes and paling skin.

"I was going to say like a skimmer or an olis," she corrected.

"An olis."

"It could be chapped skin, too."

"Chapped skin," he repeated with a scoff, shaking his head. "After all you've witnessed, after all you've seen, you'll refuse to believe?"

"Leer, it's...too fantastic. I mean, there could be a million reasons for what you're experiencing."

He narrowed his eyes. "You think this is all because of chapped skin?"

She paused, and he watched her through her silence. His skin prickled with awareness as she withdrew her hand from his face. Leer snatched her wrist with a snarl, an odd satisfaction filling him as he absorbed her unspoken shock.

Stop. You can't do this.

He loosened his grip, his head tilting down in shame. "I...I'm not..."

"Leer—" she breathed.

"I'm not safe," Leer finished quickly, adjusting his fingers over her skin with a pained sigh. "I'm not safe, Astrid. Please. Please…leave."

"Leer, you—"

"Leave," he snarled, meeting her eyes. Against his better judgment, he drew her closer to him. His body ached as she pressed up against him and he squeezed her wrist in response. "Leave. *Now.*"

"I won't," Astrid whispered.

"Stop! Just…Just, *stop that.*"

"Stop *what?*"

With more force than he intended, Leer flung Astrid away from himself with a grunt, as she stumbled backwards for a few steps. Her dark hair swung around her face, framing her confused expression. Her unique woodsy scent wafted toward his keen nose. Leer rolled his eyes upward with a groan, kicking the snow in front of him and cursing.

"Leer—" Astrid began.

"No," Leer said, halting her with a raised hand. He drew a deep breath, leaning his head back as he looked up at the darkening skies overhead. "No. Don't…Don't speak."

He watched the thick clouds swarm above him, creeping away from his sight as he drowned himself in thought.

She won't leave. I can't just…leave her to die. She's not safe. He shut his eyes. *She's not safe with me either. I might be what kills her.*

"You—" Leer paused, his words halting as he sniffed the air.

Ash…Odd ash.

"Leer," Astrid said firmly, as she took his hand. "You *need* to tell me everything you aren't saying."

Her grip was tighter than he gave her credit for. "All you need to know is that you're not safe," he replied.

"What I need to know is everything that *you* do."

"Astrid—"

"No!" she insisted, yanking on his arm, forcing him to face her. Her violent maneuver caught him off-guard. He felt his mouth drop open, the lust mounting at incalculable speed within him. "Answer me," she demanded, her nails digging into the flesh of his forearm.

His stomach tightened; his body stirred.

"I changed," he whispered.

"Into what?" she breathed. She tightened her hand, and he suppressed a shudder. "Into what?" she repeated through his silence.

"You know," he darkly countered.

She hesitated a beat. "I'm…not—"

"Don't lie," Leer growled. "You know." He stepped closer, surprising himself with how he withstood the burn of their contact. "You know *exactly* what I am. So stop denying it and *say* it."

"You haven't become some terrible beast," Astrid insisted. "Your mind…Your mind is so fixed on the idea, that it has you believing in the impossible."

He watched her, transfixed. "You refuse to believe, even after all that's taken place." He closed the gap between them, his breath hitching as his hips roughly collided with hers.

She shook her head, a slight quiver to her bottom lip. "You haven't changed, Leer. You're still the good man you've always been."

"You know better than that," he growled, his nostrils flaring as he seized her neck. "You're nothing but a filthy liar, like you've always been."

And in that moment, he knew he was his father's son.

Her throat was a twisted silver mug handle firm under his grasp. Her body, the cup holding the mead of her blood, was sinfully warm, alluring. Her delicious scent rose from it, dancing under his nose as he lifted her closer to his mouth.

I can't. I can't take a drink.

Just one...

Just one sip of her mouth.

The dark strands of her hair, silken and wild, teased his face as his fingers clamped down tighter around her larynx.

Just one—just one sip.

She moved against him, oxygen starved, her hips colliding against his stomach as he raised her higher in his hold.

He squeezed harder; he grit his teeth, saliva forming inside his cheeks.

Just one.

His eyes honed in on hers:

So blue and round. So pure.

His—so dark, so broken, now burning yellow gold around the rims of the irises.

One...One, sweet drink...

I'm my father's son...

No!

...Just one sip...
...Just one...

"Please," Astrid begged through a strained whisper. It tore the veil over his eyes.

He saw his hands eagerly taking her life away.

He felt his skin tingle from the thrill of the hunt.

He felt his fervor grow as she weakened.

He heard the calling of his soul, the longing for her death.

Leer's fingers forcibly sprang open as he released Astrid, panting as he watched her limp body quiver on the snow at his feet. As she drew shallow, strained breaths, her hair splayed like a halo on the powder around her.

He shook, trembling with agonized terror. Clarity washed over him like a harsh wave of the Sea of Zita beating against a slick jetty, residual guilt clinging with pained realization:

He almost killed her.

Leer reluctantly turned his focus from Astrid's coughing to the distant sight of the Fell. His thoughts flitted to the amulet. He was so close, so close to succeeding.

He was so close to heroism, yet so close to madness.

Movement in his peripheral vision shifted Leer's attention back to Astrid. He watched as she tried to push herself up to her knees, shaking as she sucked in precious mouthfuls of air.

His mouth opened, his arms moving slightly toward her. He froze, his feet grounded from shock and fear.

You did this to her, Boxwell.

You.

He willed himself to speak, to beg her forgiveness.

He couldn't.

Leave.

Leave before you do it again.

Leer watched Astrid rise to her feet, turning to him. His chest constricted when he saw the redness around her neck.

His fingers, etched in her skin. Her eyes, bloodshot and weeping. Her face, pale and marred.

He felt her silent fear of him growing larger with each moment. His guilt and self hatred rose beyond what he could bear.

He *was* his father's son. But now, instead of hiding behind a basket to get away from the horror his father caused, *he* was the cause.

Leer swallowed back the bile that lurched up his throat, catching Astrid's eyes as they locked on his. His breath hitched; he stepped away from her, his hands flattening by his sides.

"I…I…"

Words failed him.

But he knew action wouldn't.

He scanned the entire length of her petite frame, memorizing each detail of her:

The subtle curves of her thighs, hips, waist and breasts; the frenzy of her dark, tangled hair; the alabaster skin of her cheekbones dusted with freckles; her curious, crystalline eyes; her dewy lips, parted in question.

He closed his eyes. It was better this way. Whatever he now was, he needed to take every precaution he could. He had enjoyed the process of killing her far too much to keep her close. He would abandon her, and the rest of humanity, for the entirety of his days. After all, he could never harm something he would never see again.

He drew a shaky breath through his nose as he unsheathed his sword, tossing it to the ground in front of her. He didn't want to leave her unprotected.

He tried to ignore how sensual his first name sounded on her lips as she whispered it repeatedly. He saved her portrait and voice to his memory, both conjuring mental images that began the sickening stir within him once more.

And then, he ran.

-20-

Leer's hands trembled at his sides when he arrived at his long sought destination—an imposing iron gate shrouded by thick vines of ivy, flanked by two vast stretches of stone walls on either side, each at least three men high.

Enter the gates, but do not fall.

He didn't fear the aged blood staining the pores of the rocks, nor the erratic collection of broken bones that peeked out from the snow at his feet.

Rather, his terror came from the vivid imprint of his long fingers in her neck he saw in his mind's eye.

Whatever was on the other side of the iron gate couldn't be nearly as frightening as the unadulterated ecstasy he derived from throttling an innocent woman.

Leer sucked in a shaky breath, his sweaty right palm colliding with the ice-cold iron bar in front of him. He examined the detailed lock at eye level.

Child's play now, I suppose.

The desolate, woodland world around him was still and calm, wildlife hidden away from sight. He knew he wasn't alone, though. He could feel its presence, sense its pleasure at his arrival.

With a determined yank, he defeated the lock and forced open the gate. The gate creaked, aged metal groaning in protest from years of remaining idle. Leer ducked as snow and ice particles crashed from stretched ivy overhead, vines snapping as the entryway swung open on its hinges.

He brushed his tunic off, shaking his cap free of fractals as he stepped through with a cautious breath.

How many have made it this far from the other side?

Leer jumped when the gate slammed itself shut and resounded with power against the lock. The sound startled a small flock of nearby blue-footed grupes from their resting place among the branches of a wispy, naked hewen tree. The grupes ascended into the heavens with protesting shrieks, cawing as they accusingly cast their red eyes at Leer.

"Stupid grupes," Leer growled, fixating on one particular bird before training his eyes to the north. He wet his lips, feeling their smoothness with the tip of his tongue.

He swallowed, realizing the significance of his healed physical pain and scarring:

This was who he now was —a man able to heal. A man with power, a man who wielded magic.

A man with Vei blood.

Leer squinted as spied a path he saw cutting through the coppice directly toward the Fell. Instinctively, he crossed his right arm across his waist, pausing midway as he realized he was without his sword.

"Dammit," he muttered, as his arm flopped to his side. He pursed his lips in disgust, striding through the thicket, his boots crunching through the crusted snow as he wracked his mind for a plan.

No sword, no backup weapons.

Leer wiped his mouth with the back of his hand, sighing as he remembered the softness of Astrid's skin under his lips and fingers.

No one to trust myself with ever again.

The earth suddenly gave way under Leer's left foot, his right kicking out behind him as he fell into a sinkhole.

Leer gasped in surprise, yelling in pain as his hips and limbs twisted as he sank into the hallowed ground. The snow collapsed into the hole, revealing the mouth of the pit. It grew larger by the second, sucking brush and leaves down with him into the dark belly of the earth. He groaned, his backside scraped along the snow and ice on the chute, propelling him toward the seemingly endless black bottom of the pit.

Leer tried to brace himself, his arms outstretched to pin himself inside the tunnel, but the pathway was far too large. He only succeeded at gaining more speed, tumbling half onto his side before knocking his head into the opposite wall, bouncing backward onto his back.

Still sliding downward, Leer's eyes fluttered against the blast to his head, his fingers desperately clawing at his sides, his heels kicking inward to try to control his descent. Before he could stop himself, he landed onto the ground at the base of the chute with a violent thud, his already tender head banging again onto more rock.

Leer moaned in pain, rolling slowly onto his right side in the cavern. He panted, his eyes squeezed shut as he curled up into the fetal position; he could feel the heat of the blood that ran down his forehead.

"Dammit," he cursed as he flattened his palms, pushing himself upward onto his knees as his body re-energized.

Enter the gates, but don't fall. Right. Failed that one.

The cavern's clearing was easily as tall as any normal cottage he had been in. The space was open and round, a pathway adjacent to him illuminated with soft, yellow light that flickered and spilled out around the edge of the tunnel and filtered over the rest of the area.

Torchlight. Has someone been down here?

Leer cautiously felt his forehead. He had lost his cap somewhere along the way, and was only half surprised at the lack of presence of any wounds on his skin. He withdrew his hand, glancing at his bloodied fingertips before stepping toward the pathway ahead of him.

He momentarily paused, his breath hitching in his throat. He glanced over his shoulder, attention torn between the oddly diagonal chute he'd fallen down, and the wavering glow of the torchlight.

With a deep breath, Leer crossed the space and snagged the knotted wooden torch from its holder on the stone wall, the flame swaying as he dragged it down to eye level. He blinked, his vision adjusting to the sight. The earthy pathway wove through on a sharp eastern curve, narrow with imposing stalactites punctuating the route. Moistening his lips, he set his jaw.

Only one way to find out.

Water sloshed up on his boots from the many puddles he trekked through in the tunnel. He was mindful of the dripping limestone overhead, sharp points protruding from the underground pathway he was now deep inside of like the knives he had once inserted into a habbersnitch trap for fun as a boy.

Leer froze as his right eye was nearly impaled by a peak he somehow failed to see; sudden empathy filled him for the little rodents he had tortured so many years ago as a child. He carefully sidestepped to the left with a white-knuckled grip on the torch. The tip of his boot knocked into an object below him, rattling as it clattered against the opposite wall.

He swallowed with dread, pausing mid step.

Slowly moving the torchlight, he cast the glow to the ground, examining the graveled dirt below. It didn't take long before he spotted what he suspected was the source of the noise:

A partially shattered human skeleton complete with skull was slumped against the moist interior, the bones unnaturally splayed from his disruption. Leer felt his jaw go slack, the back of his throat drying up as he moved the light forward.

His stomach felt sick as he recalled Looney Luke's tale in Junivar a few nights ago, the details resurfacing into his subconscious.

"Ishma and Tyne," Leer breathed, his eyes fixed on the skeleton highlighted by flickering flame light.

Princess Maegan's high-pitched scream rattled Leer from his thoughts. His eyes shot toward the stretch of darkness that waited ahead of him. Her voice was faint, but near.

She was overhead.

With renewed determination, Leer darted through the tunnel, the torchlight wavering wildly. He couldn't let the Grimbarror kill her. She was an innocent woman—she didn't deserve a fate like this, a fate he felt he had somehow sealed for her.

Her second scream made Leer's stomach growl with primal appetite.

So long as I am not her undoing.

His heart thudded erratically in his chest as he sprinted, the orange-yellow flame spreading shadows that danced along the rock as his feet pounded into the dirt below. The musty stench of the atmosphere caught in his throat as he breathed, sucking in hurried gulps of air as the hot fire teased at his hairline for a taste of his locks.

Leer skidded to a stop when he saw the outline of a second skeleton ahead. The victim, gruesomely appropriate for how Leer imagined it must have perished, was sprawled on the ground on its back, right arm outstretched toward the wall next to it.

Not an ounce of flesh was left on the bones, or a shred of material in sight.

Burned at high heat, Leer grimly concluded.

Fighting his instinct to move on, Leer's eyes followed the path the victim's arm made toward the cave wall. He blinked, sniffing the air.

He smelled something that didn't belong there.

A light, woody scent pierced his nostrils. He distinguished notes of creamy spice assaulting his senses as he took a step closer to the skeleton's hand.

The same scent that lingered in Astrid's thick mane.

His heart racing, Leer crouched down after switching the torch to his left hand, his right hovering with trepidation above the skeleton. He ran it up the length of the victim's outstretched limb, his palm colliding with the wall.

He rocked forward on his toes, his fingertips pushing into the wall for support; the peppered fragrance filled his nose, stone giving way with a gentle gliding motion under the pressure.

Leer's eyes widened in awe as he moved the torch closer, examining the sliver of vault he revealed. He applied more pressure, eagerly exposing the hiding place to discover it held a finely crafted bow, next to it a quiver stocked with arrows. In the dim light, the heads of the arrows glinted with an odd purple hue.

Leer snagged the weapons, silently praying that doing so wouldn't cause his death. As he slung it over his free shoulder, he took note of a small pouch that remained. He glanced back at the skeleton for a moment—its hand outstretched, desperation evident in its grotesque form—then snatched it, securing it to his belt and replacing the vault wall. Princess Maegan's whimpered voice above him coupled with the Grimbarror's indecipherable speech churned his stomach in dread and excitement. He didn't have time to examine the contents.

Whatever it was, at one time, possessing it was worth the risk. Maybe it would be worth it again.

Leer soon came to the end of what he assumed was the escape route of the Keeper's Hold. Using a last puddle, he doused the torchlight and tossed the stick aside.

With a heavy breath, Leer loaded an arrow. He kept his aim taunt as he climbed the winding staircase that led toward the surface. He took the narrow stairs two at a time, pausing when he reached the top. Pressing his back against the wall, he listened, waiting for what he knew would be his opportune moment to strike.

His enemy was just on the other side. Leer was ready to destroy the beast once and for all.

Steady and balanced, he coached himself with a deep, practiced breath.

This was the moment he had waited for.

He would not fail Finnigan.

-21-

"Leave her be!" Leer shouted as he darted around the wall. His thick fingers held sure around his draw, his aim precise and his stance clean. He simultaneously pleaded a silent prayer to the heavens, but he couldn't help but feel it was hypocritical with the evil that flowed so willingly through his veins.

Leer knew he was the rogue pawn from the right side of the game board, the one who had crept up on the king. He saw that reflected in the Grimbarror's eyes when the beast turned to face him.

Princess Maegan stood in a far off corner of the room. Next to her was an elegant, large fireplace that was lit by a roaring fire. Leer's nostrils flared, evaluating her condition. She was obviously frightened, given her tight grip on the fire poker she held. Beyond that, though, she looked perfectly put together, her dress clean and flowing. She appeared unharmed.

"I said, leave her be," Leer commanded with emphasis. He sidestepped, matching the Grimbarror's deliberate pace, circling in the opposite direction.

"Interesting," the Grimbarror said with a growing smile, the thinly veiled initial shock washing away, replaced by ever-growing golden rims on the outer edge of its dark irises. "I saw things happening differently."

"Let her go," Leer growled, his knuckles tightening ever so slightly against the bowstring.

"What, exactly, do you intend to do with that toy?"

"I intend to use it to send you back to the hell you came from."

The beast laughed. "Then I suppose it's the same hell you now descend from," the Grimbarror replied with a cool smile forming across its thin mouth. He noted that the Grimbarror didn't have a visible weapon.

It didn't matter. The beast was the weapon.

"Tell me, Private Boxwell, aren't you the least bit curious about it all?" the Grimbarror asked, its tone dripping with arrogance. "About anything I've said?"

"I don't listen to liars," Leer spat, lifting his bow a little higher.

The beast's grin widened with satisfaction. "You are. You're barely concealing your desperate interest behind this charade of heroism you've adopted."

"Then enlighten me," Leer challenged as he took a bold step forward, "since you deem yourself so 'wise' to my thoughts."

It chuckled. "Yes…Well, then—allow me the utter privilege of tearing apart everything you think you know."

The Grimbarror's slowly arching wings blew a puff of cold air over Leer's face. Its expression changed as it examined Leer. "All he ever wanted was power. We believed in his rule, in truth and justice, in honesty and good natured people." Its eyes glanced at Princess Maegan. "We believed in blood."

Leer swallowed, his reaction barely visible; he knew the Grimbarror caught it, though.

Steady and balanced. Steady and—

"He suffered greatly, your mentor," the Grimbarror noted, its expression surprisingly solemn. "He suffered for what he knew."

"You killed him," Leer snarled.

The beast smirked. "Is that what you believe?"

"I saw you there."

Its laugh was cool and rich. "Why do you think I've been fighting? Protecting what little I have left? You're governed under a regime of lies."

Leer's eyes narrowed. "You're the only liar I see here."

He saw the shift in the beast's demeanor, how its face changed as it continued. "He wanted power. He was willing to do whatever it took to keep it. And even if in the end he denied the piper its price, he still made the deal." The beast's nostrils flared. "Now, his power—all of their power—is mine." It smiled. "Ours. Yours. It's ours to exact the revenge we deserve. To pay the penance for what you've lost."

"I'm nothing like you," Leer objected darkly. "You've killed in cold blood."

It laughed. "And you haven't killed men?" it asked. "Tell me, Leer—what do you think makes you so different than me?"

"I've killed for the good of others," Leer defended.

"As have I," the Grimbarror countered.

Leer's pulse rose as he sidestepped, his heart racing as he saw the gap closing. It made him ill that his appetite peaked as he caught Princess Maegan's sweet scent.

"I know why you kill," Leer continued, ignoring the feelings as best as he could. "You kill because of the thirst that courses through your veins. You kill because you *can't resist* killing."

It smirked at Leer. "Are you speaking from experience?" it teased.

Leer shook his head slightly. "It doesn't matter."

"Oh, but it does," the Grimbarror objected. "I sense the change in you." It smiled with unmistakable pride. "You're a strong man, a true warrior. You've done what others have never dared to. I've chosen you, Leer. You will be the leader of my army. Together, we will take Hiline back from the liars who betrayed us."

"My choice is to fight for the truth," Leer corrected. With a waver in his fingers, he loosened his grip on the bow, the color returning to his knuckles with the relieved tension. Keeping his focus on the Grimbarror's eyes, Leer relaxed his arm, his impromptu decision of slow surrender making his stomach queasy with doubt. "It's all I wish to fight for."

"What truth?" it asked, its voice turning soft. "There is no such thing as 'truth.'"

"There is," Leer insisted, his bow halfway lowered. "And I won't rest until truth and justice both reign."

The Grimbarror fell silent for a few uncomfortable heartbeats. It wore a rueful smile, still preoccupied. "You think you know what is true. You think you understand. You see much, but nothing at all." Its haunting yellowed eyes met his; they sliced through Leer's facade of resolve. It was nearly like gazing at himself in a looking glass. "Soon, when you are able to listen to the hearts of men, you will then know as well as I do that 'truth' does not exist. Only revenge."

"And what have you to avenge?" Leer challenged mockingly. "What could you possibly know about loss?"

Silence spread between them, the Grimbarror's eyes locked on Leer's. "Go, sister," he murmured to Princess Maegan. "I don't wish to harm you."

Leer relaxed as he digested the words. "Sister?" he breathed, staring at the beast in confusion. Off to his side, he saw the princess drop the hot iron to the stone floor, her eyes wide in horror as she considered the Grimbarror for a moment before scurrying out.

"We do what we must to protect our blood," the beast replied, drawing Leer's attention back, a solemn smile tugging at its mouth. "The blood that deserves it."

The voices swirled in his ears, this time without any pain.

"The truth awaits you."

Prince Edward.

"It can't be," Leer whispered, his bow arm relaxing with the revelation. The air heated and thickened around him. "You're...You're dead."

"And who told you that?" The beast grinned. "My father?" He narrowed his eyes. "His accomplice?"

"Your body was taken to the crypt by cart. The king..."

"My father is a liar!" The Grimbarror snapped its wings, the sound echoing off the stone floor. "I was expendable for his gain." It stalked away a few paces, snarling under its breath. "How can you be so intelligent, yet still not see?" It glared at him. "They are all afraid of you, you know. They fear what you're capable of. Why do you think you trained since you were a lad? Why do you think you were accompanied on your quest?" It stepped back toward him. "Do you believe all you've experienced thus far is pure coincidence?"

"The truth awaits you," the voice reminded Leer.

Leer shook his head. "What could you know of what I've experienced?"

The beast lifted its chin, its expression softening, warming to something close to empathy. "Because I can hear the drum of your heartbeat; I can see the secrets of your mind." It laughed to itself. "Whether I'd care to or not. I've no choice in the matter." It squared its shoulders. "But I made my choice, Leer. I took the power for myself. They might have made me into a beast, but they...they are the real monsters. Never forget that."

A door to Leer's right swung open, and Leer whirled toward it. His chest constricted when he saw Lieutenant Doyle brandishing a weapon—a shoddy and crude looking knife; it looked like it was made in desperation. Hardly imposing enough to challenge such a creature.

"You," the beast growled, stalking toward the Lieutenant. Its eyes fixed, wings arching, it bellowed, "You're the lowest monster of them all."

The Lieutenant merely smiled, retracting his arm and throwing the knife squarely toward the beast's heart.

"No!" Leer yelled as time slowed.

The beast seemed unaffected at the Lieutenant's move, sure of itself to the point of letting the purple-hued blade lodge into its flesh. Its expression soon changed, though, confidence draining from its features.

"How?" it breathed, its clawed hand clenching around the hilt of the knife. It shuddered, its grip lessening.

"You've Private Boxwell to thank for confirming that," Lieutenant Doyle replied with a sly grin. "Or should I say, Finnigan Lance's journal? Though naturally, I came prepared."

Leer froze, looking at the tip of his drawn arrow for a brief moment.

Purple stone. Like the knife.

Maloden.

Maloden—suppression.

The Grimbarror shrieked as it clutched its chest and tipped backward to the cold floor, blood painting the stone underneath it.

It was dying.

But if he could heal, why wasn't the beast?

The maloden. It draws away the power.

The Grimbarror rustled, shaking Leer from his stupor. He dropped his weapon and rushed over, desperate for the knowledge that would soon die with the beast.

The prince.

The Grimbarror's face contorted in pain as the blade penetrated his sternum. The beast convulsed, growing shock visible across its scaled face, blood pouring from its chest through its clothes. Leer desperately tried to withdraw the blade, but it seemed to have partially fused itself into the beast's body.

It gasped for sips of air. "The Vei has awakened in you," it whispered breathlessly, shaking. "The truth you seek is still hidden." It coughed, blood sputtering from its lips. "The truth about you." Its clawed hand reached for Leer's, but fell short. "They have withheld much. They have kept you from your true self. Embrace your power and take revenge on them, *Naetan*—Son of Night."

Leer watched the Grimbarror weaken, the color draining from its face, its final gasp of air escaping as it died.

Trembling, Leer stood, his hands by his sides. He felt the familiar stiffness between his shoulder blades— the same stiffness he had felt in the woods. He swallowed, blinking as he focused on the Grimbarror's body. He caught a glimpse of his own left forearm, at the array of gray-green scales scattered across his skin, at the line of them creeping up under the sleeve of his tunic.

His fingers slid across his stubbled face as he stood over the Grimbarror's body. His breath hitched when he felt the same scales across the burn on his left cheek and surrounding the outside of his left eye.

"Now," Lieutenant Doyle said; Leer turned to face him. "It's your turn."

"*You*," Leer growled when he saw the Lieutenant's blade lift.

"You seem surprised," Lieutenant Doyle smirked.

"You set me up, you whoreson," Leer argued. "You killed the prince!"

"And now, I'll kill you to gain the beast's power."

The Lieutenant lunged at Leer, who leaped to his right to dodge the attack, tumbling over himself before coming to his feet. His bow was too far away, and nothing remained but the poker near the fireplace. Leer rushed to it and lifted it over his head just in time to block a strike from the Lieutenant's sword. The red hot iron sparked with the collision.

With a groan, Leer pushed against the iron rod he held, throwing Lieutenant Doyle backward against the wall. He scrambled to straighten up, bracing himself as he watched his enemy stand and laugh. For the first time, the Lieutenant's purple hued sword made sense. It had been made with maloden.

He knew all along.

"The truth will be known," Leer said, his eyes fixed on Lieutenant Doyle.

"What truth is that, Boy?" he asked, smirking. "The one we create? You're a fool to think you're anywhere other than right where I want you to be. Perhaps you should've paid more attention to what Finnigan taught you." The Lieutenant's satisfied grin enraged Leer; he growled, grounding his stance.

They parried, the Lieutenant proving himself a worthwhile opponent. Leer's concentration split between staying out of the hot fire behind him and the weapon Lieutenant Doyle held. Leer tucked and rolled away from the fireplace, panting as he saw the Lieutenant turn to face him.

Within a moment, Leer went back on the defense, the glowing iron slowly cooling. Sparks rained over the stone floor as Leer blocked the Lieutenant's strikes, the two equally matched in strength and skill. Except, Leer's foot slipped on his discarded bow, giving enough opportunity for Lieutenant Doyle to take the advantage. The Lieutenant knocked the poker out of Leer's grip. Leer groaned as the Lieutenant slammed him against the stonewall.

"Once you give me what I want, the entirety of Hiline as you know it will perish," Lieutenant Doyle said, pushing his blade toward Leer's neck. Leer braced against him, straining to slow the blade's approach. "In her place, I will birth a new nation of indestructible men. Everyone you know will die—Aldred Lance, that pathetic blacksmith and his family." He smirked. "Even your little thief."

"Not if I kill you first," Leer growled.

The ground under them trembled, quaking in sudden protest. Leer felt the burn of his anger rise through himself, his breath evening as he pressed against the Lieutenant. The candelabras dotting the nearby mantle swayed with the quiver, crashing to the stone floor as furniture and other decor rattled and collapsed.

Leer seized the brief moment of opportunity he created when he saw Lieutenant Doyle's attention turn toward the chaos around them. He shoved the Lieutenant away, watching with satisfaction as his body crashed into the back wall next to the fireplace. Energy renewed, he swiped up the iron poker and raced toward Lieutenant Doyle, ready for the kill.

Through his guttural snarl, Leer heard Princess Maegan shriek, "Edward!" Heat spread through Leer's chest as he halted his approach on Lieutenant Doyle, his eyes turning toward the doorway where Princess Maegan stood. She stared down in horror at her brother's bloodied body, clutching the doorframe as the earth rumbled under them.

"This beast killed your brother," the Lieutenant lied, nodding to Leer as he moved to Prince Edward's body and removed the maloden blade from it with mock horror. "He wanted Edward's power for himself."

"Lies!" Leer spat, frozen in place as panic swirled within, slowing the quaking of the floor.

"Yet, you ready yourself to kill me."

"You—"

"Go, Princess," Lieutenant Doyle ordered. "Wait by the moor for me. He shan't harm you."

Leer was momentarily distracted by Princess Maegan's hasty exit, failing to keep his eye on Lieutenant Doyle. Before he knew how, Leer's thigh burned with a powerful ache as the Lieutenant's maloden knife lodged into his quadricep. He groaned and sunk to his knees, the earth under him stilling with his lost concentration.

The stone seared through his muscle and tissue, the pain greater than he ever felt before in his life. Water clouded Leer's eyes as he screamed and gripped the hilt, slowly prying the nearly fused knife from his thigh. His hands shook, and he panted when he finished, looking at the jagged wound the blade left in its wake. Though it momentarily tormented him to do so, he managed to stand up. He grimaced as his body rejuvenated itself, the pain lessening with each second he concentrated on healing.

By the time he was fully mended, he saw he was alone in the room once again.

Then, another feminine voice punctuated the air.

Astrid.

He bolted toward the doorway, pausing briefly to retrieve his discarded bow. Astrid's voice in the distance was motivation, his power resurfacing with his renewed direction.

Leer raced through doorway and into the corridor. His heart thudded in his chest as he honed in on the sound of Astrid's voice. He could finally hear what she was saying as he burst into the courtyard outside of the abandoned Sortarian palace:

"Shoot, Leer! Shoot him!" she pleaded, her voice raspy and raw with desperation.

Leer froze; his boots sunk into the snow as he considered her words. He shut his eyes briefly against the pit that grew inside of him.

It's a trap.

Of course she would try to do the honorable thing, the bloody fool.

Tightening his grip on the bow, Leer swept across the thick powder in the courtyard. Heat began to spread from his chest to his fingertips when he spotted Astrid in the distance a few moments later.

The Lieutenant gripped Astrid near the edge of the ravine, his sword resting against her throat. Leer swallowed when he saw the pouch he recovered from the Keeper's hold swinging from the Lieutenant's belt.

-22-

Purple and red rays of dawn's sunlight filtered from behind Leer, illuminating snow and trees around them. Leer quickly loaded his bow and drew back on the string, aiming for Lieutenant Doyle with disdain. He made a mental note of his low supply of arrows in the quiver strapped to his back.

"I'm going to presume that you understand the choice you need to make," Lieutenant Doyle said, as he pressed Astrid close. "Despite your...'power,' you simply can't have it all, can you?"

Leer glanced at Astrid. Seeing her struggle made him burn with anger, but her plea for him to abandon her made him ill.

"Don't," Astrid breathed. "It's is more important than my life, Leer."

"How noble," Lieutenant Doyle commented with a laugh. Leer looked back to him. "Quite surprising, coming from a professional thief."

Leer heard Astrid whimper. Flames of heat spread across his chest, but he kept his eyes on Lieutenant Doyle.

"You'd kill her for a purse?" Leer challenged, shifting his weight forward a little more on his toes.

Lieutenant Doyle smiled. "Nice try," he replied. "Do you really consider me that daft?"

"I consider you a dead man," Leer snapped, watching as Astrid tried to maintain purchase on the slick snow.

"Make your choice, Private," Lieutenant Doyle warned.

Leer's nostrils flared as he drew short breaths through them, his fingertips digging into the bowstring. His heart thudded in his chest, a sheen of sweat breaking over the skin of his palms.

He could hear Astrid softly pleading with him to take the shot he had. She was begging to die, to die for something she didn't even know the importance of, something he could hardly prove was even worth sacrificing her life for. His throat ran dry at his vivid mental image of her lithe body collapsing to the ground, her doe eyes wide as her blood sputtered from her throat and dripped through her dark locks.

I can't let her die.

Leer squeezed his eyes shut with resignation. He reluctantly loosened his biceps, his arms sinking, his weapon lowering. A cold pit of dread churned deep within. He opened his eyes, surrendering.

How many others will now die because of it?

"No, Leer!" Astrid shouted. "You idiot. *Kill* him!"

Leer ignored her and kept watching Lieutenant Doyle, whose mouth turned up on one side as he examined Leer's face.

"Bound by honor," the Lieutenant remarked. "I would expect nothing less from you. Put your bow on the ground, Boxwell. Or should I say, *Naetan?*"

Leer squeezed the wood of the weapon in consideration, swallowing back his disdain; he growled, fuming as he tossed it on the ground.

A satisfied chuckle flowed over the Lieutenant. "Oh, Private," he mused, his eyes still closed, "you made the wrong choice."

The Lieutenant shoved Astrid toward the edge of the ravine. Leer gasped, watching as Astrid slid toward the edge on a patch of ice. She screamed wildly as her hands clawed at the ground, finally taking hold of a small rock, keeping her from falling.

"You son of a bitch!" Leer yelled at Lieutenant Doyle, picking up his bow and firing off an arrow, just missing the Lieutenant as he disappeared into the thick wood, the arrow lodging in a hewen trunk. He snarled and tossed the bow on the ground, turning toward the ravine edge.

With every ounce of strength he had, Leer scrambled toward the edge to Astrid, wasting no time as he wrapped his arms around her arm and pulled her to safety. She was weightless, no more than a kulipe's feather cradled in his grip. The all-too-familiar ache rushed through him as he felt the vibrant warmth of her skin under his fingertips. He took a deep breath as he guided her to stand, steadying her as she leaned on him.

She met his eyes, shifting her weight forward and she lost her balance on the ice. He was caught off-guard as she tripped and fell on top of him. Leer's back crashed into the crusted powder underneath them. Astrid's chest collided with his, her face falling into the nook of his shoulder and neck. Air whooshed from his lungs; he braced his hands against her ribs to keep her from sliding off.

Her hair swept across his cheek. He drew a deep breath and turned his face in toward her. His lips brushed over her velvet-soft skin below her earlobe; his stomach groaned with fervent pain. His mouth dragged a little further down her neck as she lifted her head.

She looked into his eyes. He held his breath.

Damn.

He watched her for a moment as she stared down at him, losing himself in the hypnotic scent of her skin. Where a part of him hungered for her destruction, another was at peace under the contact. She was a soothing balm to the burn of his existence, the healing to the deep pain that resonated within.

"Leer," Astrid breathed, her chilled fingers coasting over the scales on his face with innocent curiosity, sympathy in her eyes.

Let her go.

His eyes shut against her touch; he let her examine him, drinking in her heat selfishly. The pads of her fingers glided along his jaw, hesitating where the scales ended at his gently parted lips.

But she caressed them with innate fear. It reminded him of when he was a boy and he saw a girl in the Vale with a dying olis:

The slithering creature was scaled as he now was, beaten with sticks at the well behind a tavern for no good reason by the high and mighty Elistair and his minions. In an effort to be included, Leer too had beaten the olis, running away when a peasant girl fetching water saw it. Leer was afraid he would be caught and switched, so he hid behind a wall and watched her.

The girl stroked the beast's skin with methodical sadness, her tawny face wrinkled, her stubby fingers caked with dirt and likely making its wounds worse. The creature watched with unblinking eyes under her ministrations, its lower half flicking angrily in protest while its bloodied upper rested in odd peace under her gentle caress.

The girl made sense in its world when nothing else did.

Just like Astrid.

Yet, despite the girl's attempt to soothe the olis, the creature wanted to rip at the girl's hand.

Just like Leer.

You need to let her go.

Leer opened his eyes and swatted Astrid's hands away. "Don't touch me," he warned through clenched teeth.

He stood with suddenness and pushed Astrid off of himself. He turned away as she fell onto the snow. With a deep breath, he crossed the space to retrieve his discarded bow, stooping low and swiping it from the ground. Standing straight, he looked into the distance where Lieutenant Doyle had once stood. The woods were lifeless beyond Astrid's small voice behind him.

"Leer—"

"What do you *want?*" Leer snapped, turning to face Astrid.

His expression rendered her speechless. "Leer," Astrid finally breathed, "you shouldn't have—"

"*Don't,*" he warned, taking a step closer to her. "Don't tell me what I should and shouldn't do, you filthy thief. You're nothing but a liar and a roach, just like your dead brother."

Her jaw quivered as it dropped. "Then why did you bother to save me if you think my life is so useless?"

"Because I didn't want blood on my hands."

"So you let that maniac have a brilliant source of magic instead?" she challenged. Leer shut his eyes, turning away as he adjusted the quiver on his back. "What other lies would you like to tell me, Leer?"

"Leave me be, Astrid," he warned under his breath.

"No, I won't," she insisted; he heard her step closer to him. "I care whether you live or die, and judging by the incredibly daft decision you just made, I'd say you care about me the same way. So tell me, Leer—what else might you try to say to deter me from following you?"

Leer turned toward Astrid, his heart clenching at the pain he saw in her beautiful clear blue eyes. He breathed, his pulse racing, his stomach sick. He wanted to throw himself into the ravine. Still, his fate was sealed. It was as sure as the stiff scales that littered his body and the growing veil that settled over his mind. There was no turning back.

"It's Naetan Lance now, Astrid," he replied, a rueful smile playing about his lips. "And you shouldn't follow me because everything you believe about me is wrong. Especially about me caring for you."

The deep snow sloshed over Leer's boots with each step he took further into the wilderness of Sortaria, the crystals melting immediately upon contact. Never before in the middle of such vast, open wilderness in the dead of winter had he felt so warm.

Too warm.

His skin was on fire. Every inch of him burned with a scorching heat he couldn't flee. His brow was damp with sweat despite the minimal clothing he wore.

His stomach rose and fell, waves of guilt, anger and grief ebbing and flowing through the silence of journey. Where he was headed, he didn't know—he only prayed that with each step, with each mile of distance, those he had left behind would be long gone from his mind's eye.

Aldred.

Jarle.

Astrid.

Leer paused, pressing a hand to his ravenous stomach as he peered over the endless green ripples of hewen and lingan trees. At the elevated height, he spotted a group of graceful nim. The females feasted on strips of bark they raked from the trees with their elongated teeth, their two front hooves steadying themselves as they performed acrobatics to reach the next bite.

He let out a puff of air as he saw the lone male nim dart to the side and grunt furiously at another approaching male before locking into a tangled mess of golden twisted razor-sharp horns.

You'll lose, he idly warned the challenging rebel male. *He saw you coming a mile away.*

The irony didn't escape him. Leer's hand lifted from his hungry stomach to touch his face, pushing the pads of his fingers into the hardened formations around his left eye and down his cheek.

For so long, he had fought to be the exact opposite of the man he thought was his father—the monster he saw as a boy while hiding behind baskets. He would be better, he promised himself. Stronger. Braver. He would stand for truth.

Yet, every truth he ever stood for was nothing but a cruel, calculated lie. And now he, himself, was the biggest lie of them all.

Leer squeezed his eyes shut and groaned, screaming against his fate. His torment shuddered outward through him in a charged blast, his voice echoing ferociously off of the surrounding rock. The ground rumbled, trees swayed and rocks burst as his agony penetrated into Sortaria itself, the power he now contained shaking the earth around him to its core.

The two male nim ceased fighting immediately with innate terror, each forgetting their differences over their mutual horror. They joined the herd as it stampeded for cover into the thickened brush, disappearing out of sight.

In his mind, Leer saw Lieutenant Doyle's smug satisfaction as the king declared his former guard, Leer Boxwell, to be an outlaw of Hiline. He saw the Lieutenant taking Princess Maegan as his bride for a reward.

Leer imagined Jarle would mock him for his stupidity.

He could hear Astrid's gentle voice asking him what truth really was, and if it was worth his life.

The ground ceased shaking as his dark eyes flashed open. He drew a few sharp breaths through his nose, observing the barren world around him that he now knew was his home.

He couldn't care. Caring was what was killing him. Caring was what would kill everyone.

By being someone else, he would protect the innocent. By sacrificing himself to the darkness, he would save them.

He felt the ring of heat around his eyes burn as the outer rims of his irises glowed yellow.

Leer Boxwell was dead.

It was time to be the beast.

-Epilogue-

Three weeks later, Prince James Shelton Doyle ran his fingertips over the cool wall of the Vale castle as he shifted his weight forward onto the balls of his feet. His hand fell from the stone to his tunic, smoothing the deep blue fabric over his chest as he waited patiently in the solarium.

He drew a steady breath through his nose, taking in the room in the wavering light of the fire that whizzed and crackled beside him. Its heat radiated over his freshly shined boots as he stepped closer to the hearth and the hewen-wood table in front of it.

A tafl board rested on the table's surface, the pawns of the set positioned for play. James sighed, picking up a black game piece with his left hand and examining it. The light of the adjacent fire glinted off his polished wedding band. He rolled the smooth bone between his fingertips.

Though he didn't want to admit it, Leer had been more of a challenge than he originally gave him credit for.

He heard the king's footfalls behind him but kept his back turned, still twisting the bone in his hand.

"Ironic, isn't it?" he asked, clucking his tongue.

The king straightened as he closed the gap between them. "It's a shame to see such talent wasted."

James pursed his lips. "Talent," he said. "A man who can trick people into revealing their weaknesses isn't talented. Just devious."

The king sighed. "Yes, well, his deviation has surely halted our plans."

"I have it under control," James assured.

"So Boxwell having the upper hand is your idea of control?" King Gresham growled.

"He has *nothing*," James replied through a laugh.

"He has power! The Vei awakened in him. Who knows now what force he has unleashed in not only himself, but in others."

"You forget that there is a sizable bounty looming over his head for capture alive, the same one the people now are aware of, thanks to your rousing speech earlier." James smiled. "One person hardly equates to an army."

The king's eyes narrowed. "One person is all it takes to begin one."

James lifted his chin. "Boxwell doesn't have any credibility."

"Yes, but…" The king paused; James shifted.

"What?" he snapped. King Gresham paced away. "What do you not speak of?"

"He…" The king sighed, lowering his head in shame. "He couldn't have been the one."

"What do you mean?"

"Edward," King Gresham sighed, rubbing his temples. "He couldn't have been the one she wanted."

"What are you talking about?" James scoffed. "Surely you don't have another child."

The king nodded, his eyes vacant. "I must. If Edward were the one she wished, she wouldn't have turned him into the monster." He smiled ruefully, understanding washing over him. "She would have wanted it for herself. The monster was a punishment." The king looked at James for a long moment. "It can all still be undone."

James shook his head. "It doesn't matter. I took care of Emelda, as I did Lance and Bilby. Your power, and the control of the amulet, is safe. If there is no debtor, there is no fear."

"You are blind. You may have eliminated Emelda, but you didn't eliminate the true threat to control."

"What is this threat you speak of?"

"It makes sense now," the king mused. "Why she should have come to me, chosen me."

"I don't understand."

"Purity." King Gresham turned toward the window he stood near, looking out onto the courtyard. "Her blood heir. The one who can wield the amulet over all."

"So, there's another she was truly after? And this child has the Vei?" The king nodded. James huffed. "Well, it might have been nice to know that little tidbit prior."

"Mind your tone," the king warned, glaring at him. "Despite your named succession, I am still king."

The Lieutenant closed his fist around the black game piece. "Of course," he replied, bowing his head humbly. "Forgive me, my lord." He looked up and watched as the king turned back to the window. Exhaling, he set the piece down thoughtfully next to the white king pawn. "May I pour my lord a drink, to celebrate his victory? After all, the possessor of the

Amulet of Orr surely has cause to celebrate." James moved toward the decorated jug that rested on the mantle, snatching a glass near it and filling it halfway with currant wine before crossing the distance to the king.

With remnants of annoyance, the king took it and sipped at the scarlet liquid, looking back at the courtyard through the window.

"The people seem eager for justice," James noted behind him.

"As well they should be," the king replied coolly, drinking a deep portion of wine.

"So the amulet...It's said to be able to reveal what you wish to know."

The king nodded. "Yes, through blood. But it should be used with caution. One should possess the amulet, not let it possess them."

James gave a small nod. "Of course."

"All this time," King Gresham sighed. "I thought she wished Edward for a mere debt payment. His death was in vain."

"Perhaps. Though without his death, you would have never learned the truth regarding the heir. There's always a sacrifice to ensure the larger victory. Pawns are lost before the game is won."

"He was more than a pawn," King Gresham snarled, facing James with wild eyes. "He was my son."

"Yes. And also a weakness. A potential threat to your power."

James watched the king's mouth open for rebuttal before catching the way his jaw stiffened midway; a sudden jerk overcame the older man, a wheeze escaping his throat. He observed with satisfaction as the king's empty cup fell to the stone floor.

The king groped the wall for support in frenzied shock. James blinked slowly as he watched the older man sink to his knees, his face pale and hands clutching at his throat through his struggle to breathe.

"There are many kinds of weaknesses," James whispered, stooping over the king, whose bloodshot eyes teared up, clinging to life despite the poison flooding his veins. "But do you know which is the most toxic to power?"

The king tried—and failed—to speak, his dry mouth open as he shuddered violently, falling to the floor. James squatted down and thumbed the end of the king's robe, wiping drops of currant wine from the man's parted lips before returning the cup to its place on the mantle.

Turning back toward the king, Lieutenant Doyle watched as the king convulsed against the wall, silence spreading over the room moments later. The king's body fell slack, his eyes rolling into the back of his head in defeat.

"Humanity, my lord," James murmured, examining the body. He slid his fingers into the pocket of the king's cloak, withdrawing the purse he had taken from Leer at the Fell. "The deadliest of them is humanity."

Straightening, James stood over the king's lifeless body, stepping over the dead man's legs as he withdrew the amulet from its bag with his left hand. The brilliant green stone glowed against the light from the fire, its malformed face a satisfying sight to James as he took a moment to observe it dangle from its cord. He gripped his sword with his free hand, raising the blade to his palm and slicing a clean line through it. Inhaling, he lowered the sword and pressed the stone into his bloodied grip, a smug smile blossoming over his lips.

"Show me the heir of Emelda's blood," he commanded, closing his eyes.

He waited for what seemed like an eternity, his grip tight around his sword and the amulet. His mind's eye was dark, silent. Still, he knew it would come. Drips of blood trickled down his arm. He remained, eager for the dark veil that would embrace him.

A surge struck his brow; he braced himself against the infiltration, nostrils flared as he squeezed the stone tighter. The dark Vei slowly grew stronger within him as he embraced its murky hold, feeding it with the grim promises of his mind. It twisted and churned, volts of power coursing through his veins. Through flares of light, he saw the answer.

With a gasp, he opened his eyes.

"Astrid Falstad," he breathed before letting go a guttural scream.

ABOUT THE AUTHOR

Lyndsey is a brilliant author you've likely never heard of, Superwife, and award-winning mother living life in leggings in the expensive and overcrowded state of New Jersey. She is fluent in Spanglish and Sarcasm and enjoys watching Arrow, Supernatural, Psych, and The X-Files repeatedly. You can find her either in the grocery store buying laundry detergent, Tylenol, and cat litter; hovering near her Keurig coffee brewer; or shaking her fist at the heavens in front of her computer. Occasionally, you may spot her on the beach or out shopping (when she actually has money to spare). However, you should avoid approaching her at such times as she is likely enjoying a rare moment of relaxation and can become moody if interrupted. If you decide to engage her during any one of these activities, approach with caution and a sizable cup of Starbucks in hand to avoid any ill effects.

Facebook:
www.facebook.com/authorlyndseyharper

Twitter:
www.twitter.com/lyndseyiswrite

Website:
http://www.lyndseyharper.com/